THE CAGED
Butterfly

Also By Marian L. Thomas

Books In A Series

Color Me Jazzmyne
My Father's Colors
Strings of Color

Stand-Alone Titles

Aqua Blue
Blue Butterfly
I Believe In Butterflies

Children's Book

Things Sasha Learned From Her Dog Winston

THE CAGED Butterfly

MARIAN L. THOMAS

ESTD 2009

L.B. PUBLISHING

CREATING BOOKS WORTH BUZZING ABOUT

Copyright © 2018 by Marian L. Thomas

L.B Publishing
400 West Peachtree St NW
#4-858
Atlanta, GA 30308

www.lbpublishingbooks.com
Printed in the United States of America

First Edition: October 2018

For information about special discounts for bulk purchases, please contact L.B Publishing at info@lbpublishingbooks.com

Library of Congress Control Number: 2018948898

Thomas, Marian L.

The Caged Butterfly / Marian L. Thomas - 1st. ed.
ISBN-978-1-17324880-0-7

1. Women's— Fiction. 2. Romance—Fiction. 3. Domestic—Fiction. 4. Family secrets—Fiction

*To My Supporters In
Life, Love, and Laughter*

My Husband
My Family
My Friends
My Readers
My Publicist

Thank you

When I ran, I felt like a butterfly
that was free. -Wilma Rudolph

Prologue

To the child inside me,

I ain't never gonna look in your eyes, see your smile, or hear the sweetness of your laugh, the doctors say.

It's funny how we go through life looking for the commas, but in the end, all we get is a period. One single dot at the end that becomes the sum of our life. I would have sworn I'd have a life full of commas.

I would have sworn I'd see my child.

The thought of not getting a chance to see you grow is like a knife that keeps stabbing me over and over. Reality can't pull it out. Doctors can't do anything but leave it in.

When they first told me, I sat in this here hospital bed and stared at the May moon, knowing it was the last time I would see it. It has been quite a journey to get to this road of acceptance. But I reckon I got both feet planted on it now, and it doesn't look like I got any other routes I can take. Doctors say my small hips can't bring you into the world without help, and while my bones are healthy, my young, almost twenty-year-old heart isn't.

I can hear the rain outside my window. Good thing, I reckon, so folks in other rooms can't hear my tears. You'll be coming by the time the sun comes up and the rain stops, and I'll be closing my eyes for the final time.

My forty-nine-year-old mama, Mildred "Millie" Mayfield, always said I had strong bones and small hips. She spoke about it like it was my downfall. I would never have guessed she'd be right. Although I can't remember a time, Mama wasn't right. I never minded having small hips. I could wear just about anything. Things most girls wouldn't dare. For instance, I could wear a polka dot skirt without it looking "meaty," as my mama called some of the girls.

While I'm a fan of my hips, I believe in inner beauty.

When I turned eighteen, Thomas Gray Livingston and I were sitting by Bear Creek, watching the butterflies float by and soaking up the sun, when I told him about my belief in inner beauty and how if you don't believe in your inner beauty, then you ain't nothing but a caged butterfly. I told him that if you ain't showing the world your colors, you ain't correctly giving life something it can use. I believe that everybody got colors inside them that are as bright and vibrant as the colors of God's rainbow and they should never allow anyone, and I do mean anyone, to allow their God-given colors to be caged. They should let them fly. Let them glide along the edges of life and breathe in all the possibilities of doing great things with their colors.

I believe in God. In love. In butterflies and in giving life something it can use.

That's what I believe, and you'll see one day that I was right.

Thomas is a thin-framed, full-faced, freckled boy with red curly hair and vibrant green eyes. He's smart, kind, and deeply in love with me. That was never a revelation. I'd been knowing it since we were five. He lived just on the other side of the railroad tracks that, at one point, ran clear across three counties, including Winder, Georgia.

Now, I'd like to tell you a little about where I'm from, 'cause I think it's essential. I reckon you ought to know something about the ground I used to walk on.

Winder, Georgia, (the first syllable of Winder is pronounced like "wine") is a small town located within the realms of Barrow County. It's about east of the big city, Atlanta, but filled with folks from all walks of life. Most people, however, were taking the poor step—daily, if you ask me. At least, that was how my young eyes on the colored side of the tracks always saw it.

I was born a month early, on December 29, 1930. Mama said it snowed something awful that day, but then the snow stopped and she could see the icicles inside my eyes.

Mama is always dramatic in that way. I guess it's from all her book reading.

She and I lived in a small brown-wooded house with a porch that wrapped around it. The bottom of our stairs was covered in flowers of all kinds that Mama planted. Mama said that the flowers gave the house a beautiful personality.

Mama cooked and cleaned for the Princely family. They lived just up from Broad Street, not that far from the center of our small town.

I suppose I should tell you something more about Thomas. Your father.

Now before you go getting all hot-headed and thinking bad about him, he doesn't know about you, so don't go blaming him for not being around. His parents thought they could use their money and influence to pay Mama to take me away. They were right. That's how we got back to Mama's family roots here in Chicago.

Chicago ain't the South, no sweet tea or collard greens with cornbread. However, folks in Chicago do know how to fry up some chicken and fish, and the pizza is just downright excellent, so Mama and I tried to make it home.

But Thomas—he was my best friend, and leaving him wasn't easy.

We'd been knowing each other since birth, as they say. We were even born on the same day. Thomas and his parents live in a modest but attractive house with tall white columns. His father, Thomas Gray Livingston Sr., owns the grocery store just up the road from Bear Creek over in Statham. That creek got the most significant trees I've ever seen growing around it. Birds use to love those trees. Thomas's mother, Joann, is a housewife; although she has never cooked, never cleaned, and wouldn't know how to fry chicken if someone paid her to do it. That's why they paid me to do it.

I started going to the Livingston's house four times a week, right after school, when I was thirteen. Every dime that Mama let me keep, I saved it for college. I was going to be the first in my family to go.

"Inner beauty and intelligence, that's what makes a woman," my mama always said.

She'd also say that it "wasn't right for a colored girl to walk around dumb when life gives you books." Those were the words I heard all my life. They stuck to my soul and helped me find my goals.

I never knew my father. He died just before I was born. Mama never talked about him. Never. I can't tell if it's the pain of losing him or the pain of loving him. Perhaps both.

I saw a picture of him once. He was tall with skin that had barely been touched by the sun. I had to hold the picture of him up in the light to try to make out if he was white or colored. I'm still not sure, but he was handsome. I got his light hazel-brown eyes, some of his height, his black wavy hair, and his skin.

In the picture, he was standing on a stage. Both of his feet were up in the air, about to touch, and I could see metal taps on each of them.

I can't tap. Perhaps you'll be able to. Maybe that will be in your blood. Mama always said that the good stuff about people in your history is what travels to all the generations that come afterward.

I'm telling you all this so that you know the history of your bones and those before you.

Mama is gonna put you up for adoption, 'cause she says she can't afford to raise you. I honestly believe she wouldn't be able to stand how much you'd remind her of me. Don't hate her for it.

In fact, be careful about hate. Dislike things, maybe even people because of their actions, but never hate anything. Hatred is ugly, and you don't want that ugliness in your soul. It takes away your ability to walk through life with peace in your heart. Let it go. Don't let hatred cage you in. Hatred can keep you from flying free, and when you ain't flying free, then you ain't living free either. Listen to me.

I speak from experience.

For six months, I hated Thomas's parents. Then the day came when I finally realized that I got myself into this mess, not them. They acted out of fear. I acted out of lack of restraint, as my mama told me.

She was right. Took me a while to face that fact. Yes, I loved Thomas. Still do. I see him every night when I dream about that creek back in

Winder that he and I used to put our feet in when we were kids. I reckon if I were ever going to marry a man, it would have been him—if the law and our parents would have allowed it.

He and I were going to find a college that accepted whites and colored. We'd heard that there might be some up North. We had plans. We had hope, love, and all the things that wide-eyed and naive young folks like us dream about.

We let one fall night in September of 1949 rip all that away.

That is what I regret. Thomas and I allowed our feelings to cloud out what was right and proper. But know that you are loved, my dear sweet child, and not a regret. Even though Thomas won't be able to see if your eyes match his, he would have loved you too. I'm quite sure of it.

I'm starting to cry now. The top of my hospital nightgown is soaked in the agony of all of this. I feel like the starch-white walls in this hospital room are crying with me. Even the spider that sits in the corner got tears in his eyes.

I pray that you love your new mama and that your new daddy helps you to become a fine young man or woman. In my mind's eye, I can see you giving life something it can use. I can see you graduating from college. I can see you loving someone with all your heart. I even see little ones sitting by your feet, looking up into your eyes with smiles of happiness and hearts filled with love.

I want you to laugh.

I want you to laugh a lot. I believe that laughing is like a sweet-smelling aroma for the soul and the heart. I used to laugh all the time. Back when life was good and innocent, and I was good and innocent.

Don't prove my dream a lie.

Don't be a caged butterfly.

Become something and someone that is even better than what I could see.

I don't know what your new parents will call you, but in my heart, I whispered Thomas Gray Livingston III in your ears, if you be a boy. Mama thinks that you are and like I said before, she ain't never wrong.

If I could give you one piece of advice, I'd tell you this—love the skin you're in.

Believe in inner beauty. Even a man has it.

Love,

Addie Mayfield,
your mama

Part One

Chapter One

Mildred "Millie" Mayfield - 1958

A slight wind blows against me and sends my black pleated skirt up in a flutter. I know that if I slip my hand underneath it to try to straighten it out, somebody will see me. If I were in my neighborhood of Beautifuls, I'd do it, but not here. Now ain't the time to go fishing.

I feel a few drops of sweat glide down the side of my neck. The June sun has my white blouse clinging to my body like it was holding on for life. Lord knows I want to pull what's underneath it off and allow that sun to touch my dried up bones and give them some life again.

I stop for a second or two to watch the "L" go rushing down the track just a bit from the corner of Lake Street. I haven't been in this part of Chicago before. They call it Oak Park. The West Suburbs.

I call it a neighborhood full of rich Wonderfuls.

My weak, overly greased knees are aching, and my back is throbbing from sitting on that darn train for the last hour or so. Trains got the most uncomfortable seats, and I don't have much cushion in the places where I reckon some cushion ought to be.

I always was a small woman.

Back in the day, when I was a child, folks use to say that my skin looked like it had been dipped in a scarf of creamy hazelnut. I'll admit that it has a few wrinkles now from the experiences of life—mostly around the eyes. My hair touches the mid part of my back. I keep it wrapped up in a bun since I ain't looking for no one, and frankly, I don't want anyone checking me out either, as the young folks say these days. My hair is sprinkled with strands of wisdom that seem to be sprouting up every time I open my eyes and look in the mirror. Truth be told, I've never minded getting old. I ain't never seen it as heading to the grave as some folks say, but I see it as somewhere between being able to speak your mind and knowing when speaking your mind is gonna get your behind chased down the street or thrown into the back of the paddy wagon.

I stop to take a deep breath and take in my surroundings. I've walked two blocks and I still got five more blocks to go, but I'm not going to let the agony of that reality keep me from this day.

This day.

A Wednesday.

This day got my nerves all up in a bunch. My hands are shaking. My feet feel like steel is sitting on them 'cause I'm too cheap to buy myself a new pair of shoes. My black pleated skirt is still all twisted up, and I feel another round of sweat running down my chest.

Just as I go to do what I say I wasn't—go fishing—I see the police driving by. They give me the side-eye, but they know there's only one reason why I'm in these rich parts...

Work.

I reach into my pocketbook and pull out my little white lace napkin to dab my forehead some before taking a moment to smell the trees and the fresh-cut grass. The grass here ain't like the green grass in Georgia. The trees here ain't the same either, but I'd swear that when my nose gets a whiff of the wind, everything out here in Oak Park smells like no worries.

I reckon that's how life should be.

I know I'm putting a heavy load on this day. But I believe as far down as my kidneys that this day is gonna have me smelling like no worries too.

This day is gonna set me free.

It's gonna take away the guilt and help ease the pain that's been choking me.

The possibility of it all puts a spark in my walk 'cause I feel like I'm finally gonna get a chance to make things right. I reckon that's what we're all stepping into life to do, whether we're a Wonderful or a Beautiful. We're all just trying to make the decisions we done made right.

In fact, I suppose that each one of us is just trying to find that light.

Live that dream.

Be that free.

Stop those tears.

The tears that I've been shedding for eight long years.

Truth is, I never reckoned this day would come, but low and behold, Jean, my neighbor from two floors up, told me she had heard of a family looking for a nanny. I wasn't much interested at first, but then Ms. Jean told me the name of the family, and I'd swear that my heart stopped beating for a moment or so.

Now here I am, standing at their kitchen door, trying to get the nerve to place a few formal knocks on the thick stained glass. I feel like the birds up in the trees are sitting there just watching me. Laughing perhaps. But I don't care. I'm here with both feet pointed in a direction I never thought they'd be.

Eight years is a long time to look into the eyes of the past and feel like you can't do anything to change it.

I take a deep breath, clutch my pocketbook, and finally do what the birds have been waiting to see—I knock. Nothing loud, you know. Soft and gentle like, 'cause I'm not trying to see that paddy wagon come back. A few minutes later, a tall colored woman with a head tinted with hints of gray hair comes to the door. She has on a black dress and a white apron that's hanging from her thick waist. She doesn't offer me no smile, but kind words are spoken even though her lips don't move.

She guides me past the kitchen covered in elegant floral wallpaper. My eyes search for a dish in the sink, but there ain't none. We travel down a long hallway, and she points me toward the living room where I'm told the Missus is gonna meet me.

I smile at the tall colored woman before she walks off and leaves me standing there, but at least I now know how to refer to the woman of the house. The Missus. Although her birth name is Lena.

Lena Taylor.

I did my research.

There's a white leather chair near the sofa, so I take a seat there and cross my legs. Just over my head is a chandelier that feels like it's trying its best to intimidate me. Its arms are stretched out and dangling with fancy crystals and sparkling glass. I ain't threatened by the elegant furniture though. I've been in rich folks' homes all my life. I don't envy them. I don't want to be them. Rich folks got too many issues just trying to stay rich.

I'm not dirt poor either, but I let everyone who thinks they know me believe that. Jean, my neighbor, thinks I need a job since she sees me with an apartment but no steady source of income. I've cleaned a few homes here and there since moving to Chicago, but I ain't felt like killing myself.

In the past, I had a reason too. The money I made fed into a purpose.

That purpose died eight years ago.

Life can be hard when you lose your purpose.

When I lost my Addie, I felt as if I lost my purpose for breathing. It seemed that life and I had become strangers. Like we only shook hands those moments when I had to step out of my apartment and into the world to buy my groceries.

Find a new book.

Try to forget what life had taken.

Every day I'd see my Addie's eyes staring back at mine, so forgetting hasn't been easy. Remembering her sweet, hazel-brown eyes has been downright hard for me.

While I wait for the Missus to come in, I take in the beige walls and the cream carpet. The imported white velvet sofa and the gold accessories that have been carefully put in their places. No dust anywhere. Not even in the corners. When you've been cleaning homes all your natural life, you take notice of things like that, 'cause dirt is like life—they both tend to hide in small spaces.

Ten minutes roll by before the Missus finally comes strolling into the room. Her thin-framed body is covered in expensive white clothing. White silk blouse. White silk pants. She even got on white satin-like pumps. She looks as I expected. Showy. Long pearls draping down the front of her body. I ain't never seen a Wonderful without her pearls. I supposed it's in their handbook, written down as law, I reckon.

The Missus is tall. I'd say about five-eight or so. She has long red hair that has just a hint of curl to it. Big blue eyes. She smiles at me, but I could read her.

Struggle recognizes struggle.

It's her hands that tell me her story. She married into money. I can see the hard life she came from under her perfectly painted red fingernails.

I wait for her to take her seat before I reach into my pocketbook and pull out my reference letter. She smiles again as I hand it to her. She has straight white teeth that I can tell came from years of being worked on.

I glance at the fireplace, running my eyes along the top of its mantle, as she pretends to read my reference letter. My eyes search for his photo. All night I stared at the bare walls of my small apartment, wondering what he looks like now. I can't help but wonder whose eyes he has.

The Missus clears her throat to get my attention, although I'm sure she thinks I'm looking around 'cause I was impressed with what she has. Perhaps she thinks I'm sitting in this here chair trying to determine what's gonna walk out with me.

I'm determined not to hold any of her foolish thoughts against her. For now anyway.

"So have you ever been a nanny before?" she asks.

"Not directly. However, one of the families I cooked and cleaned for, back in Georgia, had four children. I looked after them when needed or asked."

"I see." She places my reference letter on the coffee table and neatly folds her hands in her lap. "Mrs. Mayfield—"

"My mama named me Mildred, but my papa always called me Millie."

"All right. Millie, it is. We're looking for someone to assist with Timmy."

"Timmy," I say slowly. "That's what you—I mean, that's the name of your son?"

"Yes, that's right. Timothy Taylor. But he prefers Timmy." She glances toward the door, and I try not to look too hopeful that he might come running into the room at that moment.

But of course, that doesn't happen.

"My husband—Mr. Taylor—is out of town a lot and I...well, I need someone who can watch after him. Eight-year-old boys can be such a handful."

"I reckon they can be. Most ain't nothing but balls of energy at that age."

"That's right. Anyway, this will be a live-in position. My husband thinks we only need someone here during the day, but I get home late sometimes. My husband never understands how hectic my day can be."

"You work outside the home, ma'am?" I already know the answer, but I ask anyway.

"Dear Lord, of course not. But I have my charity work and hair appointments. These things take a lot of my time. I was, of course, hoping for someone with more experience with actually raising children. This position is very hands-on, you see."

"I reckon that I have about nineteen years of hands-on experience, ma'am."

She picks my reference letter back up, although she and I both know there ain't nothing on it about my hands-on experience with children.

"I raised my own child, so I reckon I was hands-on every day."

"Oh, so you have children of your own?"

"My daughter was a smart girl. I kept her in the books. Taught her to read and write before any in her class could."

"It's good you can read. How far did you get in school, back in Georgia?"

"I made it to the sixth grade, but I like to read a lot. There's not much that I figure one can't learn from a book."

"Well, at least you had a little bit of education that you could pass on to your daughter."

I had to catch myself. I had to catch myself from leaving that chair and running my hand across the face of the Missus. The only thing that held me back was remembering that this was...my day.

"Did your daughter finish school?"

"Yes, ma'am, she did. Graduated from high school and wanted to go to college."

"I see. I heard that colored folks are being allowed to go to college with white children. My husband doesn't have a problem with it—he's always been like that—but I'm from Virginia. Where's your daughter now? Is she working for anyone I know? If not, I can refer her to a few people in this neighborhood."

I grasp my hands together and try to fight the pain and anger that's boiling inside. "No, she ain't." I take a deep breath. "She isn't working for anyone. She died a while back."

"Oh, I see." The Missus leans back into the soft white velvet sofa. "I never could have children of my own. That's why..." She looks toward the door again, but this time I don't get my hopes up. "That's why we adopted."

I sit there staring at the woman who doesn't know what she's had living under her roof these last eight years—my redemption.

Silence enters the room. I welcome it as I try to control my emotions 'cause I feel like they got a hold of me and ain't about to let go any time soon.

"Well, I guess I should tell you about Timmy," she says, after a few more minutes go by and neither of us is talking.

"Your son?" I need to hear her say it. I need her to claim the precious gift she's had for eight years as her son. Although I know, she ain't seeing him like that.

I can tell.

Actions don't lie, and today her actions are telling me what's in her twisted heart.

She looks at the floor like she done dropped something, but I know she's just trying to hide the slight aroma of annoyance that's brewing in the air, from both of us.

"Is Timmy here?" I finally ask, after realizing that my need for her to acknowledge him as her son ain't gonna be met.

A relieved look floods her face. "No, he's away at school. He's been going to a private school, but now my husband feels it's time for him to come home and be here with us. In our home."

"I reckon that's a good thing. I'm sure he'd like being here…in his own home."

She moves toward the edge of the white velvet sofa as if she and I are about to be best friends and swap secrets or something. "Mildred, if you're going to be Timmy's nanny, I think it's best that I tell you—"

"You can call me Millie."

"That's right. Millie. Well, Millie, when my husband and I adopted Timmy, we didn't have all the facts about where he came from."

"He's from outer space or something?"

She smirks, but she knows I wasn't saying it to be funny. "Of course not, but I think it's important for you to know the truth about him. You see, while Timmy looks like Mr. Taylor and me—meaning, that his skin looks like ours, he's not…"

"You're saying that he looks white, but he isn't?"

She takes a long deep breath as though it's just too painful for her to talk about. "That's correct. We found out about a year or two after we adopted him that his real mother was some colored girl. We were given that little bit of information because when Timmy got sick, my husband and I inquired about his medical history. Of course, that horrible adoption agency didn't disclose the full truth about Timmy to us in the beginning. In fact, I doubt that they ever intended to tell us. I, of course, wanted to send him back."

"He ain't a package."

She sneers at me. "I, of course, wanted to send him back to the adoption agency, but my husband wouldn't allow it, for whatever reason."

"So does he know that he isn't a Wonderful—I mean, does he know that he isn't white?"

She leans back on the sofa and wraps her hands around her pearls. "No, he doesn't." She glances at the chandelier before cutting her eyes toward me. "A Wonderful. That's an interesting term to call white people. Do all colored folks call white people that?"

"I don't reckon anyone says it but me."

"I see. So what do you call your people, you know, a colored person?"

I fold my hands like she's done so many times during our conversation, and I try not to smile too much so that when I say what I'm about to say, it don't come off too smart-mouth-like. "I call them as I see some of them, I reckon—Beautiful."

I watch her body language as I grab hold of my purse, 'cause I know Miss Thing is about to throw my colored behind out of her fancy house. But she doesn't. She laughs.

It's a loud and eerie kind of laugh. One that scares me 'cause I can't tell if it's a warning to me or not. So I try to think of something to say to get her to stop, 'cause I know that if I don't, her wicked laugh is gonna be stuck in my head for the rest of the day.

"Well, I reckon we all got our secrets, ma'am. It's probably best that Timmy doesn't know. For now, at least."

"It's a lie!" she says, jumping clear out of her chair.

I reach for my purse again.

She makes her way over to the fireplace and grabs hold of the ledge like she needs it to balance herself. As I watch her fighting to regain her composure, it hits me that there aren't any pictures on the fireplace mantel. Now, I've been in plenty of Wonderfuls' homes with people who didn't like each other, but they still had some pictures of their fake smiles sitting on their mantels.

"I think he should know. He should know that he isn't a...a Wonderful, but he doesn't know anything. He doesn't even know that he's adopted," she says as she starts pacing the floor.

She stops and stares at me. Her crooked smile confirms what I'm thinking—she's either up to her elbows crazy, or she's been drinking. Either way, it's clear that I need to keep my grandchild out of her reach.

She walks back over to the sofa, takes a seat slowly and crosses her legs. "You should know that this family has many secrets. You might say that we sleep on beds filled with them, if you understand what I mean."

"I do."

"Good, because anything you hear or see in this house must never leave this house. Do you understand?"

"So you're saying I got the job, ma'am?"

She hesitates for a second or two. "Yes, that's correct, but are we clear on what I just said?"

"Yes, ma'am. I reckon we're clear."

"Perfect." She claps her long fingers together as she uncrosses her legs. "Now, Timmy will be here next Monday. I expect you to be here first thing Sunday morning so you can get settled in before he arrives.

"Now, when you get here, be sure to come to the kitchen door. You are never to use the front door. Not ever.

"Our housekeeper's name is Margaret. She's the one that let you in earlier. She'll also be the one to help you get settled. She doesn't talk much, but she's good at what she does. However, I guess she would be, seeing that she doesn't know how to do anything other than clean."

I clench my lips together, real tight-like and smile as she stands up again and begins making her way towards the door.

"I expect you to handle Timmy like he belongs to you. He will be your total responsibility, Mildred. I don't want to see or hear him. Ever. Do you understand?"

"Yes, ma'am. I understand completely. It's Millie."

She cuts her eyes at me again as I watch her stroll her thin-framed body out of the room with her nose up in the air and her pearls dangling.

As I make my way out the back kitchen door, I can feel my blood boiling still, but I ain't gonna let it take away from the fact that today...is my day.

Chapter Two

*M*orning comes in like it has business to take care of. It seemed as if my eyes had barely closed when I felt the heat of the morning sun shining on them. No breeze. I can tell 'cause my windows are open and ain't no wind hitting my skin. I sit up on my bed and stare at the faded blue walls. No wonder I always wake up feeling like the blues done got me.

It's about five in the morning, I reckon. I hear the floors creaking out in the hallway, which tells me folks are moving about. I reckon I ought to get up and move about myself. Jean's gonna come knocking on my door in another hour or so, and I like to have the coffee perking and the toast ready just before then.

The two of us have been eating Saturday breakfast together since we met. It's hard for me to accept that today will be our last one.

Jean's got the apartment on the very top floor. She calls it her penthouse. I laugh every time she says it, 'cause in her mind, that's as close as she's ever gonna get to having one. Her apartment is also the biggest one in the building, so I reckon she may have a bit of truth in her words, but I'll never admit that to her. She already thinks she's got more than most colored folks around here.

Jean is always pointing out to me that she ain't never had to clean or cook for nobody but herself. She comes from a long line of seamstresses. She can make a dress sing and pair of pants walk like some old country funk.

I try to tell her that everybody got a gift. She keeps asking me what mine is, but I ain't telling her. I let her think that her hands be the only ones that can make something beautiful.

My gift, they say, is the piano. But I ain't played in too many years to count. My Addie loved to hear me play when she was just a young thing. She'd sit for hours with her ears glued to the music I'd send to her heart. It was our unique way of making a connection.

I stare at my fingers. Nothing but wrinkles and stiffness ruling them now.

My thoughts travel back to Jean as I stare at the little brown chair in the corner of my bedroom. She's been eyeing that chair since she and I became friends. I'm going to give it to her, but I'm not sure how she can fit anything else in that apartment of hers.

Jean's apartment got bright yellow paint and mauve carpet. She done put plants just about everywhere. They're growing from the ceiling to the floor. You don't find many women waving at fifty years old that into plants.

Jean also done put up yellow-and-pink wallpaper in her little kitchen. I don't go up there much 'cause all that brightness she got going on in that apartment hurts my eyes.

She got two bedrooms. One for her and one for her sewing room. Her sewing room looks like someone done set off a bomb in there. If she weren't such a mean cook, I'd think twice about eating her food.

My one-bedroom apartment barely has a bath and a kitchen. Most of it is nearly empty now. Boxes sit in the center of it, waiting for me to finish putting the last of my stuff in them. I ain't got much furniture. Never needed much. Jean's gonna take my sofa and that old brown leather chair that I love to sit and read my books on.

I got a small square metal table and two red-and-white vinyl chairs in the kitchen that my neighbor, two doors down, gonna come and get. She got five small children. Her oldest ain't no more than six. Her husband done run off after the fifth child was born, 'cause he couldn't take the responsibility of raising his own, anymore.

Most folks in the building call her Mae, but her birth name is Charlotte Mae Summers.

Every night, right after supper, I go down to her apartment and teach her children how to read and write. I enjoy them. The noise they make keeps the evening silence from consuming me.

I saw an old picture of Mae one night when I was in her apartment. Her hair was about as long as mine. She was thin. Not as thin as me, but close, I reckon. Not like now. Mae is a big woman now. She just about done cut off all her hair and wears a wig most days. In the picture, Mae had her hands wrapped around the waist of her husband. Her smile was the smile of a woman in love with a man who isn't.

That be the real reason he left, I believe.

Mae started drowning herself in food and her children, the moment he walked out the door. When her feet hit Chicago by way of South Carolina, she was almost three hundred pounds. She thinks he took with him anything that might have been special about her. I always have to remind her that I ain't gonna listen to such foolishness, but truth be told, my lips done spoke a similar kind of silliness. Mae and I are twins in that way, I guess.

She says she's damaged.

I tell her that we all are. I ain't no different, in that regard, I reckon.

Addie's bed is still a few feet from mine. I said today I wasn't gonna run my fingers over the pillow that my dear sweet child once rested her head on.

The night before we left for the hospital, she complained about that bed. She complained about this apartment. About this here neighborhood. But the second the doctor came in and told her that she wasn't going to see any of it again, her only complaint was that she wouldn't be able to listen to the snores of her mama again.

My feet finally move, and I find myself walking over to her bed. I pick up her pillow and hold it close to my face. I know my tears are searching for a fresh spot to rest on. After eight years, they're having a mighty hard time finding one.

I said I wasn't gonna cry today.

But that was a lie. I knew it the moment I allowed my fifty-seven-year-old lips to whisper that foolishness.

I said I wasn't gonna allow the sadness to grab my bones and hold on, but it seems the sadness has me wrapped around its little fingers.

Holding on for dear life.

In fact, I was still in that state when I heard Jean knocking on my door, and that's when I remembered I hadn't started the coffee or the toast yet.

Chapter Three

"*G*irl, it's so hot out there, I think my lipstick just about melted off!"

"You already been outside this morning, Jean?"

"I went out for a few minutes to get my walk in. That sun is fierce. I swear this June weather is going to be the death of me."

Jean follows me to the kitchen with a basket in her right hand. Her shoulder-length hair is pulled back in a ponytail. She has on shorts and a light shirt, so I know that all the male folks in our small neighborhood had their eyes glued to their windows this morning.

The old and the young ones.

"I saw Mae and the children getting on the bus just now," Jean says as she takes a seat. "Mae's skirt was clinging to every inch of her, and you know her wig was crooked. Always is. Mae looked like she was going to bust out of that white blouse. She really ought to try losing a few pounds, or at least let me make her some clothes that fit. Come to think of it; they don't make many clothes for people Mae's size."

"Maybe you ought to make some and sell them," I say as I put the coffee on.

"It's a thought. I could open a small clothing store and have a nice section for women that are bigger than you and me."

"You could, or you could just open a store for bigger women. That way they'd feel more comfortable, rather than feeling like they got to compete with the smaller women who come in, staring at them with their noses up in the air."

I see a small crease form across Jean's forehead. "My nose is never up in the air just because a woman is bigger than I am, Millie. You know that isn't the case. I just think a woman should wear clothes that fit her body. That's all. Mae always looks a mess. A hot mess at that. I guess that's the seamstress in me talking."

"Maybe," I say as I turn the flames up on the coffee so it can get about its business of getting good and hot for us, "but we all can't make our own clothes."

"True." Jean pulls a few napkins out from my napkin holder, and places them on the table, as I lean against the counter, waiting for the coffee to start boiling. "Anyway," she continues, "Mae told me to tell you goodbye, just in case she doesn't get a chance to stop by tomorrow. I know those children of hers is going to really miss you. "

I sigh and nod my head in agreement. "I reckon I'll miss them as well. I'm sure Mae is on her way to work. Shame she got to work every Saturday. At least she can take the children with her on the weekends. In my eyes, Mae is a hardworking woman. I don't know why you ain't seeing her like that. Why don't you like Mae?"

I watch Jean knowing that she's allowing my question to roll around in the air for a moment before she responds. "It's not that I don't like Mae," she finally says, "I just don't like to see women who allow a man to bring them down so much that they forget who they are."

"We all deal with the tragedies of life in different ways," I say.

Jean leans forward in her chair a little and rests her hands on the table. "If a man leaves you because he doesn't want to raise the children he helped make, I say it's his tragedy, not yours."

I placed my hands on my hips. "You gotta admit, Jean, that it's the woman that's always left with the children. She's the one who got to deal with finding a way to raise them. Look at Mae. She's the one who got to raise them, children. Her husband done run off and made himself a life out there—probably with someone else, I reckon—like he ain't never made them babies with her in the first place. It's a downright shame. You can't blame her for being down, letting herself go some. You just can't."

"Maybe," she says as we hear the coffee starting to percolate. "But just remember that a woman always knows when a man isn't staying."

I let my hands drop to my side. "How you figure that? I don't reckon it's written on his forehead."

"Relax, Millie. All I'm saying is that a woman knows when his heart is already out the door. His actions tell it, even if his words don't. You and I both know she only kept having them babies in hopes of keeping that no-good man around. That baby-making game never works. I've seen many women try that to keep a man, and they all end up like Mae." She pauses for a second and smiles at me. "But you're right; it really is a shame because, in the end, no one wins. Especially the children. I think they suffer the most."

I return the smile 'cause there ain't no hurt feelings between us and I'm just glad that the conversation about Mae ended where we both stood on common ground. "Well, I reckon it's like my mama use to say—if you got to lay down in wrinkled sheets, just remember who did the wrinkling."

Jean laughs and relaxes back into her seat. "Girl, I'm sure going to miss your southern way of talking."

I join her in the lightheartedness of our conversation. "Child, you and I both know it's like the North versus the South every time the two of us get together."

"Not when it comes to my cooking! You know I always let my frying pan do what it needs to," Jean says as she touches the top of her basket.

"Well, you ain't never lied about that. What you got in that basket? It smells good!"

A sly smile comes across Jean's face, and I get excited because that can only mean that Jean got my favorites in her basket. "Nothing much," she says as she slowly opens the top of the basket and begins pulling out some of its contents. "Just a few made-from-scratch, fluffy biscuits, a jar of my homemade gravy, and some strawberry jam that I made the other day for you."

I clap my hands together like a child getting the best present their parents can afford. "Child, let me get the coffee so we can eat!"

We both chuckle as she pulls out the rest of the food while looking around.

"Most of my stuff is packed and ready to go. I still got a few more things, but I'm almost there," I say as I follow her gaze.

"I thought you'd have more boxes than that."

"No, ma'am. I only got a few." I place the small metal coffee percolator that I got from a lady I cleaned for back in Georgia on a towel in the middle of the table.

"You know, things aren't going to be the same without you," Jean says as she smothers some of her homemade strawberry jam on her biscuit. "But I'm glad you got a good and steady job. At least you don't have to cook or clean for anyone."

I place two biscuits on my plate and cut each one down the center so they can lay flat on my plate. "It's like I done told you before. Cooking and cleaning put a roof over my and Addie's head. Just like your frying pan does what it needs to do for you, cooking and cleaning did what it needed to do for Addie and me."

Jean chuckles and nods her head in agreement, but I can see the tears in her eyes as I pour a good amount of gravy over my two biscuits.

"I miss her, Millie. She was such a sweet young girl."

I use my fork to move my biscuits around in the gravy 'cause my heart needs a moment to move from the thought of Addie. "This gravy looks better than the one you made a couple of weeks ago," I say as I finally glance at Jean and see her dabbing the corners of her eyes with one of the napkins. I place my fork down and slap my hands gently on top of the table. "Child, don't you go doing all that crying on me this morning. I already done did enough of that before you came this morning, trying to make me fat with all this good food."

She sniffs a few times and reaches for another napkin. We both let a few seconds of silence sit on the table. "So, what are you going to do about Addie's bed?" Jean finally asks.

I reach over and touch the top of her hand before picking my fork back up. She smiles. "Well," I say, looking in the direction of the bedroom. "I reckon I can't take it with me, so it and my bed will stay here. I reckon whoever rents this place next can use them. I'm just gonna take the pillow Addie always slept on."

Jean places a scoop of jelly on her plate. "I have a client that could use them. I'll tell her to come by and pick them up after you leave tomorrow if that's alright with you?"

I put a little sugar in my coffee and take a sip. "That'll be alright, I reckon. Glad someone will get some use out of them. Them beds weren't expensive, but they weren't free either. "

Jean nods in agreement, and we both just sit and drink our coffee. My windows are open so we can hear the birds outside. They seem to be singing a sad song this morning. Like they know what we know about this day.

"Millie."

I look over at Jean and see this rather severe look on her face. That's when I know the question that she's been waiting to ask me for eight years is about to slip off her lips.

She says slowly, "I know it isn't any of my business, but I've wanted to ask you something. Of course, you can always just tell me to mind my own business."

I set my coffee cup on the table and brace myself for the journey into the past I know I'm about to take. My history has been buried deep for so long that I'm not sure if I can get my shovel out and tell her some of it.

"Go ahead. Ask the question you been waiting eight years to ask," I say.

Jean jumps into the hole of my past; I feel like I'm standing six feet in. "Where is Addie's father?"

I adjust myself in my seat, pour myself another cup of coffee and let her question roll around the table for a few minutes as I search for the strength to answer it.

"He left me," I say, allowing the words to roll firmly off my tongue.

Jean lowers her eyes for a second. "Well, love ain't for everyone." She grabs the gravy and another biscuit. "Girl, look at me. I have never been proposed to. Not that I'm bitter about it."

I'm shocked to hear that from Jean. She's a looker, as the young folks say nowadays. She keeps herself up—unlike her apartment, mind you. I ain't never seen no woman wear lipstick just to go to the store or for a walk, but Jean does. I reckon she figures it ain't proper not to.

"I used to think that love was for everyone," I say.

"We all have a fairy tale we want to believe in, Mille. Even grown women like us, I guess."

I take a moment to allow Jean's words to settle in my mind, 'cause there's some real truth to them. "You're right, I reckon." Jean looks up from her plate, surprised that I agreed with her so matter-of-factly. I lean back into my seat some. Jean does too, as she waits for me to continue.

"I remember a time when I used to think that love was like the softness of the wind when it wraps its arms around you and rocks your heart gently. The way it holds you. Makes you feel secure.

"When you're young and dumb, it never dawns on you that the wind can turn into something ugly. Something forceful. That it can hurl your colored behind clear across the road and take away all the love you have inside.

"I would have never thought life could be that way until the day came when it was my love being carried away. I was mighty grateful that it didn't get it all.

"That it left some for what was growing inside me."

"You're talking about Addie?" Jean asks as she moves her plate from in front of her. I nod my head slowly 'cause the tears are building up inside me again. Jean reaches across the table, and I give her my hand. "I'm sure losing her still hurts, Millie. That kind of pain is deep. One of the deepest kinds of pain a mother can feel, they say."

I remove my hand and reach for a napkin. As I dab my eyes some, I look at the wall behind Jean, as a face comes into my thoughts. "There's another pain that comes pretty darn close though," I say slowly 'cause the face in my thoughts ain't leaving. "However, I ain't spoke of that pain in almost thirty years or so."

"What kind of pain was that?"

"For a short time, I called it—my husband."

Chapter Four

"*W*e met on a day when soft blankets of snow had covered the Georgia roads with a gentle kiss, and the sun was slowly drifting off to sleep.

"January 12, 1930, to be exact.

"I stood on the corner of a street, by the railroad tracks, waiting for the bus to come. I was mighty tired that day from cleaning the silver at the home of Mr. and Mrs. Matthews. They lived nearly forty minutes away from the small two-bedroom house in Winder that I shared with my mama.

"I was twenty-nine years old then.

"I was a young woman full of nothing but the longings of freedom from the hand that life had done dished out to me. Mama had made me come out of school when I hit the sixth grade and go to work cleaning homes because Papa couldn't hold down a job the same way he could hold down his liquor.

"It was the liquor that took him from Mama and me. By then, Mama was just waiting for her turn, 'cause she couldn't take breathing in a world where the stink of Papa didn't exist.

"As I stood there waiting for the bus, I remember feeling like I was waiting for life to give me something to run away to. Truth be told, I had been looking under rocks for it. Fishing down the deep Winder rivers for it. But it always felt like my soul came up empty.

"That seemed to change, the day I saw a pair of eyes that I wanted to be looking back into mine, forever.

"Bailey was his name. Bailey Boy Johnson.

"That's what everyone called him. He moved to Winder a couple of months before the snow had done settled in. He was the first person in

Winder to come all the way from Los Angeles, California. I remember the moment his feet hit the Georgia gravel, although I didn't see it. I had done heard about him...and his mama.

"His mama was a kind woman, but she didn't have a husband. She stood around five feet, five inches in height. I reckon you could say she was a well-toned, aesthetically-pleasing white woman with ear-length, wavy blond hair and the greenest eyes I'd had done ever seen on a Wonderful.

"She also was the only Wonderful I'd ever seen live on the colored side of the railroad tracks.

"You can best believe, most of the Wonderfuls in Winder didn't take too kindly to that.

"My mama told me that she did it for her boy, so he'd understand where he came from and learn to love the skin he was in.

"Love the skin you're in. Those words have always stuck with me. I carried them in the pockets of my thoughts and used to remind Addie of them, every chance I got.

"But I ain't gonna lie. Back then, living in Winder was gonna be hard for them, no matter which side of the railroad tracks they closed their eyes at night on. Ain't much changed over the years, in that regard, if you ask me."

Jean nods in agreement as she gets up to place the coffee pot back on the stove. She opens up one of my cabinets but then remembers that everything is packed, so I point to the one container I got on the counter that I left out, 'cause it got the coffee in it. Jean places some of the coffee in the pot and then adds the water. After turning up the flame, she retakes her seat and looks at me to continue the story.

I glance again at the wall behind her, and I can still see his face. Bailey's face, staring back at me. I let out a soft sigh. "Bailey was the one who put the food on their table. In truth, he was the one to do everything. His mama didn't know how to do nothing but sit on their porch, even in the dead of winter, and look pretty, as some folks around town said.

"It was rumored that her health and mind was leaving her and real fast-like. Her name was Betty. Betty Johnson.

"People liked to gossip about her. Talk that I reckon had some truth in it. Folks said that she came from famous parents, but they had done cut her off when she got pregnant by a colored man. Mama said that she'd seen

Betty one time, dancing on their front porch with a tutu on. Mama said it was so beautiful that she sat under a tree and watched for ten minutes or so. It would have been longer, but Mama said that the cold had gotten into her toes and forced her to leave.

"I reckon that's how Bailey got the love of dance in him. It was as if it was attached to his kidneys.

"Bailey had slightly broad shoulders and strong hands that could easily wrap themselves around you. He had my papa's height, which in my mind meant he could look down into my soul and tell me all sorts of good things about life and peaches and ice cream. The kind of things that every woman dreams of hearing from a man. The things that smell good, but frankly, ain't good for you."

Jean chuckles some and glances over at the coffee pot to make sure she done turned the flame up high enough.

I wait for a second or two before continuing. "Most of the colored men in Winder didn't like him, 'cause of his skin and the fact that he was able to get a job at the plant down by the courthouse that didn't involve picking up dirty trash and a mop. He wasn't a cotton-picking man either.

"My mama told me he was a hoofer. That's what they called tap dancers back then. In fact, the day we met, he had just picked up a pair of tap shoes that had been delivered to the wrong post office, that also served as the general store for that area. The shoes were dangling by their laces, across his left shoulder. I could see the metallic taps on the foot and the heel of the wooden soles. I imagined myself playing the piano and Bailey tap dancing his way into my heart. Like I said before, I was young, dumb, and I guess eager to find myself a savior.

"I needed somebody who was gonna make my thirties look and feel better than my previous life had ever been.

"I remember the moment my eyes followed the tips of his shoes to the wave of his black hair. That day was the end of my work week, a Friday. Folks were busy around me, trying to get home, I reckon, but I didn't take any notice of them. I only saw the light.

"Bailey came walking up toward me. He was like a tall bright light full of handsomeness, and I figured the sun had just been jealous.

"Girls around town, be them colored or not, would say that he had a swagger that was as smooth as butter, and so when he stood next to me at the bus stop, I was praying that the bus would take its time.

"He smelled good. Like good, sturdy leather. I tell you, my heart ain't never beat so fast in my life. I was a plum mess, but I was determined to make something out of that moment. Scared that I'd never get it again. On that crisp winter day, it was the closest he and I had done ever shared a space.

"When the bus did finally make its way down the dirt road he and I were standing on, he sat down next to me, once we got on. My hands were trembling 'cause I was sitting there trying to find a way to open my mouth. Utter a word that would lead to him getting down on one knee.

"I remember trying to say something about his newly purchased tap shoes, as they sat in his lap like a prized possession, but he didn't hear anything I said 'cause every word I tried to utter sounded like I was trying to whisper in his ear.

"In truth, Bailey was the one who finally said something that we both could hear.

"'As soon as I get the money, I'm gonna make my way up to the Hoofers Club in Harlem. You ever heard of the Hoofers Club?' he asked me as the bus passed a few streets on the way back to our side of town.

"'No, I ain't familiar with a lot of places in New York. But I've heard plenty about Harlem. A place where colored folks sing, dance, paint, and even own their own homes,' I finally managed to say in a tone that sounded like a grown woman was talking. I was so proud that I knew something of the place that had his eyes lit up like firecrackers in the sky on a bright blue night.

"He started laughing at me.

"'You make it sound like colored folks are just living the life up there in New York. I'm sure they got it just as hard there as colored folks got it hard here. Even with all that singing, dancing and painting, you're talking about,'" he said.

"His words and tone hurt my feelings 'cause it was like he was trying to make me feel like I didn't know nothing, but I knew that wasn't true, so I said to him, "'You don't know if colored folks have it hard in New York, you ain't ever been there, yourself. From what I done heard about you, you don't know much about colored folks either, which is why you and your mama moved here. Here, you can't pass as nothing but colored.'" Bailey laughed even harder at those words, and it made me smile, instead of getting all caught up even more so in my feelings.

"'Wow, I like the way you came back at me. There was some real southern flair in those words. But despite the rumors, my mother and I moved here because it was hard for a grown man, like myself, to find work in California. I barely finished school, and the only real skill I have is sitting in my lap,' he said to me as he looked down at his tap shoes.

"'What's the Hoofer's Club?' I asked to change the subject, and when I saw his face light up again, I knew that he and I had done found our way back on the road that I hoped would lead to forever.

"'It's a place I'm going to get to one day. A place I've been dreaming about since I was a boy and first heard the sound of a tap shoe. The Hoofers Club is really just a small room in the back of a comedy club, but for those who are serious about their craft, their skill—it's more like a club for tap dancers. The Hoofers Club is located on what they call 'Swing Street.' People like Bill Robinson, Warren Berry, and even Dewey Washington go there to show off their steps, challenge other dancers, and to teach young cats like me. You ever heard of any of them?'"

"I shook my head like the little girl his dreams had me feeling like.

"'Then you don't know nothing about tap.'

"'I know the piano,' I snapped back at him. 'I can play jazz. Ain't that what you tap too?'"

"I remember the look he gave me. I couldn't tell if I had uttered something impressive or something that he felt didn't live up to the kind of woman that he could be with.

"When my stop was near, I stood up but he reached out, and he grabbed my hand. It made me nervous. I could feel his skin on mine. It was warm. He examined my fingers, like he could tell if I had done told a lie or not just by looking at them.

"'You have long and lean fingers. Good hands for the piano,' he said as I pulled my hand away.

"'When are you going to play for me?'"

"Jean, I swear his touch, his eyes, his everything...had me blushing and acting like a schoolgirl waiting for her first kiss.

"'I'm at the community center on Saturdays sometimes, after I help Mama with the laundry,'" I said to him.

"He stood up and grabbed the rail above our heads to brace himself. "'So, are you going to be there tomorrow?'"

"I nodded.

"'What time will you be there?' he asked.

"'I reckon I'll be there around seven.'

"'Perfect. I'll meet you there.'"

"He walked me to the bus door, and I had to force myself not to look up at him as the bus drove by me. Child, I tell you, he had my heart fluttering and my knees wobbling. I thought I was gonna trip over both as I made my way down the street that day."

Chapter Five

*J*ean gets up to take the coffee pot that I done forgot about off the burner. I was sure the coffee was too strong for either of us to drink, but Jean moves the pot to the center of the table anyway. "I know how it sounds," I say as I stare at the coffee pot for a second or two.

"You do?" she asks as she pours some of the rather dark coffee into her cup.

"It sounds like I was chasing him, especially after the way he had spoken to me."

Jean takes a sip of her coffee and then gets up and adds some water to it. "You know I'm not the one to judge," she says as she sits the cup back on the table and retakes her seat.

I give her the side-eye.

"Okay, maybe a little." We both chuckle. "But like you said, Millie, you needed a savior. Aren't you the one always saying that everyone needs saving from something?"

I pour myself some coffee and take a sip. Surprised that it ain't as strong as I thought it would be, but I get up and add some water to it anyway. "You ain't never lied, but needing saving wasn't the only reason I wanted him, I reckon. There was just something about him, Jean. Something mighty special that seemed to be lurking behind his eyes. That day, on that bus, I felt like I was the only one that could see it."

Jean leans back in her chair and crosses her legs. "So, what happened that Saturday? Did he come to the community center?"

I look off toward the door, and I can see the community center again. I can see myself standing in front of it that day, anxious and eager to impress. "He and his tap shoes showed up right around seven."

Jean uncrosses her legs and grabs her coffee cup.

I sigh. "I wish you could have been there, Jean. That day was something..."

"Special?" Jean says, completing my sentence with a sly smile.

"I know you're messing with me, but I tell you, my heart ain't never looked at a man in that way again. Never, I tell you."

"So, what happened? What made that night so...so special?"

I laugh at her. "It ain't like what you're thinking."

Jean takes a few sips of her coffee. "Trust me, Millie, I'm not thinking that way about you at all. I've come to know you pretty well in the last eight years. I don't think a person could be as 'pure' as you are." She throws her hands into the air and moves her fingers, to put emphasis on the word pure.

I laugh again, but then I take a deep breath because now I got to tell her what happened that night.

That night that had me trying to determine what my wedding dress would look like.

Chapter Six

"*I*'d say it was a poetic exchange between piano keys and shoes. A rhythmic movement that had done worked its way from his legs and moved down my fingers. Child, the walls of that community center ain't never heard such masterful combinations as the one they witnessed that night.

"It was a testament to a real southern girl and her West Coast love.

"Bailey stood in the center of the small stage that center had. The piano was tucked in the corner. I remember the first note I struck and how he responded with the tap of his heel. With every note I sent into the air, a series of flat-footed stomps from his shoes sent them back to me.

"He danced with his eyes closed until the music I played began to flow like a sweet melody of country flair mixed with jazz and a few keys of blues that my papa had done taught me.

"His smooth toe-tapping made the floor vibrate.

"When the last note was struck, I saw them. The tears that had done come down the sides of his face. Bailey wasn't dancing to win my heart. He was dancing to win his own, I reckon. Every step he took was like he was telling himself that he was good. That he deserved to be in that world. The world of tap.

"When we were done, he came and sat down beside me.

"'Everyone said you could play that thing. They said you could make a grown man cry. I guess that was true tonight,' he said as he leaned over and rested his hands on the top of the piano.

"'Where did you learn to play like that?' he asked as I sat there trying to stop floating on the clouds.

"'My mama played the piano and so did my papa. Although, my papa played it better. Real smooth like. They always fought about who gave the gift to me. I reckon I'm just grateful to have it.'

"'You ought to do something with it.'

"'I ain't looking to do something on a professional level if that's what you mean,' I said.

"'Why not?'" he asked.

"I shrugged my shoulders. "'I don't know. I guess it just ain't ever interested me. Plus, I don't think I could stand all those folks staring at me.'

"'You didn't seem to mind me staring.' He placed his hands on mine.

"I could feel the warmth of his hands traveling up from my toes to the center of my heart. "'That's because I knew you were just watching for my cues,' I said.

"'No, I was watching you. I've been watching you since I came to Winder.' He moved closer to me, and I saw the sweat dripping off the corners of his eyebrows, but I didn't mind.

"'You were pretty good too. I ain't never seen someone tap like that before,' I said as I moved my body closer to him.

"'It'd be a new kind of tap. It's call rhythm tap." His hand glided slowly along my cheek. "I can feel you trembling. You aren't afraid of me, are you, Mildred?"

"'I ain't afraid of you. But you can call me Millie if you want.'

"'Good, because I'm going to kiss you. Is that all right?'"

"I felt his hand slip around my neck as he drew my lips closer to his. Child, I didn't know if I should've kept my eyes open or closed. It didn't much matter really, 'cause the moment his lips touched mine, I had done handed him my heart and was praying that he never returned it.

"Two months later, he and I were married."

Chapter Seven

"It was downright hard leaving Mama. Becoming a wife. For twenty-nine years, I'd seen Mama's face every morning. After Bailey and I were married, I traded in Mama's morning routine for Betty's.

"I still can remember Betty's smile the day we told her that I was expecting. Prior to that, I had done figured she didn't much like me. Most days, she just sat in a corner and stared at me or sat on the front porch and stared at people as they walked by. It was like she was listening to something, but at the time, I couldn't figure out what she was listening to. Truth be told, every time I looked into her eyes, I thought I was looking at someone that had done gone crazy.

"To me, nobody could understand Betty except Bailey. He spoke to her through his tap dancing. As soon as he put on those shoes and she heard the sound of his front heel hit the wooden floor of our little kitchen, her face would light up, and she'd close her eyes and just listen to the sounds that his shoes made. If he made a mistake, she'd know it. She would point toward the floor, and he'd stop and do the step over again.

"Every night they'd do this. Every night they'd talk.

"But the moment she learned that I was carrying her son's child, she became the kind of woman who stroked my hair every day and rubbed my belly as it grew. In a way, I guess, my having a child gave her life meaning.

"The idea of life coming into the world brought her back to the world where she would dance every day, just about. It was just as Mama had described. Graceful. Pure. I tell you, watching that woman move across the floor of our small home was like watching a swan dance on the crystal waters of Winder. Those days were some of the happiest days of my life. Bailey was the type of husband that had you believing in fairy tales. Child, I was so in love with him. But that changed the day Betty died.

"It happened in late November. I was just going into my eighth month.

"It seems that Betty wasn't crazy. She knew that she had something the doctors couldn't cure. A rare form of a brain disease.

"Doctors told us that she couldn't see nothing but darkness. I reckon that's why she always looked like she was staring. She was just fighting to remember the light. To retain the sunshine. That was the reason she was always on the porch, even when the sun was barely out.

"Remember I told you that it was rumored that she come from famous parents? Well, they were not only renowned but rich as well, and when they caught wind of their only daughter's death, they come riding into Winder on their California bound chariot.

"Bailey fought to have the funeral in Winder, but for them, money solves all problems, and so they gave him their solution, and he took it.

"The second that money hit Bailey's hand, I learned something about the man I had married. It was something fearful.

"See, I knew down to the core of my soul what he was gonna use that money for. That fear stared me in the face for a month after his mama's funeral. The one that Bailey wasn't even allowed to attend.

"I was coming home from the grocery store when I slipped trying to get the groceries in the house. The fall caused Addie to come a few weeks early. Bailey blamed me, but by that time, Bailey blamed me for everything. He blamed me for breathing. For living. For being his wife. But most of all, he blamed me for bringing something into the world that he felt would hold him back from giving me back my heart.

"The day I brought Addie home was the day that he left me. He left a note saying that he was gonna be gone for a short time and that now that he had the money, he was gonna go to New York and dance at the Hoofers Club in Harlem.

"He swore he'd come back. I knew it was a lie the moment my heart read it."

Chapter Eight

"Nothing had prepared me for the pain that came afterward. Late in the night when the dogs outside were howling. When the moon looked down at me with pity. I'd sit there like a fool, holding the heart that he had done given back to me. Every bone in my soul ached. Every tear I had shed tore at me. Ripped apart my insides and left me dry.

"Left me bitter.

"Left me full of hate.

"You see, I was right back there. Back in the life, I had before he was a part of it. Before I had done ever heard the tap of his shoes. I was back in the filth of it all.

"Alone.

"My mama had to come with her cane and all. It was mighty sad actually. The woman I had wanted to run away from all my life became my savior.

"To my shame, I had grown a hatred for my own child. I couldn't stand to look into her eyes and see Bailey's staring back at me. I couldn't stand to hold her 'cause it felt too much like the way he would hold me. It wasn't anything like the strength of having his arms wrapped around me real tight-like. His arms always felt like they were securing me from the world.

"I'll admit it, Jean. I'll admit that I had done become the woman you despise the most. In fact, I reckon that I had become the kind of woman who let a man tear her down to the point that she thought she wasn't worthy of walking the good ground without him. Not worthy of breathing the air that he used to share with her.

"I got so low one day that I had given the idea too much thought. My mama had to fish my naked behind out of the bathtub. She had to dry off the tears and wipe the blood that put me to shame from my arms.

"She slapped me. It was a good slap if there really is such a thing. But it was one that I needed. That slap allowed me to finally take a breath on my own. A breath of life that didn't involve him.

"She put Addie in my arms and forced me to look at her. She pushed me to see my child for who she really was. A part of me. A part of me and every woman that had done come before me. Women who had done loved. Women who had done cried. Women who had done dealt with no-good men and still went on.

"She reminded me that I ain't the only one. She forced me to see what I had. A daughter who didn't need a world without her mama in it.

"It wasn't easy to come back from that dark place.

"When Mama closed her eyes about a year after that, the struggle had become almost unbearable. How does one find the kind of strength that a child can take something from when they look into your eyes?"

When I finished speaking, in came the silence. It was the first time it had come in and sat with Jean and me for such an extended period of time. It was as if it had done come with a suitcase and was prepared to stay a while.

"Millie," Jean finally said, "you're talking about the Bailey Boy Johnson? The same Bailey Boy Johnson who died from sudden heart failure back in 1940 after performing with what they called a 'swing band' at the Harlem Savoy Ballroom? I remember the papers spoke about him. They called him a true hoofer, a tap legend in the making who didn't get a chance to show the world what his shoes could really do. You telling me that you were married to him?"

"I was."

"Did you ever hear from him after he left to go to New York?"

It was my turn to lean back in my chair. To sip on my cold coffee and stare at the ceiling 'cause I was trying to hide the pain that his name had done stirred back up inside me. "When Addie was about five, my heart stood face-to-face with him once more. A lack of sensibleness had done consumed me, and I packed myself a suitcase, left Addie with a friend, and traveled the dirt roads of Georgia all the way to New York. My feet landed on Striver's Row on West 130th Street after I had done walked four blocks or so from the subway station to find the colored folks that I'd heard about. The Great Depression had done taken away the glamour I had dreamed of seeing, but my eyes got a good glimpse of the buildings they lived in that seemed to be stuck together. There were small patches of grass and one or two trees that tried to give air to the place.

"Bailey wasn't hard to find. All I had to do was ask a pretty girl about him, and she pointed me and my foolishness in the direction of where he laid his head.

"When I had finally came upon his building, I remember the feeling I got in my legs. They felt like the strength of them was leaving me, but I walked up those steps, and I pushed the button next to his name like I knew what I was doing.

"A woman answered. She sounded mighty young, but even that didn't make me take my colored behind back home to Winder. Something in my kidneys was fueling my determination. Had me feeling like a mad countrywoman.

"I gave her my first name and told her I was a relative from Georgia. A few minutes later, I was standing in front of his apartment door, waiting for the hatred I felt for him to settle down.

"The child that stood in front of me was about fifteen years younger than me. No more than twenty, I reckon. She had owl-like brown eyes and a very skinny waist. Short hair. Deep brown skin. Nothing attractive, as they say. She invited me to have a seat and told me Bailey was in the shower.

"We sat there for a few moments, sizing each other up. Only it ain't woman-to-woman, in my book. She asked me my name again, and I gave her my full name this time, including Bailey's last name.

"'You're his wife?' she asked.

"'That's right. And the mother of his daughter.'"

"She wasn't at all taken back by the sharpness of my response.

"'I saw a picture of you. It was hidden in the back of one of his dresser drawers. You're even prettier in person,' she said.

"I smiled and prayed to God that my southern roots didn't cause me to lash out at her."

Jean bursts out laughing.

I laugh some too as I slap my hands down on the table and try to get the memory of that moment from having such a firm hold on me. "Jean, I tell you, that young thing had me wanting to snatch her up by her tiny little waist. I swear, as I sat there, I could see it happening in my mind. You understand what I'm saying?"

Jean nods her head. "Yeah, I think I do. In fact, had it been me, I probably would have."

I point at her in a joking kind of way 'cause she ain't lying at all about that fact. She is a kind woman, but not one to take much foolishness. "But here's the ironic thing," I say after a few seconds have gone by, "as soon as I stopped focusing on her, reality came knocking me upside the head in a not-so-gentle fashion. There I was, my eyes resting on his expensive furniture and brightly painted walls. Taking in the artwork on the walls. Feeling the warmth of the rug, he got covering the floor and suddenly realizing that everything my eyes took in wasn't like the home him and I had shared back in Winder. Nothing like it at all."

Jean leans forward and gives me a puzzled look. "What do you mean?"

I stand up and move over to the counter, still facing Jean but not really looking at her. I'm looking at his apartment. The apartment that I can see as clear as if I were still standing in it.

"Millie, are you going to tell me?" Jean asks, bringing me back to the reality that she and I are in.

I fold my hands across my chest and cross my legs, as I lean back against the counter. "I guess what I mean is that there weren't no creaking floors. There weren't no holes in the walls or ugly paint colors on them, 'cause that's all we could afford. His apartment was really lovely. Fancy like. Like the kind in the magazines. It was at that moment, it became clear to me that he would never have had any of that with me.

"With me, he was never gonna be 'The Great Bailey Boy Johnson.'

"Just Bailey.

"That reality, the reality of his current situation, had me caught up in my feelings so much that I couldn't shake it. It had me feeling real guilty-like. So, I picked up my pocketbook and walked toward the front door.

That's when Bailey came into the room, and our eyes met somewhere in the center of the past and the present.

"He still looked like my Bailey. Like the bright light of handsomeness, I had done seen the first time we met at the bus stop. He had a towel wrapped around him, and his hair was wet, but I saw the man that I had loved and believed in.

"As I stood there, I felt my heart breaking. I reckon a few tears had done fallen from my cheeks and splashed on the part of the fancy rug I was standing on.

"Jean, he could barely say my name. He just stood there in all his shame, and I stood there in all my pain. I realized there wasn't any need in me to ask that one question all us women got to ask in a moment like that—Why? The answer was all around me.

"So, I did all I could do. I reached into my pocketbook, pulled out a picture of Addie, and handed it to him. When his fingers touched mine as he reached for the photo, I felt the need to capture that touch. To store it in a place that could help me to remember the good days.

"The days when he had my heart and never thought about giving it back.

"'How are you two getting on?' he asked, almost in a whisper.

"'We're doing okay,' I said as strong and as secure in my words as I could.

"'I've meant to send you some money. I'll start doing so right away.'

"'I didn't come here for your money,' I snapped back at him.

"'I know.'

"'No, I reckon, you really don't,' I said.

"'JoAnne,' he said to the girl who to me was nothing more than a child, 'Go get that photo of me that's on top of the dresser.'"

"I watched her leave without asking any questions or feeling any sort of way about me seeing her man with a towel wrapped around him.

"'Millie, you look beautiful. Are you still playing? Are you still playing the piano?' he asked after he was sure she wasn't in earshot.

"'I play when I get a moment. Mostly blues now.' He looked down at my hands like he knew that I was lying.

"'Millie.'"

"He tried to come near me, but I moved away from him. That's when his little young thing returned with the picture. He quickly took it from her and handed it over to me.

"'Give this to her,' he pleaded with me.

"'Her name is Addie,' I said as I opened his front door and allowed it to close gently behind me."

I shift my weight some as Jean sits there studying my face intently. "That was it. That was all the conversation he and I had, from that moment on," I say, moving back to the table. "Five years later, I read the same thing you did in the papers."

Chapter Nine

"**D**id you ever give Addie the picture?" Jean asks in a not-so-subtle way.

I shrug my shoulders in regret. "I reckon I should have. But I never did."

"Why on earth not?"

I stare at the coffee pot with cold coffee now in it. "As I came out of his building that day, I looked up and saw a tree with one leaf on it. It was all dried out and shriveled-up-like—being fall then. Most leaves had already done fallen to the ground. But not that one. It was still holding on. The wind had done come and shaken it a few times, but it didn't let go. I looked at that leaf, and I saw me. I saw me holding on, but unlike the leaf, I knew I had to let go.

"So, I made a decision right then and there. I decided to let Bailey go. I remember whispering to the leaf, telling it that it was okay. It was time. Time to let go. As I went to walk away, a strong gust of wind came, and I saw the leaf let go. I saw it floating. I know it sounds crazy, but I swear that it happened, just like that. That day, I came to the realization that I had to let the New York wind do the same for me. Carry off the memories of him and me.

"Now, New York wind ain't like the wind here in Chicago, but it got the job done. It did what it needed to do. However, the lesson I needed to learn wasn't finished. Once again, I looked at that tree. It was bare, but its strength hadn't left. It still had the ability to go on. I knew that when its time came, it would produce new leaves.

"Jean, as I walked back toward the bus that was gonna take me back to my Addie in Georgia, I realized that every day with her was gonna be a new memory, a new leaf. Bailey had done made my heart feel bare in a sense—like it had been rubbed plum dry actually. But it was still strong. Still had the ability to go on.

"I decided I was gonna do that too. For Addie. I was gonna go on. From that point on, everything I did was for her.

"I ain't gonna lie and say that I wasn't downright angry when she got herself pregnant. By a Wonderful, at that."

Jean shook her head. "You don't like white people, do you?"

I shrug my shoulders again. "It depends."

"Depends on what?" Jean asks.

I look Jean dead in the eyes. "If I got to cook and clean for them."

"Millie!" Jean says as she hits the table with her hand.

"What?" I ask with a sly smile on my face, this time. "I'm kidding," I say as I get up and dump the cold coffee in the sink, turning the water on to wash it down the drain. When I turn around, Jean gives me the side-eye.

"Stop it, Jean. I really was only kidding. I done worked for some really nice Wonderfuls."

"Millie."

"I did. That's why I call some of them Wonderful. Now, you have to admit that I don't call all colored people Beautiful. Some of us act like we ain't been reared right and all of us ain't beautiful or wonderful on the inside at all. I guess, in the end, the real problem I had was that I never expected my Addie to get in trouble like that with any young man. I was angry at her. Angry that she gave away what I'd always taught her was precious. I didn't raise her to do that. I tried to teach her right."

Jean nods in agreement as I reach for a napkin 'cause I can feel the tears welling up in me again.

"I'll put on some more coffee," I say as I grab a few more napkins and dab the corners of my eyes, before walking over to the sink to wash the coffee pot out.

"We'll both watch it this time."

We both chuckle and the laughter feels kind to my bones.

I place a spoonful of coffee in the pot, put the water in it, but then I sit in on the counter and turn toward Jean. "You know, it wasn't until Addie was almost six months into her pregnancy that I stopped being angry with her. It took me that long to understand that a child got to drink from their own well of mistakes. No matter how full that well comes to be. You try to help them see that it ain't got to be that way. But sometimes they just can't see that reality. It's just too far off for them. Too far from the moment they think they're in."

Jean nods her head firmly. "That's truth, right there. The real truth," she says.

"These past eight years have been downright hard, Jean. Downright hard without my Addie." I pick the coffee pot up again but then slam it on the counter. Jean jerks at my sudden outburst, but understands the depth of where it's coming from. "They've been sort of like staring at the world but not seeing the world 'cause all you can see is a world without her in it."

Jean stands and walks over toward me with a few napkins in hand. She reaches for the coffee pot and places it back in the sink after handing the napkins to me. "I don't think either of us really needs any more of that. We're worked up enough, don't you think?"

I try to smile through the thousands of tears I have shed in front of her. "You're probably right, I reckon. I'll wash and pack it up later," I say.

Jean looks over at the table. "You want the rest of those biscuits? There are still a couple left."

"I might eat them later this afternoon."

"Alright, I'll leave them then," Jean says as she walks back over toward the table and begins stacking our dirty plates on top of each other. She stops suddenly and looks up at me as I continue to lean against the counter, holding the napkins tightly in my hand. "You ever think about trying to find the child? Maybe the adoption agency can help? I know some people who might be able to help."

I glance down at the floor 'cause I ain't got the nerve to tell her why I'm really taking the nanny job. Although, I know she'd understand. "I reckon I done thought about trying to find him, since the day I made the decision to put him up for adoption," I finally say while trying to not show the guilt in my eyes as I look her way.

"So it was a boy. I never knew that, because you never talked about it."

"Yeah, it was a boy. I reckon he's about as tall as his age will allow and mighty handsome, I'm sure."

"I'm sure he is. Addie was a beautiful girl," she says as she hands me the dirty plates and I place them in the sink with the coffee pot.

"I did go down to that adoption agency about a year or so later, but they didn't have all the information that I wanted from them. They tried their best to assure me that he was in a good home. You know how they can be about things like that," I say as I put a few drops of soap in the sink and turn on the water again.

"Actually I do. I was adopted."

I turn the water off and turn around to face Jean. "You ain't never told me that before."

"Just like we all have our fairy tales, we all have our secrets," she says this very matter-of-factly, but I can hear the tremble in her voice.

"You ain't never lied. Some folks got closets full of secrets." I give her a wink.

"I don't have closets full, but I have my share."

I wipe my hands on a towel and take my seat back at the table.

Jean lets out a sigh. "From what I heard, my mother got hooked on the bottle, and I never knew my father. She put me into the system when I was just a year old. I was adopted about two years later. My adoptive mother, as you know, was a seamstress. She taught me everything, from cutting to pattern making. Just about every woman in her family had been a seamstress.

"My father custom-made men's leather shoes. It was a skill that had been in his family for over five generations. He owned a small shop not too far from here for a few years when I was young, but let it go after the landlord kept going up on the rent. After that, he did most of his work from our home. It was a small home that my parents rented.

"My parents had deep family roots and big hearts. They just couldn't have children of their own. My mother passed away when I had just turned forty, and my father followed about three years later. They left me some money after they died. I used it to buy this building."

My eyes open wide and I stare at Jean for a second or two. "Child, you trying to tell me that you own this here building!"

Jean shrugs her shoulders like it ain't no big thing, but I ain't buying that or letting her off the hook for not telling me years ago. "How come you ain't mentioned this here revelation before?"

"It's not a revelation," she says.

I give her the side-eye.

"Besides, if I had told you, you might not have paid your rent on time." This time, I burst out laughing. "Child, you're probably right."

Jean points her finger at me. "See, I knew it! Besides, we're friends, and I've learned that you don't mix money with friendship. It creates too many problems. In fact, no one here knows I own the building. I pay the guy you see each month to collect the rent and handle the maintenance."

"Well, that was mighty smart of you, I reckon." I give her the side-eye again.

"Stop that. I'm sure you got secrets you aren't ever going to share with me."

"You know just about everything," I say with a hint of sarcasm in my voice.

"Just remember that you said 'just about.'"

I give her a smirk and move around in my chair. I can't cross my legs as comfortably as she can.

"That's what I thought. You want the rest of this gravy, it isn't much left?" she asks as she points to the gravy bowl.

I shake my head. "Naw, I'll just eat my biscuits with what's left of the jelly, I reckon."

Jean gets up to empty the last bit of gravy into the trash and then walks over to wash the bowl in the sink. "You know, I tried to find my birth mother. It was a few years after my parents died," she says as she makes her way back to the table and places the gravy bowl in her basket, before retaking her seat.

"Did you find her?" I ask.

"In a way. I found her grave."

I reach over and give her hand a squeeze. "I'm so sorry."

Jean lowers her head for a second but then looks up with a smile on her face. "So was I. I was sorry I never got a chance to thank her.

Thank her for letting me go. Thank her for letting me have a chance at a better life. That's what you did for Addie's boy. You gave him a chance at a better life."

"Wouldn't it be nice if that was true?" I say as I reach for the small jar of jelly, scrape what's left of it on the plate with the last few biscuits and cover them both with a napkin.

"I'm sure it is. I bet he has a great family." Jean gives me an assuring look and gets up to wash out the jelly jar.

I frown 'cause I know that ain't the case. "Like I said earlier, there ain't a day that goes by that I don't regret giving him up. There ain't a day that goes by that I don't regret not raising Timmy myself. Not one day. Every day is a day of regret for me. It's like it's been living inside of me, breathing so much that I swear it has a life of its own. I reckon I thought it was best, at first. But now I realize that I was only doing what was best for me back then."

Jean tries to offer a comforting smile as she leans against the counter, holding the jelly jar in her hand. "So the adoption agency gave you his name or was Addie able to name him before she..." she pauses for a second as she sees the expression on my face. "It's a cute name, actually," she concludes as she walks over and places the jar in the basket. She looks over at me and gives me a gentle smile, but we both know that it ain't a 'cute' name.

"Look, don't beat yourself up too bad over making the decision to put him up for adoption. You were probably right in recognizing that you just wouldn't be able to handle the memory and all that would have come with it. We all have limitations, Millie. There's a lot of folks that act like they don't have any at all."

I rest my hands on the table. "When it hit me that my Addie wasn't gonna leave that hospital..." I pause, 'cause I ain't sure I can finish my sentence.

"What is it?"

I look at the ceiling like it's gonna finish my thought for me, but truth be told, I was afraid that the words that I was about to spill from my lips would somehow expose my shame and leave me looking naked and raw.

Jean could see the struggle on my face. "It's okay Millie, whatever it is, you can tell me."

I sit there for a few more minutes, gathering my emotions. Looking for an ounce of courage and only finding half that. After another minute or so, goes by, I finally realize that naked and raw in front of a friend ain't the same as being naked and raw in front of a stranger, so I say to her in almost a whisper. . . "I didn't want him to come if it meant he was going take my Addie from me. I even told the doctors that. Of course, I never spoke those thoughts to Addie, but they were there."

I search Jean's face, looking for a scolding look, but there isn't one.

"But it wasn't the baby that was going to take Addie away. Addie had a bad heart," she says in a comforting tone.

I stood up. "But it was because of him that they had done found it!"

"Mildred Mayfield!" Jean looks at me in shock, but I look away.

"I know I wasn't right. I know I wasn't right to have thought that way, back then," I finally say in a calmer tone.

Jean motions for me to sit back down and I do so. She then reaches over and squeezes my hand. "No, you weren't right, Millie, but you were a mother. You were a mother about to lose her child. We all get what they call crazy thoughts in our head in times like that. You aren't perfect."

I nod my head slowly in agreement and reach over for the last of the napkins. "Shoot, Jean, there you go, getting this old country woman crying again."

Jean laughs but reaches out for one of the napkins. "Today, we're both just women, not southern women or northern women. We're just two women getting through the mistakes of life."

We both start dabbing at our eyes, allowing a little time to come in and heal the sad moment our hearts are in.

Jean looks down at her watch. "What time is it?" I ask.

"Time for me to get myself upstairs and finish a dress for a client."

"You've had quite a few to make lately. I reckon that's a good thing," I say.

"It most certainly isn't a bad thing. Maybe I'll think more about opening that store like you mentioned earlier if business keeps going like this."

"If anyone can do it, it'll be you, Jean. You got a good business mind." I stand up and give her a reassuring grin.

Jean stands up and grabs her basket. "Did Bailey ever send you the money he promised?"

"He did. Every month, just about. Sometimes he would send something more than once. I reckon those were the months his conscience got to him," I say as I grab all the napkins we done used and walk over to toss them in the trash.

When I turn around, Jean is standing there like she's waiting for something. "What?" I ask with a puzzled look on my face.

Jean places her hands on her small hips. "You're not going to tell me what you did with it?"

I chuckle."Well, at first, I was gonna use it and the money I had done saved to send Addie off to college. I had done saved enough for her books and her housing for all four years, just about. But after Addie got herself pregnant, different decisions had to be made. I didn't want those country folks putting their noses up in the air at my Addie 'cause she had done made a mistake, so we moved here to Chicago. My parents used to live here. I reckoned that I still had enough to send her to a local college, here in Chicago. That's why I picked this apartment, 'cause it was near public transportation and within my budget. I was gonna quit working and take care of the baby while Addie went to school, but not a thing went the way I had done planned it."

"So now you're just sitting on a pile of money but living like you're not? That explains a lot. Here I was thinking I was saving you when you didn't need saving."

I walk over and give Jean a hug 'cause I want her to know how thankful I am, without telling her how grateful I am...

For saving me.

That was how it be with friends sometimes.

Chapter Ten

I stand by my open window watching folks walk down the block toward the bus stop in their Sunday best. The little girls reminded me of Addie when she still loved floral dresses with big bows on them and cute white shoes with polka dot socks. I watch the mamas pulling the boys along who would rather be shooting a ball in a makeshift milk carton hoop or throwing a half-deflated ball around in the middle of the street rather than getting on a bus with a bow tie on and a heavily starched white shirt.

I've been in this here neighborhood for eight years, and I can't say that I know the names of all the faces that I see, but I'm gonna miss the possibility that once existed, in being able to match a name to a face.

I reckon it's like walking by a bed of roses and not stopping to get to know the sweet-smelling aroma they're dressed with.

We take time and things for granted, I reckon.

At least I can speak for myself in that regard. I reckoned that I would have the time to meet them, in some form or fashion, but now that ain't the case since I'm leaving today.

I glance over at the four packed boxes I finally managed to finish packing, although I ain't moved them over by the front door yet. They're still sitting in the same spot they were, yesterday, 'cause I ain't felt like straining my back to move them. Three of the boxes got my clothes in them, and the fourth one got everything I care about in it.

Jean stopped an hour or so ago, just as I had done finished breaking down the beds so we could have our last cup of coffee together before she headed off to deliver a dress to her client. My old brown leather chair and my sofa got moved to her apartment last night, just after supper, thanks to a young man Jean knows named Michael. He's the son of one of her clients that lives a few blocks up the street.

Mae came by too, not too long after Michael, and picked up all my kitchen stuff, including the table and chairs. Each of her children gave me a hug and had me crying all night 'cause I'm gonna miss them something terrible.

Mae said she's going on a diet. She said she was tired of moaning and groaning over a man that ain't never gonna come back. In fact, she talked about divorcing him. Said she went to an attorney to find out what she got to do to make it happen since she knows that he's somewhere laying up against some woman that ain't her.

I ain't never heard Mae talk like that before, but I can't say that I blame her. I told her that sometimes, as women, we got to realize that we ain't got to accept foolishness, although I'll be the first to admit that as women, we can sometimes act foolish when a man is trying to pull at our heart.

I being the foremost one.

I shut the window and glance around my apartment. It dawns on me, as I walk over to the phone to call for a cab, that tomorrow I'm gonna look into the eyes of Addie's child.

My grandchild.

I can't get over the fact that I'm gonna hold him. Eight years old or not. I know the moment my eyes look into his, I'll be begging him for forgiveness in my heart. Whispering words to him, every day thereafter, that I never thought I'd get a chance to utter.

My attention shifts to the box that's holding all the things that I care about. Addie's pillow for one.

And then there's Addie's letter, sitting near the bottom, inside a shoe box.

Every year on the anniversary of my child's death, I'd pull her letter out. I'd allow my hands to gently gaze the dried-out ink. I'd let my eyes linger on the handwriting on each page, while fighting a battle of tears— and losing the war each time.

Her handwriting was beautiful. Graceful.

I used to tell her that your handwriting says a lot about the type of person you are. So, she would practice writing her letters just about every day until they took on a form she thought resembled her.

I'd hold that letter up to my nose and close my eyes while trying to see if I could still smell some of the perfume she dabbed on it just before she sealed it. The perfume that she'd had me bring her the day she wrote the letter. The same perfume that's now wrapped up neatly in the shoe box.

She made me promise that I wouldn't read the letter and that I would try to use the rest of the perfume.

To my shame, I ain't kept either of those promises.

I can't say I'm sorry about it, 'cause I ain't. I needed that letter.

For my sanity.

To take a breath each day.

To keep myself from going back to that dark place where my own mama ain't around to save me.

As I glance at the taped up box again, I smile. I smile because I can now look forward to another day.

The day when I can give the letter to him.

To Timmy.

That day will be his day.

Chapter Eleven

*T*hirty minutes go by, and I'm still waiting for my cab to come, so I walk back over to the window, and I see Michael, the one that had done moved my old brown leather chair and sofa up to Jean's apartment, climbing out of a car that looks older than I be.

I reckoned Michael be around twenty-two, twenty-three or so, a tall young man with deep hues of brown crayon in his skin and a solid, well-built frame.

He chats with a few other young men before making his way into my apartment building. A few minutes later, I hear a knock on my door, and when I look through the peek-hole, I see him standing there with a big grin on his face.

I open the door and stare at him with a puzzled look on my face, 'cause I ain't got nothing else left for him to come and get unless Jean done sent him to get the beds.

"Good morning, Miss Mayfield, how are you this morning?"

"I'm fine, " I say as I place my hands on my hips. "What got you over here again this morning?"

"Miss Jean asked if I would come and help you this morning."

I take my hands off my hips and move out the way so he can come in. "Well, that's mighty nice of her, but I don't really need any help. I'm sure the cab driver can help me with them."

He looks past me and rests his eyes on my boxes.

"You see, I ain't got much," I say as I follow his eyes. "It's only four boxes."

He shines all his white-as-a-bar-of-soap teeth at me. "You're right, it's not as much as I thought it would be, but I can at least help with those."

He moves around me and starts walking toward them before I can object any further.

"I'm sure you got better things to do with your time than come help an old lady like me."

He laughs. "You're not old. You look to be about the same age as my mother."

I place my hands on my hips again as he picks up two of the boxes and balances them on his shoulders. "How old she be? " I ask, worried that he's gonna say that she's old enough to have two feet in the grave.

"She's forty-five."

I place my hand on my cheek. "Child, I know I don't look like I'm forty-five."

He shifts the boxes on his shoulders and gives me a rather serious look. "Sure, you do."

I try not to blush as he makes his way toward the door. "You sure I can't help you with those?" I ask like my bones got some youth in them again, just 'cause he gave me a compliment.

"Naw, I'm good. These are pretty light, actually."

Young men and their young muscles. I got so caught up that I had done forgot that my cab still ain't come yet. "Wait," I say.

He gives me a puzzled look. "You need something out of one of these?"

"No, but my cab ain't here yet. We might as well wait for them to come before we move the boxes outside."

"Miss Jean insisted that I drive you."

"In what?" I ask 'cause ain't no way I'm getting in that thing outside.

He laughs and flashes his bar-of-soap-white teeth at me again. "My car. It's outside. She's old but reliable. Trust me. I'll go ahead and put these in the car."

"You describing me or your car, child?" I say as I open the door for him.

He smirks at me. "My car, ma'am."

"Well, I reckon I ought to call the cab company. I'm sure they ain't gonna be happy with me canceling at the last moment like this."

"It'll be okay," he shouts, as he walks down the hallway toward the front door of the building.

A few minutes later, we're driving down I-90, looking for the West Suburbs sign on the left of the expressway that will be coming up in about thirty minutes or so.

"Miss Jean told me that you're from Georgia."

"You couldn't tell?"

He grins. "My mother is from Georgia. She moved to Chicago about twenty years ago, after my father passed away. I was about two years old then, so, of course, I don't remember any of Georgia."

"Georgia has a lot of trees and dirt roads, but good southern hospitality and the best sweet tea, if you ask me."

He nods his head in agreement. "That's what my mother always says whenever she talks about Georgia."

"Well, now you know she ain't lying to you. You want to move to Georgia, child?"

"I've been thinking about it. I'm ready to get out of Chicago, and I figure the South is the place for me," he says.

"What you think they got in Georgia?" I ask.

"Lots of trees and dirt roads."

I laugh. "You ain't never lied."

"See, that's what I'm talking about. I dig the way you talk. I want to hear more of that southern drawl, as my mother calls it. Plus, I'm ready for a change."

"Well, you'll find a 'change' in Georgia. Be it good or bad," I say as I glance out the window and watch the "L" zoom down the middle of the expressway, filled with folks like it's a regular workday, instead of a Sunday.

"I figure you can get bad or good from anywhere you lay your head. It's all about how you look at it. Plus, I'm tired of the cold and the snow. I hear it barely snows in Georgia."

I tilt my head and smile at him, surprised that at such a young age he seems to have a good head of wisdom on them shoulders of his. "It snows for a day or two, maybe. Then it's gone the next."

"That sounds much better than the knee-deep snow we get here in Chicago," he says.

I catch him looking at my hands.

"Miss Jean told me you can play the piano."

"Did she? She only learned that yesterday and already she blabbing about it?"

He nods his head. "She said that you're excellent."

"She did, huh?"

A car blows their horn at us as he tries to get over since our exit is coming up soon.

"You better be careful there, child. These cars coming fast," I say as we finally get in the exit lane.

"Sorry."

I give him a wink as we make a left turn on Harlem Ave. "It's okay. I hate driving."

"You know how?"

I give him the side-eye. "No, but I hate even being in the driver's seat, truth be told. That's why I take the bus or the train. Although I'll admit that the seats on the train ain't made for women like me."

"I hated taking the train or the bus, growing up. That's why I couldn't wait to get my own car. It took years of me saving my money to get her."

I look at the dashboard that looks like it's barely holding on. "Oh, so this is a she?"

"Of course." He reaches out and pats the dashboard. "This here is my baby."

"Child! Look out!"

As the car comes hurtling at us, all I can think about is one thing; I ain't gonna get to see him.

My Timmy.

Part Two

Chapter Twelve

Timmy - Eighteen Years Old - 1968

Everyone has a date in mind, at some point in their life. For some, it could be the date of their wedding or the date of their divorce.

Either one represents freedom, depending on how one sees it.

For me, that date is June 2, 1968.

Today.

I toss my cream silk sheets back and sit on the edge of my mahogany bed and listen. It's how I start most of my mornings— listening for her. Wondering if her speech will be slurred, because those are the worst mornings; the aftereffects of her previous night thinking about all the reasons why she hates me.

Lena Taylor. My mother.

Sometimes, I don't hear the clank of her heeled shoes making their way down the hallway that leads her to my bedroom door.

Sometimes, I don't hear the high pitch of her voice as she yells at me for being born.

Sometimes, I can pretend that she's a loving mother and that I'm a son who really loves his mother.

Sometimes— is not today.

Today, I hear the clank of her heeled shoes moving swiftly down the uncarpeted hallway.

A second or two later, I see the handle of my bedroom door moving. Just as I go to stand up, my bedroom door swings open and she comes charging inside, wearing her favorite summer color—white. Only she isn't pure, will never be chaste, and I doubt there's a bone of good to be found under her skin.

I look at her hands.

I look to make sure there's nothing in them. Nothing that she can hit me with. Although the five-carat ring on her left hand has been just as brutal in the not-so-distant past.

"You're going!" she screams as she stands in front of me.

"No, I'm not," I say in a firm voice.

"Yes, you are! You'd better be thankful—"

"I'd better be thankful for what? Being your son?" I can see the fire burning in her eyes, but I don't back down.

"I don't have time for this nonsense of yours, this morning, Timmy!"

"Let me guess, you have a hair appointment to get to, or are you already out of your favorite liquid?"

"As a matter of fact, I have a hair appointment," she spits back at me.

"Well, I guess you'd better get to it."

She takes a step closer toward me. "Who do you think you're talking to like that?"

I brace myself for what's coming. "I would say my mother, but we both know you've never been that." She stares at me for a second, shocked at the tone of my words, but not in the truth that's mixed within them.

Her left-hand moves into the air. Filled with purpose.

"What are you going to do? Hit me? Choke me? Which one will it be, Mother?"

She answers my challenge with a sly smile just as the sting of her ring finger slashes into my skin, piercing the skin just under my eye. A drop of blood runs down my cheek, but I don't wipe it away. I want her to see that I don't care what she does to me.

Not anymore.

After today—after today, she'll never see me again.

It's that knowledge of freedom that fuels me to say the things that a boy should never say to his mother.

Today is my day.

"What's going on in here?" My father asks as he stands in my doorway, looking at the scene from a distance—as always.

My mother turns around and glares at him. "Deal with him. I'm late."

"Where are you going this early in the morning, Lena?" he asks.

She doesn't respond as she pushes past him.

I ease down on my bed and watch as my father walks toward me with an envelope dangling in his hand.

My father is a hard-bottom shoe kind of man. His hand-tailored suits are freshly ironed each day. His custom white shirts are heavily starched, his cuff-links are always polished, and his face never goes without the proper shave.

Sky blue eyes, a runner's body, and a neat haircut that dresses a mind that can make influential business decisions but can't get to his son's high school graduation on time, or at all.

He always has a confident walk when he enters a room, one that makes him look like he's worth more than a million bucks.

Truth is—he is.

He sits down next to me and looks at my face. "You want me to have Margaret get you something for that cut?"

I shake my head slowly. "No. It's not like it's the first time."

He looks at the floor and shifts the envelope that's in his left hand to his right. It's also not the first time awkward silence has sat between us.

"Here, I know it's late," he says as he hands me the envelope.

I stare at it for a moment. "Better late than never, huh, Dad? Isn't that how it always works with you?" I take the envelope and toss it off to the side. I know the contents.

Money. It's always money.

He ignores my comment as he glances at my cut again. "What were you two fighting about just now?"

I lean back on the bed some. "She wants me to play at a graduation party some friend of hers is having for her daughter."

"Do you know the daughter?"

I look down toward my dresser and try to find something more interesting to look at on it than the conversation we're having. "I've seen her around the school."

"So, what's the problem?" he asks as he places his hand on my shoulder to draw my attention back to him.

"Mother is the problem!" My father raises his eyebrow at my sharp outburst, so I lower my voice. "She uses me. Treats me like a puppet. I'm sick of her always trying to force me to play the piano for her stupid friends."

He places his hand on my shoulder again, but I shrug it off. "She's not treating you like a puppet, Timmy. What parent wouldn't want to show off a talent like yours?"

I don't respond.

"You've got to learn to respect your mother."

I stand up and look at him. "Respect her? How could I ever respect a woman I hate?"

"Don't say that, she's your mother. She—"

"Don't say she loves me. We both know that's not true. Trust me when I say that the hatred that exists in this house is mutual."

"She has her way of doing things, but she doesn't—"

"Hate me? Really?" I pause. "Tell me something, what kind of mother tells the cook not to feed her son for days just because he came in through the front door instead of through the kitchen? What kind of mother does that? She even—"

"She even what?"

"You know she drinks, and when she's drunk, she gets even nastier. One night she got so drunk that she tried to choke me with a rope."

He stands up next to me, with a look of denial on his face as he looks into my eyes. But I won't allow the denial to live in this moment. Not even for a second.

"That can't be true," he says.

I look back at him with eyes full of truth. "It is! She brought the rope into my room, and as I was sleeping, she wrapped it around my neck and pulled on it. It got so tight, I could barely breathe. She made me swear not to tell anyone, or she'd make sure she carried it through next time."

I take a step back from him. "I was ten years old. Ten years old, Dad. How do you forget something like that?"

I looked at his face again. The denial—it was still there. "I can't believe she would do something like that," he says, almost in a whisper.

"She did it, and she's done worse!"

He sits back down on my bed and looks as if the nightmare that I've been living is finally becoming a realization for him. "Timmy, I wish I had known. I wish you would have told me this was happening sooner."

I look down into his eyes. I want to believe him. I want to see the truth in his words because what's on the surface, is not as convincing as it should be. "Whatever. I don't even know why I'm telling you this now. You're never here. In fact, you're only here now because you missed my graduation a few days ago."

"I tried to get back. Really, I did. I didn't miss your graduation on purpose."

"I was that one kid who only had their housekeeper show up for their graduation. She was the only one who cared enough to come."

He stands up and takes a few steps toward me. "I care, Timmy. I'm so sorry."

His words soak into me, but I won't allow them to travel to my heart. No distractions. That's how this day has got to be.

"Dad, I'm leaving," I say in a matter-of-fact tone.

He steps back and looks into my eyes again. "What do you mean?"

I look down at the floor for a second. "I mean I'm leaving here. This house. I can't take it anymore. I can't take her anymore. It's got to stop," I say, while still looking for a speck of depth in my eighteen-year-old voice that sounds as grown as the man I need my father to see. "I'm going to make it stop, forever."

He reaches out and tries to place his hand on my shoulder again. "Timmy, I'll talk to her. I will make her stop. I promise."

He thinks he can still save me.

It's too late for that. I will be my own savior.

I turn my back to him and put some space between us. "What good would that do?" I ask, but not really looking for a response. "The damage has already been done. Can't you see that?" I turn back around. "Maybe, you can't." I lift up my shirt and turn so that he can see my back. "This is what the woman you think I should respect did to me. Every scar. Every bruise. Every mark from a tree switch that you see was put there by her."

I turn and face him. I see tears in the corners of his eyes. "I knew she hit you sometimes, but I never imagined—I never imagined that she was capable of that."

I feel like that little eight-year-old boy again. The one who could look into his father's eyes, when he was home, and see something I didn't understand at the time. Hope. "She's been capable since I came home from school ten years ago."

He sits slowly back on my bed. His eyes never leaving me. "What do you want me to do? What can I do now to make things better for you?"

I walk over and sit down next to him. It's my turn. I place my hand on his shoulder. "Let me go."

He looks around my room as if the time I've spent in here gave either of us something worth remembering.

"You know, ten years ago, I thought I was doing the right thing by bringing you home. I was hoping that having you around would help her to—"

"Love me?"

His eyes rest on a picture of me that sitting on my dresser. I was twelve years old, sitting behind my piano.

"Something like that. To be honest, I would have settled for like," he says.

I sigh and remove my hand. "That woman doesn't know what love is. All she knows is how to drink. How to hit. How to almost kill me. She doesn't know love. I doubt that she ever has. I doubt she's even capable of it."

He nods slowly as he focuses his attention back on me. "You said that you want to leave, where would you go?"

"New York. I can get a job there playing the piano. I'm good enough, you know I am."

He runs his hand through his hair. "Yes, you're good enough, but you're still only eighteen. I can't let you go off to New York at eighteen years old unless it's for a purpose—like, maybe to go to college."

I stand up and walk over toward my dresser. I pick up the picture that he was staring at. "Dad, I'm not this kid anymore. I doubt that I was even him back then. The day I left that boarding school, that stopped." I walk back over and sit down next to him. "I know you have always wanted me to go to college, because that's what you did, and it turned out great for you." I pause and glance around my room, then back to him. "But it's not what I want to do. "

He rubs his hands together, and I know that a long speech is on the tip of his tongue.

"Timmy, I didn't want to go to college either, at first. My father forced me to go. I wanted to backpack around the world." I stare at him in disbelief. "It's true. After I finished high school, I wanted to see what life had to offer me, but my father—he saw something else for me. Another path that I didn't think I fit on." He pauses for a second. "I just want the same for you. I know you want to find your own path, make your own way, but you could be something more. You have what it takes. Today you proved that."

I shake my head. "I'm not going to college, Dad. I'm sorry."

"Just let me finish." He runs his hands through his hair again. "College became something more than I expected. It was key for me. It helped me. Because of going to school, I was able to buy a home. This home. Because of college, I was able to make money for this family. Pay for everything you see and enjoy. You sleep on silk sheets. Everything in this room was imported or handmade. You have a cook and a housekeeper. I make sure that you don't have to lift a finger so you can focus on your education. That's because I make a lot of money. Money that I work hard for. I buy companies. I sell companies. I'm a businessman. College helped me to become that. All I'm trying to do is give you that same opportunity. Playing the piano may not be able to give that to you. Going to college, I'm convinced, will. You should be happy that—"

"That I have a rich father I never see?"

"That you have a father who loves you and wants what's best for you," he says, ignoring the sarcasm in my tone.

"I don't think leaving me with her was best for me." He nods his head slowly because he can tell that I'm not going to forgive him for that. Not now at least.

"Timmy, I didn't know what she was doing to you, but I will correct it. Besides, I'm not asking you to stay here. I agree that you need to leave. Get away from her. But the only way I can allow you to go to New York is if you're going there to go to school. That's the only way I can give you my support."

"You mean that's the only way you will give me your money."

He stands up and looks down at me as if the matter has been decided.

"However you see it, son."

"That's how it is, isn't it?"

Once again, he does what he does best—he ignores my feelings. "So which school will it be?" He reaches into his back pocket and pulls out his checkbook.

I meet him, father-to-son, as I stand. "I told you, I'm not going to college. I'm going to New York, and you can keep your money. I'm tired of being beaten. I'm tired of trying to be bought. I'm just tired. I'm leaving."

"You're not going anywhere."

I don't flinch at his tone. We've been working our way toward this moment. I knew it was coming. I knew it couldn't be avoided.

It's been eighteen years in the making.

"Yes, I am, and unless you're going to become like her and lock me in my room, there's nothing you can do to stop me. Like you said, I'm eighteen."

I see the anger in his eyes, but I need him to see mine.

Even if it's for the first time.

Chapter Thirteen

When I was younger, I stood in the parking lot of my school and screamed at the top of my lungs that I hated my father. He had, once again, allowed me to be the only child who didn't have a smiling parent with a Polaroid camera at the school play. Margaret had been there, as always, calming my voice and trying to reason with my heart. As I stand here now with my backpack slung over my shoulders and suitcase in hand, I can still hear her words lingering around in my head. "Timmy," she said in her motherly tone, "just remember, baby boy, that you can love a person and still not like them." I remember shaking my head in disagreement, but now, here I am. Fully understanding the depth of her words as I think about him.

My father.

I don't hate him, but I don't like him either.

I blame him.

I blame him for everything.

Right or wrong in my life.

As I move toward my bedroom door, I can't help but wonder...Will I ever see him again?

Do I care?

I stop at the entrance of my door and look around my room. A room that I hope will never feel my breath again or the weight of my body walking upon the carpet that's filled with tiny stains of blood from the slashes and bruises that Margaret often cleaned for me.

This room has four walls. Each wall serves as my witness. Each one a witness to the pain that I've had to endure for eighteen years.

The chandelier over my bed holds every tear that I would never allow to fall.

The thick, dark blue velvet curtains covered me with darkness when my mind wouldn't allow me to escape from the nightmares.

In the corner is my first true love.

My piano.

It helped me find peace.

It will be the only thing I will miss.

It and Margaret, of course.

She is the first woman I've loved.

She was the one that taught me to save every dime my father gave me so I could use it to get away from here.

This house.

The one that I'm not allowed to come through the front door of.

I close the door and make my way down the hallway, stopping in front of my father's office. His door is closed, but I can hear them inside. His voice is filled with anger, as he tells my mother that it's because of her that I'm leaving. I wait for her response.

I'm sure the neighbors can hear it.

The bitterness in her laugh. It drips from her lips and travels through the crevices of the door, only to stand face-to-face with me. Challenging me to not allow a door to hold me back from saying words that my bones long to shout out loud, rather than whisper in my mind and heart. As I look down, I find my hand tightly wrapped around the doorknob.

I move to open it, but then I look and see Margaret standing at the top of the stairs.

Saving me.

She walks over and quietly removes my hand from the door. She strokes my chin and whispers—"Today is your day. Don't let her take that away from you."

We move down the stairs and towards the kitchen. When we get to the kitchen back door, she opens it and says to me— "Don't look back, baby boy, ain't nothing back here but the past. You get to the main road. There should be a cab there to take you to the airport."

I reach out to hug her, but she steps away and waits for me to move out into the Chicago sun. As she closes the door, I do what she tells me.

I move forward.

One step at a time, until I reach the main road and see the cab.

"Where you headed?" the cab driver asks as I climb into the backseat after throwing my suitcase into the trunk.

"New York," I quickly say. "Airport, I mean."

He grins.

A few minutes later, I hear the engine start, and I have to force myself not to look.

Not to look back.

Chapter Fourteen

*M*y one-way ticket is firmly tucked in my back pocket as I stand outside the airport exit doors, waiting for a brown Thunderbird that belongs to Margaret's brother, Boney Bass Bryan, to come and carry me off into a world that I have never known. Every hope and dream that has been the focal point of my thoughts for the last eighteen years is being attacked by a vicious virus called fear.

Margaret said it would be like this.

She'd said I'd look at my present situation and wonder if my future will be any better. As I watch people move around me, beside me, and in front of me, I find myself envious of their faces.

Their faces are draped with certainty. Purpose. Determination, even. No traces of fear. No hints of doubt. In their eyes, I see the confidence in their ability to move in the direction they need to go.

I take my hands out of my pockets and stare at them. It's something that Margaret used to do when I was younger. Whenever I doubted. Whenever I felt fear or doubt in my ability. She'd take my hands off the keys of my piano and hold them tight in her own hands. Then she'd stare into my eyes and tell me that in my fingers I will always find certainty. That the blood running through them was filled with purpose. Determination, even.

I wish she could have come here with me. "You've got to put both of your feet on your own path," she said to me one day. "My brother Bryan lives in New York. He'll get you where you need to go. Don't you worry. He'll take good care of you. I done seen to it."

Bryan.

I know something of him from the newspaper clippings that Margaret keeps carefully displayed inside a red velvet photo album.

I also know that he's been here, in New York, for over thirty years now and I read in the papers that he's played with some of the best bass guitar players to come in and out of this place.

Margaret said that he keeps a gold guitar pick in his back pocket at all times, just in case, some up-and-comer feels the need to challenge his ability.

I glance at my watch. Two hours have passed since I stepped off the plane. The cab drivers that are lined up against the curb keep staring at me. Waiting for me to make any movement toward one of them.

Just as I grab my suitcase to head back inside and out of the heat, I see a brown Thunderbird moving swiftly through traffic and towards me.

The car pulls up close to the curb, and I walk over and look inside. The cushions in the front leather seats are busting out from the seams. The steering wheel has definitely seen better days, and the rearview mirror is barely hanging on.

Bryan leans over and smiles at me. "You Margaret's boy?"

I nod my head slowly.

"Good, 'cause the way you got your head all up in my car, I thought I was gonna have to remind you that I might be "Boney" but I know how to use these knuckles. You know what I mean?"

I step back.

He laughs and jumps out of the car.

I can see why they call him Boney. He's at least five inches over six feet and slim. I mean, like, bone-slim. His small but thick 'fro is sticking out from the sides of the hat he's wearing, that's slightly tilted to the side. His plaid shirt is tucked neatly into a pair of wide-bottom dress pants that dangle over a pair of thick-heeled dress shoes. He talks fast and moves even faster as he grabs my suitcase and backpack and tosses them in the backseat.

"You waiting for me to open the door for you?" he asks as he rushes back to the driver's side of the car.

I move quickly and jump inside.

"You can roll your window up once we hit the highway if you need to. New York ain't as windy as Chicago, but she holds her own. You know what I mean?"

I didn't, but I nod my head anyway, as Bryan merges into traffic.

"So you ready for New York, kid?" he asks as he weaves around cars with one hand on the steering wheel and the other, hanging outside the window.

I nod.

He glances over at me. "You can speak, I ain't like your mama. I ain't gonna beat you for speaking your mind."

I glare at him.

"I'm sorry. I shouldn't have said it like that." He tries to smile in my direction, but I ignore him and look out my window.

"Look, kid, all I'm saying, is that it's a real shame what that woman did to you. But you're here now. In the land of possibilities, as they say. The only thing that's gonna beat you here is life. It's grown-up time. Ain't no boys in New York, you hear what I'm saying?" he says as he glances over at me.

I shrug my shoulders and keep looking out the window. "Yeah, I hear you."

"Good, because I ain't got time to babysit."

He quickly glances over at me again, but I don't respond.

"You need a lollipop?" he asks as he reaches down and grabs one from his side door.

"Dude, really?" I say as I stare at him. Annoyed.

He laughs. "I'm kidding. Lighten up. You're in New York! You ain't got to worry about nobody now but you."

I return to looking out the window. Trying not to show my anger as I hear him opening the wrapper to his lollipop.

As we move down the expressway, New York flashes by me in a blur. When the car finally stops, forty-five minutes later, we're in front of an old building located in what Bryan calls the Bronx.

"This is home, kid. Get your stuff and let's get at it. I've got to get some sleep before we head in tonight. I ain't no spring chicken like you. Tonight will be a long night. It's Friday so the joint will be packed, and I like to get there early and make sure the band is set and ready to go."

I follow him into the building, and we head up about ten flights of stairs.

"As you can see, the elevators ain't working, just like everything else around here, but they keep this building clean and folks in this neighborhood ain't gonna kill you. There are some of your folks around here, so you shouldn't feel too out of place. You know what I mean? Anyway, if anyone does give you any trouble, just tell them that you're with Boney. You got that?" He opens the door to his apartment.

"Yeah, I got it." I take in everything in a matter of seconds. His apartment is the same size as my bathroom back home.

He catches me looking. "Welcome to New York, kid, where everything is small but the rent."

"It's cool."

"It has to be. It's all we got. Now, look here, the sofa is over there on the left. It lets out into a bed. The sheets are clean. Margaret made me buy you some new ones. Don't worry, I'll take it out of your first paycheck. The kitchen is in that corner, and the bathroom is just to the right. It's about three, so I'm going to hit the sheets for a few hours. Be ready to go by six."

"Am I playing tonight?"

"We work around here. If we don't work, we don't eat." He chuckles as he heads to what I assume is his bedroom, but looks more like a closet. "Get some sleep, kid. This ain't Kansas, you know what I mean?"

Chapter Fifteen

"Who's the white boy?" A slender woman asks as she stands in front of me. Her skin reminds me of Margaret's—without as many wrinkles, of course. Gentle hints of brown mixed with splashes of cream. She has big brown eyes and a broad smile. A cigarette dances off the tip of her fingers as she stares me up and down.

"This is...What's your name again, kid?" Bryan asks, glancing over at me.

"Timothy Taylor, but everyone calls me Timmy."

"Right. Right. He's a friend of my sister. The one in Chicago. He's going to be staying with me for a bit," Bryans says quickly, giving me a wink.

"So what's he doing here? He looks like he's barely out of diapers, and he's white," she says while taking a puff on her cigarette.

"I'm eighteen, ma'am," I say.

"Ma'am? You see your mama in here? My name is Jackie Daniels. I own the place." she says, looking around the place as if she's never seen it before.

"Look here, Jackie, you said we needed a new piano player, so I brought you a new piano player," Bryan says, annoyed.

She frowns at him and grabs my hands. "What kind of music you play? Classical?"

"I can play anything, including blues and jazz. I've been playing both all my life."

She lets out a deep, haughty laugh, but I keep it cool.

"What does an eighteen-year-old white boy know about blues or jazz? You've got to have some drama in your life for that. I don't know too many white folks with that kind of drama," she says as she glances around, looking for something to place her cigarette in.

Bryan grabs an ashtray off a nearby table and hands it to her. "Jackie, the boy's been through enough to be able to deliver. Trust that, you know what I mean?"

Her eyes narrow suspiciously as she looks at him. "So you've heard him play?"

"Naw, I ain't heard the kid play, but my sister knows music, and I trust her ear."

"Well, I don't. The folks that come here expect to hear music with some soul in it. Not white folks' music," she says.

"I can play that too, Ms. Jackie. Music with soul, I mean. I grew up on it. It's all I know."

She looks me up and down again. "Well then, get on up there and let me hear it. You'd better be good. I don't have time to find someone else for tonight. We open in a couple of hours," she says, cutting her eyes at Bryan.

"Come on, kid," Bryan says as he starts to walk over to the stage.

I follow Bryan and take a seat at the piano that's off to the left of the stage. I run my fingers across the keys to get a feel for it. "What are we going to play?"

"We don't name music in here, kid. You gotta listen for your cue. I'll pull you in when I'm ready for you. You got it?"

"Yeah, I got it."

"I hope you can keep up."

Bryan reaches into his pocket and pulls out a gold guitar pick. He smiles at me as he grabs his guitar that's sitting on the side of a chair and allows a few notes to float in the air. He then takes a seat and closes his eyes. When his fingers touch the chords again, all I hear is fifty years of sweetness. His style is smooth. Raw but gentle around the edges. The sounds that come from his guitar bounce off the walls with ease.

It takes me a moment or two to hear it—my cue, but Bryan does more than pull me in. He guides me to the spot where I need to be. My eyes are glued to his movement. My ears search the air. Listening to the chatter his fingers make. I let the flow of each key I hit talk back to him.

When the song is coming to a finish, Bryan slows down. He leaves me out there. The rhythm of each note he hits challenges me, and I reply in kind.

I let him know that when I'm in front of a piano, I can handle my own.

Chapter Sixteen

"**M**an! You sound like Art Tatum. I bet you don't even know who that is," Bryan says with a slight grin on his face.

I smile. "He died about twelve years back. Your sister introduced me to his music. Called him one of the jazz piano greats. When my mother went out, Margaret and I would sit and listen to 'Two for Tea' just about every day."

Bryan shakes his head, enthusiastically. "Love that cut. My sister loves her some jazz, too. She got an ear for music, although she can't play." He pauses and smiles for a moment as if he can see her face, then he slaps his hands together to bring himself back to the present. "I played with Art once. Back in 1937." I give him a look of doubt. "It's true. Ain't got no reason to lie. I was just a young buck with a guitar back then. Barely had two cents in my pocket and yet there I was, playing with Mr. Art Tatum. You know he was blind?"

"Yeah, and mostly self-taught, like me."

Bryan smirks. "All right. So you got some crumbs of knowledge about jazz under your nails. I'll give you that." He pauses again, and I watch as his face shifts to a more serious look.

"I ain't gonna lie, kid, you can play. I ain't never in my fifty-something years heard a white boy play like you. I can't believe you're only eighteen."

"I owe most of it to your sister."

He looks at the floor. "Yeah, my big sis is something. She's ten years older than me, but she got wisdom in her bones, you know what I mean? Speaking truth, she just about raised me. If it hadn't been for her insisting,

I wouldn't have left Chicago and moved here. She always believed in me. Saw something that most didn't. Even our parents. I ain't seen her since I boarded the bus for New York over thirty years ago."

"She talked about you all the time."

"That's cool. Look here, we got to stop this going back into the past thing. Ain't nothing back there but pain, if you know what I mean?"

It was the first time I knew exactly what he meant.

He gives my shoulder a firm slap. "Boy, you can play. My big sis came through! Come on, let's grab some food before this joint opens and the rest of the band gets here. Food is the only thing Jackie gives us for free. That woman is all about business. She fine though. Mighty fine. She about five years younger than me, but I like them young. You know what I mean?"

I look at him.

He laughs. "Of course you don't."

As Bryan and I are coming out of the kitchen, I see a young woman on the stage wearing a pair of blue jeans and a white shirt, testing the microphone and warming up her voice.

"Who is that?" I ask as we grab seats near the small bar area to eat.

"That's Simoné. She's Jackie's daughter, and boy, that little thing right there can blow. You know what I mean?"

"I think so. You mean that she's a good singer."

He puts his sandwich down. "Nope, that ain't what I mean. Plenty of folks here in New York are good at singing. Heck, anybody can carry a tune if they try hard enough. Man, even the dogs and the cats in the alley can do that. What I'm talking about is having the gift."

"The gift?"

"Yeah, my sister didn't school you on that?"

I shake my head.

"Well, you got it, and that young thang on that stage got it. The gift. It's the ability to move people with your rhythm. Your style. It means you can do more than just sing or even hit the keys of a piano. It's like you can blow life into something that was once lifeless. "

"I just think she's beautiful," I say, lowering my head because I can't believe I said that out loud.

Bryan slaps his hand on the table. "Watch out now! A white boy that digs a colored girl. Well, you ain't the first, but I seriously doubt you can handle that right there, kid."

"I'm not trying to handle that. I just think she's pretty." When I look her way again, her eyes meet mine.

"Of course she is. You saw her mama. Them genes run deep." He picks up his sandwich again and takes a bite.

"Bryan...So how much will I get paid?"

"Enough," he says with a mouthful of food.

"Come on, man, what's 'enough'?"

He raises his hand up to indicate that he needs to finish chewing before he can answer. After a few seconds, he takes a sip of his water and then leans back in his seat. "All right, white boy, I like your style. All business. Let me tell you something, here in New York, you got to live that way. Every day. That's what people here know. Money. You know what I mean?"

"So how much money am I getting paid?"

He licks his fingers as he searches the table for a napkin. "Look here, I ain't gonna lie. It wasn't going to be much at first, but I think I can get Jackie to give you a little bit more now that she's heard what you're made of. Let me hit her up after we finish the gig tonight, and I'll get back to you on that. You know what I mean?"

I give him a look of disbelief.

He wipes his hands with a napkin he takes off a table near ours. "Look, kid, I ain't gonna do you wrong. My sister would kill me. Plenty of folks here would though, including that beauty up on that stage that you can't take your eyes off. Let me give you this piece of advice. A little something from Boney Bass Bryan. You listening kid or you looking?"

"I'm listening."

"Good, because I can see you're a smart kid, but don't get dumb on beauty. You know what I mean?"

"Yeah, I understand."

"That's what I want to hear. Eat your food. She'll come to find you before the night is over. Trust me."

Chapter Seventeen

*J*ackie's Jazz & Blues.

It's a joint-style place, located just on the outskirts of Harlem. Much bigger than many would expect, once inside. Autographed pictures of music legends and platinum records encased in glass line the walls.

Soft melodies of recorded jazz make their way through the chatter of people that fill the tables and booths, as they wait for the band to return to the stage. Since it's a Friday night, the place is mixed with what Bryan calls old school music heads and people just dipping their toes into the satisfying rhythm of blues after a hard day at work.

But none of this captures my attention the way she does.

Out the corner of my eye, as I sit behind the piano, I see her. It's hard not to be captivated by the outline of her presence as she makes her way up and on the stage.

Gone are the blue jeans and casual white shirt. A silver satin dress dons her body. Gentle strands of pearls dangle from her neck and hang down to her waist. Her hair is draped off to the side and carefully held in place by a cream flower. Ruby red lipstick perfects her thick, full lips.

Simoné.

"Good evening," she says as she gently grabs the microphone. The crowd hushes as the dim lights embrace her. I watch as Bryan picks up his guitar.

"Tonight, I want to sing a little Ella Fitzgerald for you. The song is called "My Funny Valentine." It's one of my favorites."

She glances back at me as I lay my hands on the keys to lead her in. A few minutes later, Bryan makes an entrance, then the rest of the band joins in, but I only hear her.

Her voice.

It has breath.

It's living in the air.

Breathing in a rhythm that only I can understand.

I allow my fingers to be guided by her voice as it points me in the right direction.

A place where we can meet. Even if it's just in the lyrics of a song.

She closes her eyes, but even in the mist of darkness, I feel her voice searching through me.

I glide my fingers along as if I'm stroking her hair. Touching her skin.

Her voice moves me to inhale the possibilities.

The possibilities of love.

It scares me.

The thought.

The feelings that are waking up inside me.

I try to pull back, but her voice reaches out to me. It grabs at my heart and pulls me along. I don't put up a fight.

As the song nears the end, I know that this is only the beginning.

The beginning of us.

It's four in the morning when the band and I hit the last note. I make my way off the stage and over to an empty booth, as Bryan begins to pack up his guitar.

I can feel the heaviness of my eyes as I slouch down in the booth, so I lay my head on the table to give them a few minutes of rest.

Ten minutes later, I hear her voice.

Simoné.

"You were really good up there," she says, as she sits down next to me. "Way better than any pianist we've had here before. What's your name?"

I sit up."Timothy Taylor. But you can call me Timmy."

"I'm Simoné."

"Yeah, I know."

When she smiles at me, every part of me wants to kiss her.

"I was surprised at how well you could keep up. Those guys have been playing together for years. Since I was a little girl, actually. Most musicians that come through here are intimidated by them."

"They're playing music. Music isn't intimidating," I say.

"It's not? What is then? What intimidates you?" she asks as our eyes introduce themselves.

"You. You're beautiful."

I see her blush as she looks down at the table.

"You're pretty confident for a white boy."

"I'm a young man with a heart that beats just like yours. Do you want to feel it?" I take her hand and place it over my heart. "What do you feel?"

"A white boy who's trying too hard," she says as she pulls her hand away.

"Maybe. But I think you're worth trying hard for."

"You're pretty smooth."

"I'm not trying to be smooth. I'm just trying to be with you."

I watch the curves of her mouth form into a laugh. My eyes drink in the sugary brownness of her skin and her watery deep hazel eyes.

"Go out with me," I say as I move closer to her.

"Like on a date?"

"Yeah, like on a date."

"I don't date white boys," she says as she looks toward the bar area.

"Why can't I just be a boy who wants to take out a beautiful girl? Why do we have to use labels? I never called you a colored girl, did I? Do you want to know why?"

"Why?" she asks, returning her attention back towards me.

"Because you're a young woman, a human being, and I only want to treat you as such."

Her eyes meet mine again. "I see," she says, slowly.

"Look, I just want to take the beautiful girl that I just met out on a date, nothing more." I follow her eyes and see her mother leaning against the bar, staring at us. "Do I need to ask your mother first? Is that how this works? I've never done this before."

"What, ask out a colored girl?"

"Any girl," I say.

"Why am I the first?"

"Because you're smart, and like I said before, you're beautiful."

"I'm sure you've been around plenty of beautiful girls before."

"Of course, but you're the only one I want to dance with."

"Hey, Romeo! It's time for us to go," Bryan shouts from across the room.

"So are you going to go out with me or not?" I ask quickly.

"I don't know."

I see Bryan moving in our direction, so I stand up. "I have to go, but let me know tomorrow, okay?"

"Where would you take me?"

"I don't know. I just got here. You pick the place. Just let me know tomorrow, okay?"

"Okay."

"So that means it's a yes, then? You'll go out with me?"

"I guess so."

I touch the side of her face with the tip of my finger. It's exactly as I imagined.

Soft.

Outside in the crisp night air, Bryan throws the car keys at me before plopping himself in the passenger's seat. "You remember how to get back?"

"I think so," I say as I climb into the driver's seat.

"Good, because I've had way too much to drink tonight. Don't drink and drive. Remember that Boney Bass Bryan told you that. It's gonna become a saying one day."

"Are you going to be all right, man?"

"What, you ain't never seen a drunk colored man before? Just drive and don't hit anything or get pulled over. You do know how to drive, don't you?"

"Yeah, I know how to drive. I also have seen a drunk person before. My mother was one and as far as I'm concerned, being a drunk is not based on your skin color, it's based on your choice."

I glance over at Bryan, and I can tell that he's thinking about what I just said.

"Man, I'm sorry. Look here, you ain't got to worry, I don't drink often, and you will never see me drunk again. I promise you that." He leans his head back in his seat for a second but then sits up again. "I thought you said you were listening, not looking."

"Huh?"

"Young and dumb. You're gonna learn, kid. You're gonna learn you can't touch everything just because it's beautiful. It's like my mama used to tell us kids—when we were young bucks, you know. She'd say as we walked into some fancy store, 'Look but don't touch.' You acting just like we did back then—young and dumb. You know what my mama used to do to us if we touched those beautiful things?" He looks at me. "She'd give us a real good whipping when we got home. That's what she'd do. You're gonna learn, and it's gonna be just as painful."

Ten minutes later, he's fast asleep.

Chapter Eighteen

Sunday night brought in a wave of people eager to listen to something that would allow them to escape the reality of having to go to work the next day. The dimly lit lights seem to give the night just the right flavor as I sit behind the piano with my ears in the air, listening for my cue.

All night, the band keeps drawing me in. Whenever I'd hit the keys of my piano, the crowd would beg for more, and I'd give it to them.

I found myself smiling. Laughing. Feeling like I belonged. Like I had a home. A place in music.

There was only one thing I longed for.

It was her.

Simoné.

For the last three weeks, I've tried to take Bryan's advice and stay away from the 'beautiful' things. But every night, I see her eyes, her smile, and it's as though she's speaking to me without ever saying a word. I can't shake it. I can't shake her, and quite frankly, I'm tired of trying to.

Tonight, I'm going to stop admiring the beautiful things only from a distance.

I wait for the tables to be cleared and the doors to be locked before I approach her. It 's been tough trying to get her alone so we can talk, but my chance has finally come as I see her sitting at the bar, drinking a cup of water. Her shoes are on the seat next to her, and she has her head down, listening to the recorded music that plays through the speakers in the ceiling.

Looking as beautiful as ever.

"Long night?" I ask as I walk up to her slowly.

"Yeah."

I pull up a chair and take a seat next to her. I can smell her perfume as I glance around the room and spot Bryan in the corner, talking to a waitress.

A member of the band walks up, just as I'm about to try to ask her out again. Miles. He plays the saxophone and has a set of lungs that never seem to run out of air.

"You got some skills, kid," he says as he stands on the side of me. Grinning.

"Thanks, you do too."

"You need to think about doing something more with that. Something more than just this place."

We both look around the joint, at the same time. "One day, sure. Right now, I'm just trying to keep up with you guys." I say with a bit of laughter in my voice.

He places his saxophone bag on the floor, next to him. "Man, please. You and I both know that we're just trying to keep up with you. Who taught you how to play the keys like that? You be on fire with every note." He moves his hands in the air like he's playing the piano.

I chuckle as I watch him. Simoné does, as well. "Thanks, man. I taught myself," I say.

He nods his head enthusiastically. "That's what's up. When you play, man, it ain't nothing but soul. You got it. It's like it's pouring out those fingers of yours. Most white boys ain't got that, but you got it. Best believe. I've seen a lot of cats come through here. None of them can touch you."

I smile and glance over at Simoné, who's nodding her head in agreement, which seems to fuel Miles' enthusiasm even more.

"You're hot, kid. I mean, like, really hot. This joint ain't never been packed as it's been these last couple of weeks. Did you see the crowd in here tonight? A Sunday at that! That's fire! That's hot. You the man." He glances at Simoné for reassurance, and she nods again. "Most of us here ain't never had any formal training. No schooling, I mean, like our little princess here. We all learned our thing from the street. That's how you learn to play real jazz."

"That's why I'm here, to learn real jazz," I say, hoping this will end the conversation.

"Ain't that right." He glances at me and smiles as if he gets the hint. He then claps his hands together and places his saxophone bag back on his shoulder. "Well, all right then, you kids be good. I'm out. I ain't like the rest of these cats—I got a wife and three babies at home." He glances over at Bryan. "Fifty years old and still trying to work it. I ain't mad at him."

Simoné and I wait for him to leave before we both burst out laughing at the same time.

I watch her for a few minutes, before starting our conversation back up again. "So you're going to some musical school or something?" I ask as I reach over the bar and pour myself a glass of water and throw a few lemons in it before taking a sip.

"Fancy," she says as she watches me.

I shake my head in disagreement. "Nothing fancy. I just like lemons."

"I see." She reaches over and plops a few in her glass and we both smile. "Actually, I go to the university here. It's my second year."

"That makes you what, nineteen?"

"It does."

"You want some more water to go with your fancy lemons?" I ask. I love to see the movement of her mouth when she smiles.

"Sure. Thanks."

I take her glass and pour some water into it. Our hands touch for a second as she takes it out of my hand.

I see her blush as she places her glass on the counter.

"So what about you?" she asks, clearing her throat. "You have any plans to go to college?"

I lean back in my chair casually. "College was never my thing. My father wanted me to go, however." I take a sip of my water. "I think I need something stronger."

She glances at me with a questioning look on her face.

I laugh a little. "I was referring to a pop. You know, Coca-Cola?"

She smirks as she grabs the line with the Coca-Cola in it. "I knew that. Give me your glass."

I hand my glass over to her.

"You should reconsider," she says, as I watch her.

"What, college? Why?"

She leans back in her chair, and our eyes connect. "So you'll have something to fall back on. A Plan B. Most don't make it in the music industry, you know."

"I will."

She grabs her glass and pours some Coca-Cola into it. "I'm sure. But it still never hurts to have a backup."

"You can be my backup."

"There you go putting it on heavy, white boy."

"How long are you going to keep it up with the white boy stuff?" I ask as I stand up, instantly seeing the remorse on her face.

"I'm sorry. Come on, sit back down."

I pretend to hesitate for a second.

"I'm sorry. Really, I am. Sit back down. Please," she says as she pats the seat I was sitting in. "We can talk about where you're going to take me on our date."

I ease back in my seat. "I thought maybe you had changed your mind or something. It's been a few weeks since I asked you out. You've been avoiding me ever since."

She looks down at the counter. "I'm sorry. I've just been busy. School three days a week and working here every weekend."

"You just weren't sure you wanted to go out with a white boy," I say with a sarcastic tone.

"Don't be like that."

"Why not? You know it's true." I look over and see her mother sitting in one of the booths, staring at us. "Your mother doesn't seem to like me, does she? Is that the real reason why you've been avoiding me?"

"She's cool. Just being a mother. You know how that is."

"Actually, I don't."

"Did your mother pass away or something?"

"I wish."

"Don't say that. That's not nice."

"It isn't. It's just true."

She places her hand on top of mine, and I can feel the warmth of her skin. We both look down at her hand on top of mine and allow a moment of silence to rest between us.

"Was she mean or something?" she whispers.

I look over at her mother again. "You could say that."

"I'm sorry to hear that," she says as she slowly takes her hand away.

I shrug my shoulders some. "It's cool. So where do you want to go?"

She sits up in her seat, and her smile brightens the mood. "I was thinking a restaurant or something."

"What's open at three in the morning?" I ask.

"I'm not talking about now."

"Why not? I'm hungry. Come on." I grab her hand. "There's got to be something around here. New York is famous for diners, right?"

"Of course, but—"

"No buts. Let's go." I start pulling her toward the door.

"Really?"

"Really," I say.

"Wait. I need to put my shoes on."

I watch as she slips her shoes on and then I grab her hand again.

When I feel the warmth of her skin in my hand, I know.

I know that I will fall in love with her.

Chapter Nineteen

*T*he diner is packed, so it takes us a few minutes to find a table, but we finally settle down at one in the corner, by the window. I can't take my eyes off her as we wait for a waitress to come over.

"Why do you keep staring at me like that?"

"I like the way your mouth moves."

She looks around the diner to see if anyone heard me.

"Am I making you nervous?"

"A little, to be honest. You sure you haven't done this before?"

"Been out on a date with a beautiful girl? Never."

There she goes . . . blushing again.

"Stop calling me that," she says.

"Stop calling you what?"

"Beautiful."

"Why?" I ask in a curious tone.

"Because there's more to me than my looks."

"That's why we're here, aren't we?" I wait for her eyes to meet mine. "To get to know each other beyond all outside appearances."

She looks away. "You know who you remind me of?"

"Who?" I ask as I wave my hand to get the attention of a waitress nearby.

"An older man. It's like you have an old man's mind in that young body of yours."

"Is that a good thing?"

"It's different. I like different."

"Good, because I like you."

"You don't know me enough to know if you like me or not," she says as she pretends to be looking over the menu.

"Sure, I do. Your eyes tell me everything I need to know."

She looks up at me. "Like?"

I lean back in my chair. "So you're just going to put me on the spot like that?"

She mocks me and does the same. "You put yourself on the spot. So let's hear it. What do you see in my eyes?"

The waitress comes over to take our order, and I wipe my head, acting as if the interruption came just in time to get me off the hook.

Simoné places her order and then glances over at me. "Don't think you're off the hook from answering my question."

I wink at her and give the waitress my order. I let a few minutes go by after the waitress leaves. I can see the anticipation on Simoné's face."

"Timmy, come on, spill it!"

"What?" I ask in a playful manner.

"Tell me."

I pick up a spoon and begin tapping it on the table. "You really want to know?"

"Stop stalling!" she says as she reaches over and grabs the spoon from my hand to stop the tapping.

"I'm not stalling," I say.

She leans over the table and cups her face in her hands, as she props her elbows on the table. "Then tell me what you see when you look at me. What you see beyond my looks."

I lean over and allow our eyes to play with each other. "Okay." I clear my throat.

"Am I making you nervous?" she asks in a flirtatious manner.

"Just a little," I say. Flirting back.

"Come on. You put yourself out there. Don't chicken out now."

"I'm not going to chicken out." I reach over and grab her hands. I can feel her pulse. I imagine that it's beating just for me. "When I look in your eyes, I see a strong woman who isn't afraid to let go. Who isn't scared to be herself. Still, even in that strength, I see traces of fear. Fear of giving your heart to someone. Fear of being kissed by someone. Fear of falling in love.

"When you sing, you sing with everything because music is where no one can touch you. No one can tell you want to do. Not your mother. Not the band. Music allows you to be you. It's your protector. That's why you belt out each note with such raw passion. It's like you're giving every lyric that drops from those beautiful lips of yours a hug. That's what I see in your eyes. That's what my heart hears when you open your mouth." I stop and fight the urge to reach over the table and allow our lips to meet.

"Wow," she says slowly, as she pulls her hands back and leans back in her chair again. "That was...that was pretty insightful. Sounded kind of rehearsed, though."

I chuckle. "Come on, you know that wasn't rehearsed."

"I don't know. It kind of sounded like it. That's all I'm saying." She starts to grin and I...I reach across the table and pull her to me. I place a soft kiss on her lips.

She looks around the restaurant.

"You're blushing," I say, watching her in amusement. "You seem to be doing that a lot lately."

"That's because of you."

"I kissed you. I'm sorry."

She gives me a non-believing look.

"Yeah, you're right. I did it on purpose. I couldn't help it. I've been sitting here, all night, trying hard not to. It's your fault, you know?"

"My fault?"

"Yes. You and those kissable lips. It's hard for a man to resist. You know what I mean?"

"Oh, my. You sound like Boney."

We both laugh as the waitress finally brings over our food. I wait for the waitress to leave and move out of earshot range. "Simoné, I meant what I said earlier. I'll never lie to you. I think you're amazing. Inside and out." I lean over and retake her hand. "Do you believe that?"

Her eyes seem to search through me as she looks into mine. I can feel her heart checking to see if mine is real. If I am real. I don't mind the examination. I'd open up my soul for her.

"Yeah, I believe that," she finally whispers.

I look down at my plate. "This looks good. It's a lot of food, though."

"It's a diner. There's always a lot of food. That's New York. It's how we do things," she says as she takes a bite of her sandwich. I lean back and watch.

She glances up at me as she takes a sip of her pop. "Please tell me that you're going to eat and not just sit there and watch me eat?"

I smirk as I grab my glass. "I'll eat. Eventually."

"These French fries are amazing. Love the way they put seasoning on top of them. Here, try one."

I lean over, and she places a French fry into my mouth.

"They're hot. But you're right, they are good."

"Sorry, I should have warned you." She gives me a sly smile.

"So now it's your turn," I say as I swallow the French fry and take a sip of my water.

"What do you mean?" she asks as she continues to eat her sandwich.

"It's your turn to tell me what you see when you look at me."

"Are you sure you want to know?"

"I am."

"All right then." She places her sandwich down.

"Hold on," I say.

"What are you doing?"

"Getting ready. A man has to be in a good position for a woman to see what's in his heart."

She laughs as I pretend to adjust myself in my seat.

"Are you ready now?" she asks as I move a few more times.

"Okay, now I'm ready. Look as deep as you need to."

She gives me a smirk, but then her face turns serious. "When I look at you, I see depth in your hazel eyes. I see thick eyebrows. Slightly broad shoulders, a slender nose, and great lips."

"Great lips, huh?"

She smiles. "Let me finish."

"I'm sorry. Go ahead."

She sits up in her chair. "I also see a young man with black wavy hair that he hates."

"I don't hate my hair. But come on, those are just my looks. What do you see when you look at me, beyond those things?"

She reaches across the table and takes my hands into hers. "I see pain. Determination. Honesty. I see a man who looks at things outside of the normal every day. Who isn't afraid to speak his mind. Who isn't afraid to get lost."

"Get lost in what?" I ask.

"In someone who needs to be found."

"Do you need to be found, Simoné?"

The waitress returns and fills up our glasses before she can respond.

"So how long has your mother owned the club?" I ask as the waitress walks away.

"Since I was born. She inherited it from her father. She's remodeled the place over the years, but it still has the same vibe. I think that's why people love it. That's why they come. I guess that's why I love it there, too."

She takes a sip from her glass again and clears her throat. "You were right about me. You know?"

"Which part?" I ask.

"All of it really. Music has been sort of a protector for me. I love music. I love it because, in it, I find a place where I can go and just be me. Whenever I sing, I find a certain kind of strength when the lights go dim, and no one can see me. They can only hear my voice. On that stage, I feel like I can put all my troubles, all my worries into the air and let them ride off and be as free as they want to be. You know what I mean?"

"Yeah, I do. It's why I love playing the piano."

"Miles was right. You should try to do more with that. I could talk to some people. My mother knows a lot of people in the industry."

"I thought you said I should go to college."

"I did. You should. But you should also follow your dream if playing the piano is it."

"It is. It's all I know. To be honest, I don't want to know or do anything else. I'm going to make it. That's why I came here."

"It kind of sounded like you came here to get away from your mother."

I look out the window for a second or two. "That too. But it doesn't change the fact that I believe in myself."

She pushes her plate forward and places a napkin over what's left. "I love singing. I do. But if I had my choice, I'd be doing something else."

"Like what? Get married? Have babies?" I give her a sly smile.

"One day," she says, smiling back at me. "But I really want to . . ."

"What? What is it that you really want to do?"

"I really want to dance. I love ballet. I used to practice all the time when I was a little girl. I know all the moves."

"Really? So, why didn't you go to a ballet school?"

She looks away from me. "Because . . ."

"Because, what?"

"My mother would kill me if I drop out of school. She doesn't believe it's possible to support yourself dancing. Plus, Blacks haven't always been allowed to go to college, you know. Movements and marches are still going on all over, to further that right and others. "

"So you're going to a school that you don't want to go to, for your mother and for the movement?" I ask, sarcastically.

"You wouldn't understand."

"Why? Because I'm white?"

"Maybe," she says as she looks down at her covered plate.

"That's nonsense, and you know it."

She looks me in the eyes. "It's not nonsense, it's just complicated." I frown.

"Stop looking at me like that."

"I take it all back."

"What are you talking about."

"Everything I said about you. About you being strong."

"I am strong."

"Then, prove it. Go after your dream. If you want to dance, do that."

"My mother is not one to cross. She always gets her way. It's how it always has been, and it's how it is now. What about you? What are you trying to prove to yourself? To the world?"

I smirk at her. "Don't try to throw it back on me," I say.

"I'm not. Answer the question. What do you want to prove?" she asks as I reach into my pocket and place money on the table to cover the check.

"That I'm worth it."

"Worth what?"

"Love."

Chapter Twenty

"Is that a park up the way?" I ask as we walk down the street with her hand in mine.

"It is, but shouldn't we be getting back? I have a class in about five hours."

"Come on," I say, pulling her toward the park.

A few minutes later, we spot a bench just under a tree. She sits down and takes her shoes off.

"Aren't your feet going to get cold?"

"I doubt it. It's pretty warm tonight. Besides, these shoes are killing me. I've been in them all night."

I stand, remove my jacket and then sit down next to her. "Give them to me."

"What are you talking about?"

"Your feet. Put them here, on my lap."

"Are you serious?"

"Of course." I lean over, grab her feet and place them on my lap, then I put my jacket over them.

"Thank you," she says.

We sit and listen to the crickets in the bushes behind us.

"I love the summertime. What's this time of year like in Chicago?" she asks.

"I don't know. I was more of an indoor person. I spent most of my time listening to music and playing my piano every chance I got."

"That's a shame. I bet Chicago is beautiful in the summer."

"Maybe one day I'll take the time to pay attention. If I ever go back."

"You had a piano?"

"What do you mean?"

"You said that you played your piano all the time, so that means that you must have had one, right?"

A couple holding hands walks by us.

"You going to answer my question?"

"Why?" I ask, watching the couple fade out of sight.

"I'm just trying to get to know you. You could be a serial killer or something. You do have me in a park at the crack of dawn."

I laugh. "I'm not a serial killer."

"But your parents have money, right?"

"They do," I say, wishing we could change the subject.

"So let me guess. You didn't take a dime of it when you left because, as you said, you want to prove to your father that you can make it without his money. Am I right?"

"You want to dance?" I ask.

She looks around the park. "Here? Now?"

"Sure, why not?"

"We don't have any music."

"We have you. You can sing for us. Be our music. I'll just move with you."

"Can you dance?"

"Let's find out." I grab her hands and stand her up. I pull her close, wrapping my arms around her waist. Her body is warm as she rests her head on my shoulders and we start to move. "Your hair smells good."

"Thank you. You feel that?"

"What, my heart beating?" I whisper.

"No." She steps back. "A raindrop."

"I don't feel—"

I look up as the sky sends warm rain crashing down on our skin.

"Oh no, my hair!"

I laugh really hard, as we stand in the rain.

"What are you laughing at? I look a mess! My hair is ruined!"

"You look beautiful. Don't worry about your hair. I'm not worried about mine." I run my hands through my hair.

She starts to laugh and I find myself desperately wanting to touch her lips as they move.

Wanting to feel the warm rain upon them.

"Shall we?" I say, reaching out my hand.

Her body moves slowly as I pull her into my arms again.

She starts to sing. Softly. Gently.

"I know this song. It's Nina Simoné," I say as I twirl her around and watch the way her hair clings to the front of her face, covering her eyes. I pull it off to the side. When my fingers touch her skin, I pull her closer to me. Our lips barely touching.

"Simoné," I whisper as the streetlights dance in her eyes. "I want you to know that I want to be with you."

"You are with me," she whispers back.

"No, I mean, as your man. You okay with that? You okay with having a white boy love you?"

"I thought we weren't using labels anymore?" she says, looking into my eyes.

"I just want you to be sure. To understand who I am and to accept me for that."

"I do."

"So is that a yes?"

She nods slowly as my fingers caress the small of her back.

"I'm going to kiss you now," I whisper in her ear.

"All right," she whispers back.

Chapter Twenty-One

"What time is it?" I ask, as I slowly open my eyes to see Bryan in the kitchen, fixing coffee.

"Well, look who finally came home. If it isn't Romeo himself."

"You make me a cup?"

"Cups are in the cabinet. Coffee is on the stove, young buck."

I stretch as I move slowly to get up. Finally making my way into the kitchen.

"So you finally got that first date, huh?"

I lean against the refrigerator and rub my eyes. "Yeah, something like that."

"I mean with her, not ever."

I don't respond as I grab a cup from the cabinet by the refrigerator. He stares at me as I turn around. Cup in hand.

"Tell me you've been on dates before."

I shrug my shoulders slowly and look down at the floor.

"You're pulling my chain here, right?"

I glance over at him as he stands there with this dumbfounded look on his face.

"Wait, did my sister give you the speech?"

"What speech?" I say, acting as if I don't know what he's talking about.

"Yeah, she did. That look on your face confirms it." He walks over to the stove and pours himself another cup of coffee. "Don't worry, she gave me that same speech, right before I moved here. The 'don't date until you're ready for marriage' speech."

"I happen to think she's right."

"Really? So what was last night?" He places his cup on the counter, next to him.

"We went to grab a bite, and then we danced in the rain at the park."

He smirks. "Oh, is that all, Mister Romeo?" He picks his cup up again and takes a sip. "Sounds like a date to me. But look here, just so we're crystal about all of this—you ain't ready for marriage or the things that come with it. You know what I mean?"

I walk over to pour myself a cup of coffee. "Dude, there isn't much in here."

"Margaret ain't here, kid. Make some more, unless you don't know how."

"I know how to make coffee."

"Really? Let's see it."

I fumble around with the coffee pot for a few minutes.

"Just as I figured. Let me show you how to do this." I watch as he measures out the coffee, adds the water and then places it on the stove. "You got it?"

"Yeah, I got it."

He leans up against the sink. "So you in love now?"

"I like her."

He slaps his hand on the counter. "Boy, please. You got whipped written all over that forehead of yours. You were in love with Little Miss Thang the moment you saw her. I saw it. Shoot, the whole band saw it. Even her mama saw it."

"Which explains why she's always lurking around, staring at me whenever I try to speak to Simoné."

"Just remember what I told you. Her mama is all about business. Not love. Her daughter ain't much different."

I give him an ambiguous look. "Meaning?"

"Look, kid, don't say that I didn't warn you. They act all innocent-like, but like I said before when it comes to Simoné, the apple doesn't fall far from the tree. You know what I mean?"

"How do you know so much about her or her mama?"

He smiles. "I just do. I've been around. Jackie and I go way back."

I shake my head. "Well, Simoné is nothing like her mother. She's got dreams and plans of her own."

"Is that right?"

"Yes. She told me."

"Well, I'll be. So now you feel like you know everything there is to know about her because she told you so?"

"I'm not saying everything. I'm sure there are a lot of things I don't know about her. But in time I will."

"Oh, so you in there for the long haul, huh?"

"Maybe. I asked her if she and I could be together."

"Together how?" he asks, looking at me with an incredulous smile.

"Not like that."

"Better not be. You're just a young buck, you know what I mean? Too young to have little feet running around here. Trust me, you ain't ready for all that."

"I asked her to be my girlfriend," I say, matter-of-factly.

"And what did Little Miss Thang say to that?"

"She said yes."

He grins. "Of course she did. Well, all right, lover boy, go head with your bad self. Got yourself a woman in just a few weeks of hitting the streets of New York. And what a woman! You do you, man! Just don't let foolish love bite you in the heart, you know what I mean?"

"It's the butt."

"I know. But I also know what I said."

Chapter Twenty-Two

"*W*hat you doing up so early?" Bryan asks as he walks into the kitchen to grab a glass of water.

"It's eleven," I say, glancing over at the small clock over the stove.

"Man, it's eleven? That was some good sleep." He looks at my plate on the counter. "Did you make that toast?"

"Stop acting surprised! I finally figured out how to use that toaster you got."

"You the man," he says as he walks over and pats me on the shoulder.

"Whatever."

"Maybe in another month or two, you'll figure out how to use the stove to make something other than coffee."

"You got jokes this morning. Hey, I need to use your car later."

"I don't know about that. My car is kind of funny about other folks driving it."

"I've driven it before," I say.

"What's up? What you got going on?"

"I want to surprise Simoné today. It's Wednesday, so she doesn't have school, and we don't have to work tonight."

He leans up against the counter. "Jackie's probably going to change that soon, so don't get settled in. Folks have been asking her about opening five days. You know she's all about that paper."

"She'll have to pay us more," I say.

"My man. I keep forgetting you be all about that business, too. I'll talk to her about it. Say, look here, you ain't talking like a ring surprise here, are you, young buck?"

"Didn't you tell me I wasn't ready for marriage?" I say sarcastically.

"You ain't been listening to me since you got here. Too busy looking. I figure why change the game now?"

I give him a sly smile. "I listen. Sometimes."

He shakes his head in denial. "Sure you do. Look here, young buck, let me get a couple slices of that toast."

"There's the bread," I say, snickering.

"Funny." He walks over, opens the bread, and slides a couple of pieces into the toaster. "So, it's been what, two months now for you and Miss Thang?"

"Something like that." I glance at him, trying to figure out where's he's going with this.

"You two seem to be stuck together," he says. Giving me a weird look.

"I guess. Why?"

"Just sniffing you out is all."

"What, I stink now or something?"

"Naw, you'll come to understand what I mean by that one day. I just hope it ain't soon, you know what I mean?"

I laugh as I finally get it. "Yeah, I think so."

"So you tell her yet?" he asks as he grabs his toast and places it on a napkin.

"Dude, you got plates," I say, pointing to the cabinet.

"Man, ain't no housekeeper in this place. Napkins do me just fine. Now, answer my question."

"Tell her what?

"That you're in love with her," he says, after taking a bite out of his toast.

"You going to let me borrow your car or not?"

"Oh, so you trying to tell me in a not-so-polite way to stay out of your business." He walks over to the refrigerator. "I need some jam or something. I can't eat dry toast, like you."

"Man, the car?"

"It's cool. What time you need it?" he asks, as he gets out the jam and proceeds to spread it on his toast. I watch as he then licks the spoon.

"I hope you don't put that back in that jar again."

"It's my place. I bought that jar, so I just might," he says with a smirk on his face.

I shake my head. "That's gross. Anyway, I need the car around seven. I'm taking her out for dinner and dancing. It's a really nice place."

"I see. Well, most real nice dinner and dancing clubs that I know of, ain't allowing jeans and a shirt."

"Yeah, that's why I bought a suit and tie a couple of days ago. Just about broke me."

"I see she already got you spending money you ain't making. That's how women do. Did you tell her about your dinner and dancing plans?"

I throw my hands up in the air. "I just told you that it's a surprise."

He looks over at me and shakes his head. "Kid, you gonna learn."

"Now what are you talking about?"

"Look here, young buck, dinner, and dancing, to a woman, requires a fancy dress, a trip to the hair salon, and a pair of shoes that ain't gonna kill her feet while you twirling her around the dance floor, you know what I mean? You can't just spring something like that on them. Shoot, they spend all day getting ready for something like that. But I guess your woman ain't like that, huh?"

I run my hand through my hair. "So, you're saying that I should let her know?"

"I just might be."

"Let me go call her."

"So you listen when you need to, huh?"

"Man, eat your toast," I say, as I head to the phone.

Chapter Twenty-Three

*H*ow do you capture beauty? You don't. You watch it walk down a flight of steps and glide over to you as if it's walking on a cloud.

Simoné.

My woman.

It was hard not to be in awe of her beauty as she stands in front of me. Hair pulled up. Earrings dangling, mixing in with the light of the moon. Eyes sparkling.

Her long, backless black evening gown obediently resting on the curves of her body.

"Wow, you clean up well. I think this is the first time I've seen you in a suit," she says as she gently plays with her earring.

"You don't look so bad yourself."

"Is that right?"

I pull her close and kiss her neck. "Man, you smell good."

"Thank you."

I take a step back from her.

"You look . . . well, you look beautiful."

"Much better," she says with a smile that melts my heart. I run my hand through my hair as I open her door and watch her ease inside.

"When is Boney going to get rid of this piece of junk?" she asks as she checks her lipstick.

"You know he loves this thing," I say. I listen to her laugh and know there isn't a thing about her that I don't love.

"I know. I think he even named it," she says.

"Bettsie."

"Yeah, that's it." She places her hands in my hair.

"You know that took all day, right?" I say, grinning.

"What took all day?"

"My hair."

She laughs and places her arm around my neck.

"You have to stop doing that," I say, playing with her.

"Doing what?"

"Laughing like that. It's too cute. Too . . ."

"Too what?" she asks, giving me a sly smile.

"That too. That smile. It's dangerous."

"So now I can't laugh or smile?"

"Exactly."

"What can I do?"

"Be my woman."

"I'm already that, aren't I?" She places a small kiss on my cheek. "So how far is this place?"

"Not too far. It's in Manhattan," I say as we merge onto I-95. "We should be there in about thirty minutes or so."

I notice that she suddenly gets quiet. "What's wrong?" I ask.

"Nothing really. It's just that for the last couple of months, I've been thinking about what Miles said."

"What did he say?"

"He talked about how he thought you should try to get something better."

I smile as I glance at her. "I like where I'm at. I get to see you and play music. It's cool."

"But you're worth more than my mother's place. Everyone knows it. In fact, my mother has a few connections with Fountain Records. You ever heard of them?"

"They're pretty big," I say as I watch for my exit to come up.

"They are. I could introduce you to someone from there."

"Maybe," I say, very nonchalantly.

"Just think about it," she says as she moves back over to her side.

"What's that all about?" I ask. Concerned.

"What?"

"Why did you move? I'm not dismissing your idea. I'm just not sure I'm ready for it, right now." I reach over and gently stroke the side of her face. "Come on, don't get mad."

"I'm not mad."

"Then smile for me."

"I thought you didn't want me to smile."

I glance over at her again. "You know what kind of smile I was talking about."

I watch her face. "That one, right there."

We both laugh.

She reaches over and flicks on the radio. "This piece of junk only has only one radio station?"

"At least it's not country music," I say with a slight chuckle.

"I've heard Boney listen to country music. He says that a real artist of music appreciates it in every form."

"That's deep," I say.

"Yeah, especially for Boney. You know what I mean?"

We both laugh again.

"I think this is what I should be on," I say, as I see NY-9A S come up. "It's only about five miles, once we get off at 79 St, I think."

She leans back in her seat as we listen to the one radio that will play. Ten minutes later, I pull into the parking lot of the restaurant. and park the car.

"Be careful," I say as I wrap my arm around her waist and we head toward the entrance.

"I've always wanted to come here. I've passed this place so many times. I heard it's hard to get in because they have an amazing room for dancing on the other side."

"That's why I made reservations."

She stops at the door. "You sure you can afford this place?"

"I don't know, I've seen you eat."

"Funny," she says with a smirk.

"Come on, let's get at it," I say.

"Boney always says that."

"I know."

"He kills me with that," she says as I open the door.

"Tell me about it. But he's been a good friend."

"You seem to trust him a lot."

"I do. I know he always has my back."

"Welcome to Michael's," the hostess says as we walk in.

"Reservations for Mr. Taylor," I say. Glad I made them since the place is packed.

"Right this way, Mr. Taylor. We have a booth ready, right by the window, as you requested," the hostess says as she leads us past a crowd of people waiting for a table.

As we follow her to our table, I fell Simoné squeeze my hand.

She waits for the hostess to leave. "Did you notice that the hostess didn't even look at me?"

"I didn't really. If you're uncomfortable, we can leave."

"And miss out on that amazing dance floor they have! I'm just going to have to show them how black folks get down, the fancy way."

"I love you." It falls off my tongue and lands on the table between us. It wasn't how I wanted to say it or even how I wanted it to happen, but there it was . . . staring at us both.

"I know," she whispers. "This place is beautiful," she says, as her eyes roam the restaurant.

"I hope you brought your dancing shoes," I say, changing the subject for the time being.

"What do you know about that?" she asks, slyly.

"Bryan schooled me, as he says."

"I've got them on and ready to hit the floor after we eat." She moves one of her legs out from the table and shows off her shoes.

"I'm just ready to get you in my arms."

"Is that right?"

"It is."

"Tell me about your parents. What are they like?"

I take a sip of my water. "Wow. Where did that come from?"

"Your mother hurt you, didn't she?"

I take another sip of my water and glance down at the menu. "She would beat the crap out of me after she drank. She was always drunk."

"I'm sorry to hear that. Is that why I haven't seen Boney drinking much since you came?"

"I didn't realize he was drinking less."

"Not that he ever had a drinking problem or anything, but now he doesn't touch the stuff. He seems to care about you a lot."

"And what about you? Do you care for me, Simoné?"

She leans over the table and whispers in my ear, "I do."

Just as I go to kiss her, a waitress comes to take our order.

"You know, when I was a little girl, I used to imagine that my father was some tall, dark, handsome fellow who came through New York, swept my mother off her feet, and then went off to war or something and was never heard from again," she says, after the waitress walks away.

"That's some imagination."

She takes a sip of her water. "I know. It's probably far from the reality though."

"You never know. It could be close."

"It could be. My mother always tries to play like she has amnesia whenever I ask about him."

"Maybe that's because she loved him and it's hard for her to talk about it."

"I considered that, but with my mother, I doubt it. She isn't the type to fall in love."

"Are you?"

"It depends."

"On what?" I say, amused.

"On if the guy can dance or not."

I stick my leg out from underneath the table and lift up my pants leg. "Good thing I brought my dancing shoes."

"You are funny."

"I try to be."

She grins at me as the waitress brings our food.

For the next thirty minutes or so, we eat and chat about our favorite music artists.

"You know, I think that's the first time I've seen you eat all your food," she says, pointing to my clean plate.

"At these prices, I wasn't going to leave a morsel."

She looks down at her plate. "I was thinking the same thing."

We both chuckle.

"So you ready to put those shoes to work?" I ask.

She nods as I help her out of the booth and we head next door.

*T*he music is intoxicating.

"Do you hear that piano?" I say as we walk in.

"Yeah, he's good but not as good as you," she says, pulling me to the dance floor.

"You know, I've been waiting all night to get you in my arms," I say as I pull her close and place a kiss on her neck.

"This isn't a slow song," she says as her body moves to the beat of the music.

I step back. "Well all right then, little mama, show me what you got."

"You 're a mess, Timothy Taylor," she says as she swings her hands in the air and moves her feet.

"Only when I'm with you," I say as I try to match her style of dancing.

Suddenly, the music slows down and the lights dim.

"I guess you got your wish."

"It's like they were reading my mind."

She rests her head on my shoulders as we move in tune.

"You can dance, Mr. Taylor."

I spin her around slowly and then pull her close to me again, smelling the sweet aroma of her hair and feeling the warmth of her back as my fingers touch her skin.

"Simoné?" I whisper in her ear.

"Yes, Timmy."

"I meant what I said earlier, I'm falling in love with you. You know that, don't you?"

"I do."

"I want to . . ."

"Let's go."

I stop and look into her eyes. "Are you sure?"

"Yes."

Chapter Twenty-Four

"**G**ood, you're up," Bryan says as he pulls up a chair.

"What's up with the heat?"

"I'll get with the landlord about it later. Simoné called you an hour or so ago. Something about you and her going to get a car. What's that about? I know you ain't buying that girl a car."

"It's for me. Now that you've negotiated all of us getting paid more since Jackie started opening up the place on Wednesdays, I can afford a car. Just in time too, since it's the middle of December and your piece of junk doesn't have any heat."

"You been enjoying that piece of junk for the last six months, just remember that, kid."

"True, and don't get me wrong, your piece of junk is great. It's wonderful. It just doesn't have any heat."

He stands up. "You go ahead and get yourself a car with your little girlfriend. Just don't let her talk you into spending all the money you ain't making yet."

"I won't."

He looks at me.

"I won't. I promise."

"Don't make promises your little girlfriend ain't gonna let you keep."

"I'm not getting anything fancy. In fact, why don't you come with us? I've never bought a car before, and I could use your experience."

"Don't try to flatter me."

I shake my head in denial. "Will you come?"

"I might think about it." He sits back down and leans back in his chair. "So what's this I hear about you talking to some dude from Fountain Records?"

"I'm not talking to him. He's just some guy Simoné knows."

He slaps his hand on his knee. "You trying to get a record deal and didn't talk to me?"

I sit up. "No. But to be honest, I didn't think I needed your permission."

"Now hold on, young buck, don't let your little girlfriend get your chest all out in the air. I'm just trying to look out for you," he says as a look of concern covers his face.

I smile, trying to lighten the situation some. "I know you're always looking out for me. I didn't mean it that way. You know I wouldn't do anything like that without talking to you first. I trust you. You're my best friend. I only talk to them for her. I'm not trying to do anything with them."

I can see him settle down some. "I hope not. This is New York. It ain't the yellow brick road, you know what I mean?"

"Yeah, I hear you."

"No, listen to me. I mean, really listen. Better yet, talk to some of the cats in the band. They'll tell you about Fountain Records and their contracts. We've all been there and got taken."

"Like I said, I'm not looking for a record deal with Fountain Records. I kind of like where I am. It's a good spot."

He stands up and paces the floor in front of me some.

"What's going on, Bryan?" I say as I pull my covers back and sit on the edge of the bed, fearing for the worst.

He stops and turns the front of the seat towards him and straddles it. "Look here, young buck, there's something you should know. Something I think I should have told you."

"What?"

"Jackie's place ain't no good spot. It's cool for me. It's cool for the band, but it ain't no good spot for you. I know you don't want to believe that, but trust me, it ain't."

"Why not?"

He pauses. "Jackie got a way of doing things, especially when she sees something in you. Something that can make her money. She ain't right and the things she tries to do ain't right."

"So why do you work there?"

"I got my reasons."

"That's not telling me much."

"Kid, if you open them young buck ears of yours and really hear what I'm saying, it's telling you everything."

I shake my head in frustration. "Now, I'm confused. Are you saying that I should just take a record deal and move on from there? Simoné thinks so. She's been mentioning it for a while now."

"That girl got your nose wide open."

"She loves me. Wants what's best for me, that's all."

"You keep believing that, kid. You keep believing that she's doing it all just for you."

I stand up and face him. "You know, you're always talking bad about her, but you never give me any real evidence to back up your claims."

He stands up and moves the chair away. "They ain't claims, kid. Just truth that you ought to recognize and listen to. I speak from experience. Best believe that."

"Well, just remember that you're the one who got me a job there, so it can't be all that bad."

He leans up against the wall. "I was hoping it wouldn't go down like this, but now I see I'm going to have to fix this."

"What are you talking about?" I ask, even more, confused than before.

"Nothing." He throws his hands up in the air. "What time are you going to get your own piece of junk?"

"In about an hour."

He starts to move toward the front door. "Cool. I tell you what, you and Miss Princess go handle that. I'll see you both at the club tonight. Come early, I want to have a meeting with the band and discuss some new music." He grabs his jacket.

"Where are you going?"

"I got somewhere I gotta go in my piece of junk."

I place my hands on my hips as I watch him open the door. "Man, I'm sorry. Don't be like that," I shout. "Bettsie and I are cool!"

A few seconds later, the door closes behind him.

Chapter Twenty-Five

"So what did you get?" Boney asks as Simoné, and I make our way inside the club, pulling our coats off and placing them behind the bar.

"A piece of junk just like you have, Boney," Simoné quickly says.

"At least my piece of junk has heat that works," I say, jumping into the conversation.

Bryan gives me a sour look. He pauses for a second or two, looking around the club as if he's looking for someone.

"Look here, Timmy, I got someone I want you to meet," he says in a hurried fashion.

"Okay," I say, searching his face. "Who is it? I thought we were having a meeting with the band."

He looks around the club again and then waves at an older man sitting at a table on the other side of the club. I notice that his hair is balding in the center and he appears to have golfing attire on.

"This will only take a few minutes," Bryan says, as he moves toward the table.

Simoné begins to follow us, but Bryan stops her. "He doesn't need you to hold his hand, princess."

"What are you doing, Boney? What's Jim Steel doing here?" she asks.

He gives her a sly smile as I stand there, trying to understand what's going on.

"Go on, little girl, this here is grown folks' business," Bryan says, looking in my direction.

Simoné glances at me. Not sure what else to do, I kiss her cheek. "Give me a few minutes, okay?" She hesitates but walks away.

"Come on, young buck. Like I said, this ain't gonna take long."

Bryan and I approach the booth, and the man stands up. I glance back at Simoné, who's heading toward the kitchen.

"Don't worry about her. Come on, let's all have a seat."

A few seconds of awkward silence joins us, and I feel like we're all just sitting there, staring at each other, trying to figure out who's going to talk first.

"Timmy," Bryan finally says. "I want you to meet Mr. Jim Steel. He's with Sun City Records, one of the biggest record labels around. Jim and I go way back."

Jim reaches over the table, and we shake hands.

"Boney has told me a lot about you, young man. He tells me you can play the piano like no man's business. Is that true?"

"I do all right," I say, glaring over at Bryan, who ignores me and keeps his eyes focused on Mr. Steel.

Mr. Steel looks at me, then he looks at Bryan and smiles. "Well, I heard that you do more than all right." He looks toward the door. "This place doesn't open for another couple of hours, and I saw folks already lined up outside as I was walking in. Word around town is that it's because of you."

"They come to see the band. I'm a part of the band." I look directly at Bryan. "What's going on here, Bryan?"

Jackie walks over. "Yes, what's going on here, Boney? What's Jim Steel doing in my place?"

Mr. Steel stands. "Jackie, long time."

"Jim," she says, rather coldly.

He gives her a peck on the cheek, anyway.

She looks at Bryan again. "What's Jim doing here?"

A severe expression of anger comes over Bryan's face, as he looks Jackie in the eyes. "You and Miss Princess got folks coming in to see my boy, so I thought I'd bring in my folks. Folks that ain't tied to the Mafia."

"Is that right?" Jackie says, glaring at him.

Bryan glares back at her. "Yeah, that's right. What, you can't dig a little competition?"

"We'll talk about this later."

"No, we won't!" He stands up abruptly and moves in front of her. "Look here Jackie, I ain't about to let you do to this kid what you tried to do to me," he says, pointing back at me. "It ain't about to go down like that. You understand me? You understand what I mean? Ain't no games here anymore, sunshine."

Simoné walks over and stands next to her mother. I try to make eye contact with her, but she won't look my way.

"What's going on here?" I ask, standing up.

They both ignore me.

"You need to think long and hard about what you're doing and saying here, Boney," Jackie says.

"No, I don't." I watch Bryan's eyes shift toward Simoné, then back at Jackie. "I don't care if she knows. You can tell her now. As a matter of fact. . ." He turns to Simoné and holds out his hand like he's introducing himself. "Miss Princess, I'm your father. It's a pleasure to meet you."

"No, you're not!" Simoné shouts, taking a few steps back from him.

"Yes, I am," Bryan says calmly, keeping his eyes on her. "I've been working here to pay your mama the child support I owe her and to be around you as much as I can. But she never wanted me to tell you the truth."

We all stare at Jackie, who doesn't appear phased by any of what Bryan has just said.

I see the tears in Simoné's eyes as she stares at her mother.

"Mother, is this true? Please, tell me that this...this broken-down, don't-have-nothing man isn't my father!"

Jackie sighs heavily and glares over at Bryan before turning her attention back to Simoné. Bryan just stands there. Smiling. Claiming a victory to a war that to me, no one wanted to enter into, except him.

"Mother. Tell me the truth," Simoné says, her whole body shaking. I move toward her, but she gives me a glaring look, so I stop and just stand there.

"You better let them work this one out," Bryan says to me.

"Shut up!" Simoné shouts.

"Hey now. Watch it there, princess," Bryan snaps back at her, still smiling.

"Mother, answer me!" Her mother glares at her and Simoné tries to lower her voice. "Is this man my father?"

Jackie folds her arms in front of her and looks around the club, as most of the staff too, is waiting for her response.

She slowly nods her head. "He is. Boney is your father."

Simoné takes a few steps back. "Were you ever going to tell me?"

"Nope," Bryan says.

Simoné snaps her head in his direction but doesn't respond.

Mr. Steel clears his throat, loudly to get everyone's attention. "Look, I don't want to get in the middle of whatever is going on here, no matter how fascinating I find it all," he says as moves toward me, trying not to grin. "Timmy, here's my business card." He reaches in his pants pocket, pulls out his wallet and hands a card to me. "Look, in case you were wondering about the Mafia claim, Bryan is right. Those guys at Fountain Records have been connected to the Mafia for years. Trust me, you don't want to have anything to do with them. In fact, you better thank Bryan here for having your back. It looks like he's the only one that does," he says, glancing at Jackie and Simoné.

Bryan looks at me and nods in agreement.

"Look, if you want a real deal with a record label that will take good care of you, call me." He reaches over and tries to shake my hand, as Simoné runs toward the kitchen.

"Thank you," I say, giving him a quick shake. "I'll think about it."

He starts to move toward the front door. "I hope so, we'd love to have you. Bryan, you know how to reach me.

"Jackie."

She nods but doesn't look in his direction.

"Call me, kid. You won't be sorry. We put out good and honest records. Always have. Always will."

I glance at Bryan, but he and Jackie still appear to be at war with their eyes. "Go get your coats kid, I'm sure she's around back, in the alley."

Walking through the kitchen and out the back door, with our coats in hand, I find Simoné in the alley, just as Bryan had said, leaning up against a wall with tears in her eyes.

I rub my hands together because it's freezing outside and the snow is starting to fall.

"Simoné."

"I don't want to do this right now," she says, not looking in my direction.

"That's cool, but can we not do this inside?" I ask as I hand over her coat and slip mine on.

"Thanks," she says as she slips the coat on, but still refuses to look me in the eyes.

I clap my hands together and stick them in my pockets. "Look, I know everything that just went down in there was a shock to you, but I gotta ask . . . did you know?"

"Of course I didn't know Boney was my father!"

I move in front of her and grab her hands. "Simoné, you know that's not what I'm talking about." The tears really begin to flow down her cheeks, but she still won't look at me.

I reach out and turn her face toward me so that our eyes finally meet. "Did you know about the guys from Fountain Records? Did you know that they are connected to the . . . to the Mafia?"

She looks down.

"Simoné, tell me the truth. Please."

"Do we have to do this now?" she asks. Her eyes pleading with me to say no.

"Yes, we do. I think I deserve to know the truth."

She looks away.

"Simoné."

"What?"

"Tell me. Tell me the truth."

She folds her arms in front of her to put space between us. "Yes, I knew. You happy now? I knew! There I said it!"

I take a step back and run my hands through my hair. Trying to stay calm. Trying to understand. Trying not to hate the woman that I love so much.

"Why would you try to get me caught up in something like that?"

She doesn't answer me.

"Why!"

I see her jump. "I'm sorry. Just . . . Just tell me why. That's all I want to know."

"Because . . ."

"Because...what?"

"Because my mother asked me to! All right! She knew you had a thing for me so she thought I could . . ."

"Make a fool out of me?" I whisper as I watch her.

She puts her hands in her pockets as the tears continue to fall. "It wasn't hard," she finally says, looking directly at me.

I pause as her words . . . her words cut deep into me.

"I loved you."

"That wasn't my problem," she says, wiping the tears away.

"But I thought—"

She looks down at the ground for a second and then looks back up at me. Her face is different. Her voice. "Timmy, you're a nice guy. Really, but . . ."

I see it. I finally get it. I finally understand what Bryan tried to tell me, but it was too late.

My heart was bitten.

I move in front of her again. Forcing her to look me in the eyes. "I was just a white boy who had something that you could use. A talent that you and your mother could make money from. That was the plan the whole time, wasn't it?"

Her eyes don't back down this time. "It was," she says, matter-of-factly.

I shake my head. The pain is hitting me in waves, so much that I look away from her, for a second.

"To think that I wanted to marry you. I was going to ask, you know?" I whisper.

"Now you don't have to waste your time," she says, bitterly. "I would have said no anyway. I wouldn't have let it go that far."

I pull her to me and kiss her hard. Then I pull away. "Too late. It was already there."

She pushes me away, and I move back from her, watching as she walks toward the door.

"Tell me one thing, Simoné."

She opens the door but then stops. "What's that?"

"Did you love me?"

She walks inside, and I watch the door close behind her.

A few minutes later, Bryan comes out.

"Hey, kid. You all right?"

"What do you think?"

"Right. Dumb question."

"Why didn't you tell me?"

He comes and stands next to me, as I lean up against the wall. "Look, it ain't no sense in my standing out here in the freezing cold, telling you—I told you so. All I can say is . . . Like mother, like daughter. They both just ain't right. Jackie, more so, though. That woman is just wicked if you ask me."

I shake my head in agreement. "You could have just told me they were trying to connect me to the Mafia."

He glances over at me. "I didn't think she would go there until I saw the guys from Fountain Records come in. That's when I knew I had to shut it down, no matter what it was gonna cost me."

I could see the pain in his eyes. "So Simoné is your daughter?"

"Yeah, as crazy as that piece of info is, that princess is my baby girl. I ain't gonna lie, it felt good to finally tell her. I've wanted to for years, but Jackie wasn't having it. She threatened that if I ever told her, she'd fire me and the band. I couldn't let it go down like that because of me. Most of the cats in the band are feeding their families from what they make from this place. Every last one of them cats are like family to me. You know what I mean."

I nod. "So what are they going to do now?"

"I gave them the heads up before everything went down. That's the other reason why I had to get here early. They had my back. Like I said, they're family. Just like you. I'm gonna always have your back and not because my sister told me to do so."

I grin. "Yeah, we're family. Always will be." We slap hands and continue to lean up against the wall. Looking at nothing.

"So, what happened with you and Jackie?"

Bryan places his hands inside his pockets. "When I first got here, I was like you. Young and dumb. Determined to make it. I was willing to do whatever it took, and I do mean anything.

"When Jackie and I first met, she saw that I had it—the gift. Man, I could play that guitar with a sweetness folks back then hadn't ever heard of. I was hot. So she pretended to be into me. Had my nose open wide, just like Simoné was doing with you, only with me, Jackie took it to another level. She got pregnant and tried to use the baby as a way to get me to sign a deal with Fountain Records.

"Had me thinking I would be doing it for us. For our family.

"She almost had me until one day, my sister calls me. Just in the nick of time, since Jackie and I were making plans for the altar, you following me here?"

I nod. "Yeah, I'm following you."

"Good. Anyway, I tell Big Sis about the deal Jackie had done hooked me up with, and Big Sis schools me. Now, Big Sis don't talk much, but she's smart, and she ain't never steered me wrong. Ever. She always had my back. She tells me to ask around, check out the folks of Fountain Records, because even in Chicago, she had heard some things about them. What they're into. So I did.

"Jackie tried to deny it at first, but finally, she 'fessed up, after I threatened to just walk. She even told me that she got pregnant on purpose. I ain't gonna lie, I felt like a fool. Used, you know what I mean?"

I look over at him.

"Yeah, kid, you know what I mean. But it's okay because we all gonna be fools in life in something. It's a fact. It's just how it is. You make mistakes, but as my sister always taught me, you learn from them. She'd always said that you gotta pull your pants up and walk like a man after you done messed up. That's what I had to do.

"I wasn't gonna be one of those dudes who doesn't handle their responsibilities. Not Boney. It wasn't going to go down like that for my baby girl. Not ever.

"So I got a band together and came and worked here. It was a way to see my baby girl. The only way. Because despite how I felt about her mama, I ain't no deadbeat father who don't take care of what belongs to him. So now you know. There it is, the messed up life of Boney Bass Bryan."

I place my hand on his shoulder. "Like you said, we all make mistakes."

He nods in agreement. "That be the solid truth. Solid."

"Bryan, man, I gotta thank you for having my back even when I was looking instead of listening."

He slaps me on the shoulder. "It ain't nothing, man. You deserve someone who really cares to be there for you. You know what I mean?"

I smile, even though, I'm hurting inside.

From her. Simoné

Bryan glances over at me. "Man, we can't both be out here crying like two little girls who got their feelings hurt. Come on, we got a set to do. Black folks will tear this joint down if we don't get our butts on that stage. Plus, it's cold as I don't know what out here. You know Boney don't do cold."

"See, that's why you need to get rid of that piece of junk. I mean, Bettsie."

He starts heading toward the door but stops. "Man, you gotta stop putting Old Bettsie down. You know she's sensitive."

We both burst out laughing, as I head toward the door.

He stops again and turns toward me. "So what you think about what Jim said? About signing with them?"

I pretend like I'm thinking about it, then I grin. "I trust you. I'll sign with him, but only if you can be my manager and the guys can be my band."

He takes a step back in excitement. "That's hot. I'm sure he'll go for that. He wants you real bad. Sun City Records been battling with Fountain Records for years. Jim is always looking for a way to stick it to them. That's why I went to see him."

I pause for a second. "Why didn't you ever sign with them?"

"I told you. I wanted to be here with my baby girl. My princess."

"What are you going to do about that now?"

"Miss Princess knows the truth now. I'm gonna leave it up to her."

I nod in agreement. "It's going to be hard to get over her, Bryan."

He reaches over and places a hand on my shoulder again. "Man, I feel you. I fell in love with that princess when I first held her in my arms. She was just a little thing, but I knew she was going to be something, even back then. Look, kid, don't worry. Music will help you. Time will heal you. You know what I mean?"

Chapter Twenty-Six

Timmy -1973

"**Y**ou ready, kid?" Bryan asks as he sticks his head in my dressing room.

"How's it looking out there?" I say, turning around in my chair and motioning for him to come inside.

"How you think? It's packed out there. You okay?"

I turn back around and glance in the mirror. "I'm cool. Just can't believe it's been five years since our first jazz record went platinum."

Bryan pulls up a chair and takes a seat in front of me. "Now look at you. On tour."

"In Chicago, of all places," I say, frowning.

"Look here man, don't let that stuff get to you. It's the past. You gotta let it go. I don't know why you don't go see a—"

"I don't need a shrink. I just need to get this concert done so we can move to the next venue."

Bryan smiles, but I can see the concerned look on his face.

"I'm good. Stop looking like that. You just need to be sure everything is handled."

"It's handled. She's here."

I glance up at him.

"You gonna be cool with this? With her being here, I mean?"

"It's cool. We need a singer since the one we always use is sick. I'm just glad she was able to get a flight here and quick."

"True, but—"

"It's cool. Really." I turn around and face him. "Look, I'm always going to love her. I just wouldn't ever trust her again. Not with my heart. Her bite hurt, you know what I mean?"

"There you go again, stealing my words," he says, as he stands up and opens my dressing room door. "You want me to leave it open?"

"You can close it. Give me five minutes, and I'll head that way."

"All right. Hurry up. You know white folks like their concerts to start on time."

I grin at him as he walks out and closes the door behind him. I glance in the mirror again and run my hands through my hair. My eyes look tired from not getting much sleep last night on the plane.

I take a sip of water from a water bottle that Bryan had brought in and as I go to stand up, I hear a knock on my door.

I swing the door open and see my father's eyes staring back at mine.

"Timmy."

I take a few steps back. Both of us taking a few moments to find the next word. I look at his face. I can see the hesitation on it as he stands there, waiting for me to say something.

"Dad," I finally say.

He reaches out to hug me, but I give him my hand instead. I see the look of disappointment, but he takes it, and we shake hands for a second or two.

"What are you doing here?" I ask as I move aside and he comes into my dressing room.

"It's your first concert in Chicago. You didn't think I would miss it, did you?" he asks, looking around.

"You missed just about everything else. Why change the game now?" I say, still not believing that's he's actually standing in front of me.

"I deserve that. Can I sit?"

I glance at the chair Bryan was just sitting in, and he takes it, placing his suit jacket on the back, as I ease back into my own.

I look toward the door. "I see you're still into wearing suits. Same haircut, too."

"It's been a long time since I've been to a concert."

I nod my head slowly but refuse to make eye contact. "You should do it more often."

"You're right. I should."

I finally look over at him. "Did she come with you?" We both know who I'm referring to.

"No, she isn't here."

I look down at the floor. "Right. Why would she be? I doubt she would be able to handle seeing me make something out of myself." I glance back up at him, and I see a look of sadness on his face.

He pauses for a moment or two. "Timmy, your mother, she . . . she passed away. About six months after you left. She had cancer. I would have called, but I didn't know where you were in New York, and to be honest, I didn't think you would have come to the funeral anyway."

I stand up and look at the wall behind him.

"Did you hear me, son?"

I can't find my voice, as I continue looking at the wall.

"Timmy. Say something."

I place my hands in my pockets, and our eyes meet in the space between us. "Look, I have to get going. They're waiting for me."

"Right. I understand. Maybe we can have a cup of coffee or something, after your show tonight?

"No," I say, firmly, but immediately regret the firmness, when I see the hurt look on his face.

He stands. "Timmy, please. Just think about it."

I walk over and open the door. "I gotta go, Dad."

He walks over and tries again to hug me, but I don't respond. I just stand there. Limp.

"Is Margaret here?" I ask, just before he turns to leave. "I didn't think to send her tickets. I—"

"It's okay. She wouldn't have come anyway. She said that she wanted me to experience this by myself." His face lights up some. "You know she would want to see you, though. Maybe you can stop by the house before you leave and say hello."

"Maybe. I'll think about it."

"It would be nice."

"Dad."

"Okay. I'm leaving. It's good to see you, Timmy."

"Thanks." I close the door behind him.

And punch the wall. When I glance over at the mirror, I see myself. A tear falls.

Chapter Twenty-Seven

I see a woman's figure, standing by the stage entrance as I walk up, but my mind doesn't really register who it is.

"Timmy, I just wanted to—"

I don't respond to the voice. Everything in my mind is a blur. On the stage, I see nothing. Only darkness as I sit behind my piano and run my fingers across the piano keys.

I let them hear it all.

The pain.

The madness.

I can feel the music wrapping itself around my anger. Digging deep into my hatred.

I keep seeing her face. Standing over me. Pointing at me. Telling me, I was nothing. Worth nothing.

My mother.

I hit the keys. My fingers moving in despair.

It isn't fair! I want to scream.

She was supposed to be here.

She was supposed to see me. On this stage.

Being something.

Even now, I can feel it.

Her hatred touching me.

The reality of my situation. Knowing that now I will never get a chance. Never get a chance to ask the question that tears at my insides every night, as I go to sleep.

"Why?"

"Why did she hate me so much?"

"Why couldn't she love me?"

Exhausted. I begin to slow down. The fog starts to lift, and I look out into the audience.

They are on their feet, as the lights come up.

I look out at the front row, and I see him. I see the tears in his eyes.

My father.

Chapter Twenty-Eight

"You sure you want to do this?" Bryan asks as we both sit outside the home that I left over five years ago—and vowed never to return to.

"We're here to see your sister and the only person in that house that I care about," I say.

He shakes his head in disagreement. "Don't say that, man. That's just hurt talking. At least he came. He reached out. You've got to give him credit for that." Bryan glances out the window for a second. "Fathers ain't perfect." He looks over at me. "Put your grown-man pants on, and go in there and talk to him. You feel me?"

I nod slowly and glance back at the house again. Taking in its calmness. The way that it sits there like it never witnessed the pain I was put through.

By her.

"She ain't in there," Bryan says as if knowing what I'm thinking.

"I keep trying to remind myself of that," I say with a heavy sigh.

"You ready?"

"Yeah, I'm ready. Let's get at it."

We both smile as Bryan taps on the window that separates us from the driver, and I hear the doors unlock.

I walk toward the back of the house, as Bryan heads to the front door. He stops once he notices. "What, you can't go through the front door of your own house?"

"Margaret will be in the kitchen. It's where she always is."

"Oh, I see."

As I stand in front of the door, I turn to Bryan. "Truth be told, I was never allowed to go into this house through the front."

"Maybe you should do it now."

I place my hand on the doorknob. "Let's just get this over with," I say, getting ready to open the door.

"Wait a minute."

I turn around.

"What's up?"

"Man, I ain't seen my Big Sis in years."

I place my hand on his shoulders. "She won't think about that. She'll just be happy to see you now. You ready?"

"You're right. Let's get at it."

I walk in first. Margaret is sitting at the kitchen table. She can barely stand up as I walk over to her, but there is an amazing smile on her face.

"My Timmy." She places a thousand kisses on me as I hug her. Then she pulls away as Bryan comes into the kitchen.

"Big Sis," he says, as they embrace.

I've never seen Bryan cry before.

I've never seen tears of joy, like the ones that are on both of their faces, as they enjoy their reunion.

I leave them to talk as I head up to my old room. Just climbing the steps brings back the agony. The pain. The hatred. I get to the top, and I glance back down. I see me, running down them. Running to get away from my mother.

Running to Margaret.

Praying she could save me.

Margaret would be there. Holding her arms out as my mother would stand at the top of the stairs, carrying a switch in her hands.

"You can't always protect him, Margaret!" she would scream in a drunken rage.

"As long as I'm breathing, Ma'am, I can and I will," Margaret would reply.

I move toward my bedroom.

I can feel my heart beating fast as I reach the door and swing it open.

The curtains are open. The bed is made.

Everything is just as I left it. Down to the paint. The carpet.

Even my piano.

I walk over toward it and run my hands across the top.

"I was hoping you would come."

I look up and see my father standing there with a pair of casual dress pants and an unbuttoned at the collar shirt.

"New look?" I ask, as I move toward my bed and take a seat.

He comes and takes a seat next to me. "I stopped wearing the business look when I'm at home, a few years ago."

I nod. "I see."

"Actually, I've changed a lot of things."

I stand up and move around the room. "Really. Like what?"

"I've been taking it easy. Running. Reading books. Going to places in Chicago that I've never been to before."

I stop and study his face. "That doesn't sound like you. How's the business going?"

"I took a break from it . . . after Lena passed away."

Hearing her name, causes me to pause for a few minutes, but I try to shake it off. I look over, and I see him watching me.

"So you don't own the company anymore?" I ask, as I walk over to my piano again and take a seat behind it.

He stands up and leans on one of the bedposts. "Of course I do, I'm just not as involved in the day-to-day affairs as I once was. Your mother's passing made me realize a lot of things."

Curious, I glance over at him. "Like what?"

"All the years I'd missed. The years of not being here when I should have. The years of not protecting you. Not protecting you from her." I could hear a slight tremble in his voice, and it scared me. It was a side of my father I had never seen before.

"I loved her, Timmy. I really did, but I didn't like her. In the end, when she was suffering the most, it was hard for me to look at her and to know what she did to you. To see her for who she was and then realize that I had to look past that. To help her."

I hit a few keys on my piano to fight the sadness that was threatening my hatred. For her. For this house.

"Dad . . . I need to ask you something," I say, making a few minutes of uneasy silence evaporate.

I watch his body shift as if he already knows what my question will be.

"Why? Why did she hate me so much?"

"That's a hard question to answer because the truth is ugly. But it's one that you deserve the answer to. No matter how much it's going to hurt me to answer it." He stands up straight, as I move from behind the piano and lean up against it.

"Let me start by saying that I love you. I love you, and you will always be my son."

I run my hands through my hair. "What are you trying to tell me?"

"The truth."

"It's starting to sound more like a confession," I say.

He moves closer. Leaning up against the bedpost closest to me. The sun pours into the window and hits the side of his face. When I look at him, all I see is fear.

"Dad, are you alright?"

He tries to smile, but I see the nervousness in his hands.

"I guess the only way to say this is to just say it." He clears his throat as I lean forward.

"Lena and I aren't your birth parents. We adopted you just after you were born."

Time stops.

The walls feel as if they are closer in. My heart stops beating as I fight to catch my breath.

"Timmy, did you hear me? Did you hear what I just said to you?"

I stand up and move as far away from him as I can.

"Timmy?"

"I heard you," I say, as I find a spot on the wall to hold me up.

"So that's why. That's why she could do all those things to me . . . because I didn't belong to her." I see his face change. "There's more isn't it?"

He nods slowly and sits on the edge of my bed. "Your birth mother was a black woman."

I take a few steps toward him. "What did you just say?"

"It's true. We found out a couple of years after the adoption went through. You got really sick, and it became necessary for us to obtain your medical records. Learn about your history. That's how we found out. The adoption agency didn't give us any other information except that. No name.

Not where your birth mother was from. Nothing. To be honest, they only provided us that little detail after I dropped a serious amount of money in someone's pocket."

"Wait, so you're telling me that I'm black?"

"I'm telling you that you're my son. My son who happens to have had a birth mother who was black."

"But doesn't that make me black?"

"I don't think your birth father was—"

"What, all black?"

"It doesn't matter, Timmy. You are mine. You are my son."

"You sound like you're trying to convince yourself of that."

"I don't need convincing. I never have."

I bend over, grabbing my stomach.

"Are you alright, son?"

"Stop calling me that!" I shout, pointing at him. "You should have told me. You let her do all those things to me, knowing that when she looked at me, she didn't see a child that belonged to her!"

He stands up. "Timmy, try to calm down."

I stand up straight and look him in the eyes. "Are you kidding me right now? You want me to stand here and be calm when I just found out that the woman I called my mother hated me because I'm not as white as she is. I'm right, aren't I, Dad?"

"Timmy, you have a right to be angry. You have a right to—"

"Hate you? Hate her?"

He lowered his head.

I move back over to my piano and take a seat behind it.

He starts to move toward the door. "There's something that I need to give you. It's in my office."

"I don't want anything from you," I say, not even looking up at him.

He stops and turns toward me. "This is important. Stay here. I'll be back in a few."

I watch him leave.

As I stand up, I feel like his words are plastered on the walls. Screaming at me.

"You're black."

I see her face.

I see her face, and it's laughing at me.

"Timmy."

I look up and see my father standing there with a box in his hand. He walks over and places it on top of my bed, and then steps back.

I move slowly toward it. "Where did it come from?" I ask, not able to take my eyes off it.

"When you were eight years old, your mother tried to hire a nanny. Her name was Mildred Mayfield. You were so young, you probably don't remember that."

"I remember it," I whisper.

He leans up against the bedpost again. "Okay. Well, as you know, that lady was killed the day she was scheduled to come here. About a year ago, a woman came to see me. Her name is Jean. She was a close friend of Mildred's and had found this box inside the car that Mildred died in."

I touch the top of the box. "What's inside it?"

"A letter. A letter that has your name on the outside envelope."

"Why did Mildred have a letter with my name on it?"

"Mildred Mayfield was, by birth, your grandmother."

I take a step back and stare at him.

He points to the box. "The letter in the box is from her daughter. Your birth mother."

My eyes move slowly from him, back to the box again. "Did you read it?"

I hear the hesitation in his voice, as both of our eyes stare at it. "I know I probably shouldn't have, but I did."

I open the box, and I see the letter, laying there as if it had been waiting its whole life for me.

"That letter saved me."

"What do you mean?" I ask, as I pull the letter out and stare at my name.

"It's the way it's written. The words in that letter are quite inspiring. If that makes any sense."

"It doesn't," I say, abruptly. I see my father flinch, but then he smiles.

"Reading that letter helped me to deal with some things. Things I was struggling with in regard to Lena. My feelings for her after she died. While she was alive."

I put the letter back in the box and close the lid. "So you know who my birth mother is?"

"It's in the letter, along with some other things. Maybe reading it will help you to think differently about things."

"Like what? What's it going to help me to think differently about?"

"Hatred for one."

I chuckle as I pick the box up. "No letter is going to do that."

"I hope you're wrong."

"I'm not." I look toward the door. "Look, I gotta go. I'm sure Bryan is ready, and we have to catch a flight back in the morning."

"Right."

I see the sadness in his eyes. "I need some time. Some time to process all of this."

"I understand. Just remember, you are, and will always be—my son."

Chapter Twenty-Nine

"Man, that's some deep stuff right there. I ain't never in my life thought I'd hear a story like that," Bryan says as he leans back into my hotel room sofa. "That right there is the kind of stuff you read in the tabloids."

I glance up at him.

"Don't worry, you know I ain't going to the tabloids. But man, this is deep. I mean like, wow, kind of stuff! You're black! At least that explains some things."

I nod slowly. "I'm just not sure what to do with all of it. It's like it's rolling around in my head with nowhere to go."

"You gotta just take it for what it is. It doesn't mean that you ain't you. You know what I mean? You're still Timmy. Being black ain't gonna change that."

"Maybe," I say, as I lean back in my seat.

"So you gonna read it?" he asks, as we both glance down at the box that's sitting in the center of the sofa table, between us.

I shrug my shoulders. "I don't know. Part of me wants to. The other part of me is, like, just burn the whole thing."

Bryan sits up. "Man, you can't burn that. That's just crazy talk."

I lean forward. "Why not?"

"Look here, man, that letter is from your birth mother. She could have written it on her deathbed or something. You don't know." He wraps his hands around his head and leans back again. "This is so crazy."

I lean back in my chair again, as well. "I know. What if..."

"What if what?"

"What if people find out that I'm—"

"Black? Why are you sweating that? Ain't nobody gonna hear it from my mouth."

I stand up and run my hands through my hair. "You and I both know that my whole career is built around the fact that nobody can believe I can play jazz like I do, being white. It's never really spoken, but it's there. What if people found out and they stopped buying our records? You know I have a huge following of. . ."

"White folks?"

I sigh. "Yeah. This could end my career."

Bryan claps his hands together. "Don't even think that way. Like I said, ain't nobody gonna hear it from my mouth. You and I are the only ones who know. Besides, it ain't like you'd be lying. I mean, your birth father got to be white. I mean, look at you." He points at me. "He's got to be as white as they come if there is such a thing. That's the only way you could look..."

"Like a white boy?"

He grins. "Hey, man, you said it, not me."

I pace the room. "I can't help but wonder, who is he? My birth father. What does he look like? Do I look like him? If so, how much?"

"Timmy, you are just going to keep stressing yourself out, man. Sit. Chill. Besides, you ain't gonna know unless you read that letter. Maybe she tells you, or at least gives you some clues about the man."

I sit back down. "I'm not going to read it. In fact, I'm going to burn it."

"Seriously?" he asks, staring me in the eyes.

"Seriously."

"That'll be your decision to make, but if it were me, I'd wanna know. Knowing who your folks are and where you come from—those things are important. You don't want to end up marrying someone you could be related to. You know what I mean? It could happen."

I glance over at him. He grins back at me, knowing he made a good point.

"I'm sure that's not the case," I say, trying to shrug it off.

"I'm serious business. Besides, you ain't never gonna feel complete if you don't at least find out if either of your birth parents is still alive. And then there's the question."

I lean forward in my chair again. "What question?"

"You know what question, man. The 'why did you give me up' question that you gonna need the answer to. Don't tell me it ain't entered into your mind."

I stare at the box. "Yeah, it's there. Along with everything else my dad told me."

Bryan smiles. "Well, I'm at least glad you still calling him that."

"It ain't easy."

"But that's who he is. Your father. Ain't nothing gonna take that away. Even if you find this cat—I mean, your birth father. You know what I mean?"

"Yeah, I guess."

He stands up and stretches. "Well, I'm gonna leave you to burn your box, and I'm going to my own room to hit those sheets." He walks toward the door but stops. "I almost forgot to tell you..." He comes and sits back down on the sofa.

I study the serious look on his face.

"Considering the day you've had, I'm not sure I should even tell you this right now."

"What is it?" I ask. Now, even more curious.

"It's about Simoné."

I place one leg on top of the other. "What about her?" I ask, nonchalantly.

"She's getting married."

I sit up. "To who?"

He leans forward. "Some cat she met after she finished school. They set the date. I guess it's going to take place in a month. You know how women like those summer weddings."

"Is he...?"

"Black? Yeah, a hundred percent."

"You got jokes."

He laughs. "Sorry, couldn't help it. Anyway, this cat is a few years older than her. I ain't crazy about him, but he seems to be a stand-up kind of guy, I guess. They've been dating for a year or so. Her mother introduced them."

I look at the wall behind him. "Does she love him?"

He leans back into the sofa. "It ain't my business to answer that, you know what I mean? But I will say this . . . we all got situations in life that cause us to make decisions we think might help make life easier."

I catch Bryan's eyes. "You mean he has money."

"You know her mother wouldn't have it any other way. He comes from nothing but it. You gonna be all right, man?"

I stand up and lean against the wall. "Yeah, it's just that . . ."

"Man, you ain't got to tell me. First love is hard to kill because all you really ever do is bury it deep. It doesn't help that situations like this come and dig it back up."

I stare at the floor for a second or two. "It's cool that you and she were able to work things out."

"It still ain't peaches and cream, but at least we talk. Like I said earlier, she ain't the same as she was—"

"The night she took a bite out of my heart."

He lowers his eyes. "Yeah, something like that. Look, don't get me wrong, she's still a princess if you know what I mean. Always got to get her way."

"I'm sure."

"Her mama, on the other hand, that's another story."

I look him in the eyes. "You still love her mother, don't you?"

"Like I said, first love is hard to kill, but I ain't looking for no resurrection either."

I laugh. "Don't I know it."

"So you cool?"

"Yeah, I'm cool."

"Hey, I need to run something else by you."

"What's that?"

"You ever think about talking to someone? I mean, like someone professional?"

I shift my body against the wall. "How many times you going to ask me that?"

"Man, I just think that after all you've been through, it can't hurt, that's all I'm saying."

"I don't need a shrink," I say, walking toward the door and opening it.

"Look, you and I both know that your mother put you through some rough stuff. Stuff that's messing with your mind. You know what I mean? And now this, this right here." He points to the box. "This right here is something else you got to deal with. Ain't nothing wrong with talking to someone."

I pull the door open wider. "You ever go lay down on some shrink's couch and tell them all your problems with life?"

"Once."

I close the door softly. "You serious?"

"Yeah, I'm dead serious. I would've gone more, but I couldn't afford them sessions. I wasn't rolling in the paper like you are now."

I walk back over to my chair and take a seat. "Why do you keep thinking that I need to see a shrink?"

"Look, man, I worry about you. You keep warring with your past and with your mother. Your adoptive mother, I mean. That's why I keep bringing it up."

I lean back in my seat. "I'll think about it."

"Seriously this time, I hope."

"We'll see." I glance at the phone that's sitting next to him, on a tall glass table. "Man, I'm hungry. You wanna order something from room service?"

He looks down at his watch. "It's almost midnight. I need to be hitting those sheets, but since you brought it up . . ." He grins. "I can't go to sleep with a hungry stomach. Ain't right for an old man like me. You know—"

"Yeah, I know what you mean."

He picks up the phone. "What you feeling like?"

Chapter Thirty

I glance over at the clock. It's six in the morning.

The box sits at the foot of my hotel bed. Staring at me. Even in the dark, I can see the outline of it.

It's got me feeling like I'm losing my mind.

Maybe I am.

Maybe Bryan is right. Perhaps I do need to see someone. Talk to someone. Someone who can't judge. Only listen.

Because right now . . . right now, all I feel is lost.

I pick up the phone and dial a familiar number. Don't pick up.

"Hello," he says.

I almost hang up. I almost . . .

"Dad," I finally say.

"Timmy? Is that you? You alright?"

"I can't read it," I whisper, as I sit up.

"You have to."

I switch on the light and pull the box to me. "What if . . ."

"Timmy, you are always going to have what if questions until you read it."

I pull out the letter and allow it rest on my lap.

"Bryan thinks I should go see a shrink," I say, as my eyes trace the outline of each letter of my name that's written on the front of the envelope.

"That might help. You've been through a lot, and you've got a lot of—"

"Hatred built up inside me?"

"Yes."

"That's what Bryan says."

"It's something to think about."

"I've hated her so long . . ."

"You've hated me too, but, here we are. Talking, although, I will say that I wish it wasn't at six in the morning."

"I never really hated you, Dad. I just . . . I just didn't like you."

I hear him turning on his light. "I understand that. Really, I do. Read the letter, Timmy."

I place the letter to the side. "Maybe, I'll read it on the plane."

I hear him clearing his throat. "I didn't mention this when you were here . . . but I'm selling the house."

I move to the edge of my bed. "Why?"

"It's too much for Margaret now, and I just don't want it anymore."

"Are you in some kind of financial trouble?"

He laughs. "No. Believe it or not, my company is doing better than it did when I was there. I'm just ready to move on."

"To what?"

He gets silent.

"Dad, what is it?"

"I got married again. A few days ago actually."

I almost drop the phone.

"Timmy, you still there?"

"Yeah, I'm here. Barely, but I'm here. It just seems like everyone is getting married these days."

"What do you mean?"

"I just found out that someone that I used to really care about is getting married."

"I see. I'm sorry."

"She was black."

He pauses as he shifts his phone to the other ear. "Are you talking about the singer at your concert?"

"Why do you ask?"

"She was beautiful."

"Yeah, she is." I stare at the wall for a second or two. Remembering when . . . "So who is this woman that you've gone off and married?"

He hesitates.

"Do I know her or something?"

"Not exactly, But you've heard me mention her."

I try to think back and come up with nothing. "When?" I ask.

"When you were at the house, yesterday. She's the woman that brought the box over. Jean. She's a . . . a black woman."

I stand up. "How did that happen?"

"Easily, actually. The day she came by, we started talking. She was so easy to talk to. We started seeing each other just about every day after that."

I listen to the excitement in his voice.

"Jean is a kind and amazing woman. I've never been able to talk to any woman the way that I can talk to her. I love her.

"To be honest, Lena and I had become strangers, way before you left."

"Is that why you were always gone?"

"Son, there was a lot going on with Lena and me that you don't know about."

I sit back down on the bed. "I'm listening."

"Lena was having an affair, and it wasn't just with the bottle."

"I don't know what to say to that."

"There's nothing to say. Lena was Lena. I just wish I had seen the kind of woman she was before I married her. After you left, I had planned on divorcing her, but then I found out that she had cancer and it just didn't seem right."

"I can't say I agree with that."

"No one deserves to be alone when you're going through something like that. You have to act human, even if they haven't."

I shift my body some and the letter moves, as I glance over at it. "So tell me about your new wife—Jean."

"Like I mentioned a few moments ago, Jean's a beautiful woman. She's kind. She's smart. She owns the building that she lived in and a few specialty clothing stores for women. She makes and designs all the clothes that she sells in her stores.

"One of her old tenants, Mae, is the spokesperson for her clothing line for bigger-sized women. Jean said that she got the idea from Mildred."

"Mildred, my grandmother?" I say slowly as the reality of my situation swirls around in my head.

I hear the hesitation in his voice again. "That's right. They were very close."

"Well, Jean sounds just right for you."

"She is. She really is. But there's something about Jean that I think you should know."

"What?"

"Jean knew your birth mother. She knew her when she was pregnant with you."

I almost drop the phone again.

"Timmy?"

"Yeah, I'm here," I say while trying to regain my composure. "You said, knew? Is she still alive? Is she here in Chicago?

"Dad, please tell me."

He sighs heavily. "Your birth mother died while giving birth to you. Read the letter. Please. She wrote it for you."

I place the phone on the hook, pick up the letter and toss it across the room.

Ten minutes go by as I sit, staring at it laying on the floor in front of me.

Twenty minutes pass. I walk over and pick it up.

Chapter Thirty-One

"You sure you want to do this?" Bryan asks as I place my packed suitcase on the sofa.

"Not really, but I feel I have to."

He nods slowly, walking over towards me. "Here are your tickets. Your flight leaves tomorrow. Man, I feel like I should be going with you."

"No, it's cool. We've been on the road for months, and this was our last stop, plus, you need to get back to New York and get some rest. You're starting to look like an old man," I say, grinning.

He takes a few steps back and looks me up and down. "I'll have you know that Boney Bass Bryan gonna always look good. You know what they say about Blacks and aging."

"What?"

"That black don't crack. Welcome to the club," he says, reaching over and giving me a slight punch in the arm.

I smirk at him. "Funny."

"You halfway there. You know what I mean," he says with a sly smile.

I frown. "Man, you're killing me. Look, you'd better get going before you miss your flight back to New York."

He lets out a sigh as he glances over at my suitcase. "Man, ain't that the same suitcase you had when I picked you up the first time?"

I quickly glance at it. "Yeah, it still works. Kind of like Bettsie."

He smirks. "Oh, so we back on Bettsie again, huh?"

"Calm down, " I say, punching him back. "Bettsie will always be cool with me. Although, I can't believe she's still putting along."

He gives me the side-eye. "Well, look here, I best be getting on with it. You know I hate flying. But don't forget to ring me when you get to Georgia. I'll have a car there to pick you up and take you out to the country. I mean, Winder."

"No limos or drivers. Just a regular rental car, okay?"

"You sure? It ain't like you can just follow the yellow brick road or something."

"Man, I can handle it."

"All right then, young buck, I'll set it up on my way to the airport. You gonna call your dad and tell him?"

I shrug my shoulders.

"You think he might be hurt that you're going to see your birth father, huh?"

"Something like that," I say as we walk toward the front door of my hotel room.

He places his hand on my shoulders. "Look here, man, I think it's cool what you're doing. I think you need this. Every man needs peace. We don't always find it, but that shouldn't stop us from the journey. You dig me?"

"It that something new?"

"What?" he asks.

"'You dig me.'"

He gives me a sly smile again. "You always trying to steal my stuff, so now I got to change it up. You feeling me?"

"Bye, man."

Chapter Thirty-Two

elcome to Downtown Winder, the sign reads as I pull over and park my car in front of a barbershop. I watch as people casually walk past me, smiling, as I sit here holding the letter in my hand.

An older man, with a head full of gray hair, knocks on my window after an hour has passed.

"You lost there, son?" he asks, as I roll the window down.

I stare down at the letter. "I'm looking for a Mr. Thomas Livingston."

He leans over and glances at the letter.

I place it on the seat next to me.

"Senior or Junior?" he asks.

"Junior, I guess."

"You related?"

"Something like that," I say.

He looks me over for a second or two. "You look like you could be one of them. You got that curly hair, just like them."

I'm not sure how to respond to this, so I don't.

He smiles. "Well, I reckon it's alright to point you in the right direction."

I smile. "Thank you."

"Where you from? You sound like you're from up North."

"I live in New York." I glance up at him, trying not to sound anxious but desperately wanting the directions so I can finally move on.

He glances around for a second or two as I sit there wondering if he's crazy or not. "I ain't never been to New York," he says as he looks down at his watch and then back at me. "It's about two, so I reckon Thomas is at his law office round about now. If he ain't, just head over to the courthouse.

You'll find both of them, the office and the courthouse, just around the corner. Five blocks up. Off Broad Street. His wife works in Statham at his parents' old grocery store, if you think you might want to head there first."

"I really just came to see Mr. Livingston."

"I see. Well, I reckon you ought to call him Thomas since Mr. Livingston was his father. I used to cut his hair up until he passed away, a few years back. The wife, Thomas' mother, passed away about five years prior. They were nice folks. Raised a good boy."

"Thank you again," I say as I start my car.

"You mighty welcome, young fellow. I'll let you be on your way. Welcome to Winder."

"Thanks," I say, as he begins to move away from the car. I wave and pull off slowly, glancing for a second in the mirror to see him standing there, looking in my direction.

I drive about five blocks and turn, just as the old man told me to do.

Livingston, Baker, and Garner Law Office, the sign reads.

I pull up to a building that looks more like a house. The gravel road leads me up the side where the parking is. I take a deep breath as I climb out of the car. My knees wobble as I straighten the collar of my white dress shirt and make sure that it's tucked neatly inside my jeans. I feel my legs tremble as I move toward the front door.

A young lady welcomes me as I step inside. "Welcome to LBG, how can I help you today?"

I run my hands through my hair and try to act casual. "Hi, I'm here to see Thomas Livingston."

She pulls a small book from her top drawer. "Your name, sir?"

"Timothy Taylor," I say as I watch her quickly scan through the names written down in her book.

"I'm sorry, Mr. Taylor, but I don't see your name in his appointment book. Do you have one with Mr. Livingston today?"

I glance at the door. Every part of me wants to turn around and walk back out. "I don't," I say slowly, but with a smile.

She frowns.

"I just came in from New York to see him. I'm related," I say, running my hands through my hair, hoping that she will notice.

She glances up at me and grins. "Mr. Livingston does that all the time with his hair. It's quite annoying."

I take a step back.

"I'm kidding. It's adorable, but don't tell him I said that. Have a seat, and I'll go see if he's available."

I sigh in relief. "Thanks, I really appreciate that."

I watch her move quickly down the small hallway and out of sight, as I take a seat.

The foyer area is simple.

A couple of leather chairs. A few old paintings on the walls and a coffee table. I glance around, hoping to see a picture of him. Most attorneys have a picture of themselves on the wall of their office. But there isn't one of him or of the other attorneys.

I sit for ten minutes. Fumbling through magazines. Watching the hands of the clock on the wall across from me move at a turtle's pace. Fighting the desire to get up and run.

Back to New York.

The young receptionist finally comes back and takes a seat at her desk. She looks my way. "I'm sorry for the delay. Mr. Livingston is in a meeting, but he said that if you don't mind waiting about ten more minutes, he'll see you then. Can I get you something to drink while you wait? We have coffee, tea, and Coca-Cola, of course."

"I'll take a Coke."

A minute or two later, she hands me the Coke just as a man with red curly hair and green eyes comes around the corner. He walks up to me and extends his hand. "Hi, I'm Thomas Livingston. Grace here tells me that you came from New York to see me today."

My hand is sweating as I search for my voice. "My name is Timothy Taylor."

"What can I do for you, Mr. Taylor? Grace said that you told her we're related." He glances at my hair and smiles.

"We are," I say, running my hand through it. "Can we go to your office?"

He hesitates. "Well, all right then." He looks at Grace. "Do I have any appointments coming up?"

She walks back over to her desk and scans the appointment book. "No, sir."

He tries to hide his disappointment. "Okay then," he says, clapping his hands together in a nervous fashion. "I guess we're going to my office. Why don't you follow me?"

Just as we start to walk off, Grace walks from around her desk quickly and stops us. "Hey, aren't you that pianist? The one who plays jazz with that black band?"

"You listen to jazz?" I ask, surprised.

"No, but my brother does. He plays the saxophone. Tries to anyway. He has all your records. In fact, he went to see you once, in New York. Said the show was amazing. Couldn't stop talking about it. Since then, all he talks about is moving there. To New York, I mean. He's convinced it's the only way to become famous in the music industry."

"Grace." Thomas looks at her.

She glances over at me and then back to him again. "I'm sorry, sir. I just had to ask. My brother would kill me if I didn't."

He chuckles. "That's all right. Why don't you head on back to your desk and Mr. Taylor and I will go have ourselves a little chat. I'll come find you if I need anything."

I can see her disappointment. "Yes, sir."

We walk to his office in silence. My eyes trying hard not to stare at him as we walk.

"Have a seat," he says as he closes the door.

I look around. His office is like the foyer. Simple. I take a seat on the leather sofa.

"Seems you're pretty famous. I take it from Grace that you play the piano," he says as he sits down in a chair across from me.

"I do," I say, trying hard not to start asking all the questions that are floating around in my head.

"I love the piano," he says, glancing over at me with a friendly grin on his face.

"You play?" I ask, as our eyes connect in this moment of awkwardness.

"No, I couldn't play an instrument even if my life depended on it. I'm more of a books person. Which is why I became an attorney. I use to know a girl though, years ago. Her mother played the piano and boy, was she something to hear. Her mother's name was—"

"Mildred Mayfield," I say.

He looks at me, stunned, and leans back in his chair. "Why, that's right. You knew them?"

"I'm originally from Chicago. Mildred and her daughter lived there."

"You knew Addie, Mildred's daughter?" he asks, leaning forward in his seat with an anxious look upon him.

I shift in my chair some. "I never actually met either one of them."

"I guess I'm confused here."

"I was too, at first, to be honest. Addie Mayfield was my..."

"She was your what?" he asks, studying my face.

"She was my birth mother."

I watch him. He doesn't move. In fact, he doesn't say anything. He just sits there . . . staring at me. I don't say anything either. I want him to speak first. I don't know why, but I feel like that's how it has to be.

I can feel him looking into my eyes.

It's like his eyes are seeing me for the first time. I follow them as they roam from my head down to my shoes.

I don't know how to take the inspection, but I continue to watch his face.

I'm waiting.

Waiting for the disappointment to appear.

I'm waiting for the realization.

The realization that I'm his son.

He leans back in his chair, slowly. "You said was. Is Addie still alive?"

"Did you know her well?" I say, angry that there is no acknowledgment.

He stands up and walks over to the window. "Back in the day, over twenty years ago, Addie and I were..."

"In love," I say.

He turns toward me. "Yeah, I guess you could say that. Actually, you could say exactly that. Back then, things were very different between Blacks and Whites. Especially here in the South." He sighs as he glances out the window. "Addie and her mother just up and moved one day. I didn't even know where or why."

"They left because she was pregnant. By you." I know I'm pushing, but I need to hear the words. I need to hear him say them.

He walks back over and sits down. He stares down at the floor for a few minutes and then looks up at me. "Are you trying to tell me that you're my son?"

There.

There they are. Sitting between us.

The truth.

"I am," I say, as I slowly pull the letter out of my pocket and hand it to him.

He walks over to his desk, puts on his glasses and then sits to read it.

I watch as the tears flow down his face as he takes in each word.

It was the first time I saw it.

Love for my mother.

My real mother.

"My Addie is dead," he whispers, as he puts the letter down and begins to wipe his face. "What about her mother?"

I clear my throat. "She was . . . killed in a car accident about eight years after I was born."

"I see." He leans back in his desk chair and runs his hands through his hair.

It was a gesture that brought the reality of our situation home. Made it real. Made it raw like an open sore. I felt like we were both searching for some sort of healing ointment.

"I know it's a lot to handle," I say, looking over at him.

"It is, but it has to be handled," he says as he picks up the letter and comes and retakes a seat in the chair in front of me.

"How?"

"One day at a time, I suppose. We have a lot of catching up to do," he says as he hands me the letter back.

"I thought you'd be mad or try to deny it or something."

"Why?" he asks, studying my face again.

"I don't know," I say, as I fold the letter back up and stick it in my pocket. "I didn't really know how this would play out as I drove here from the airport."

"How long have you known?"

"I just found out. My father told me."

"I see." He pauses for a second and then looks me in the eyes. "You mean your adopted father."

I ponder over the meaning of his words for a moment. Allowing them to sit in the pit of my stomach. "He's my father."

He smiles. "Of course. I'm sorry. I know it's too earlier to expect you to consider me like that."

I don't respond.

"It's a beautiful day out there today," he says to break the silence as he stands up and walks back over to the window.

"It is," I say, standing up and moving toward the window next to him. "Georgia is beautiful. Not at all what I imagined."

"What did you imagine? Cows and overalls?"

"Something like that," I say, grinning.

He chuckles a little. "I suppose most would. I've been in Georgia all my life. Always wanted to go to New York."

"You should come for a visit. I own a great apartment, right in Manhattan. You could stay with me or something."

He nods. "That would be nice."

I can hear the sadness in his voice as he glances back out the window. "There's a creek back there. It's a ways back, of course, but it reminds me of the one that Addie and I used to sit at."

"The one by Bear Creek," I say.

He grins as he touches the glass with the tips of his fingers. "She was so beautiful. Full of inner and outer beauty. She made you want to be something. A better person. She was inspiring like that." He glances over at me. "I loved her. I really loved her."

I walk over to him and place my hand on his shoulder. "It's good to know you loved her."

"I did, and after reading that letter, I now know how much she really loved me."

"Did you doubt it?" I ask as I lean up against the window.

He lets out a heavy sigh as he places his hands in his pockets. "Our parents, her mother, and mine, had us doubting all sorts of things back then. Let me just say that being prejudiced is not just a white person's thing. Addie and I got it from both sides. But if I had known she was pregnant, I would have married her, even if it meant leaving Georgia." He glances out the window again. Toward the creek. Toward the past. "I would have married Addie even if she hadn't been pregnant."

"I'm sure you would have." I watch his mannerisms. The way he shifts his body as he stands. I can see myself in him. "Addie spoke about the house she grew up in. Is it still around? I'd like to see it."

He nods in disappointment. "It's not. I wanted to buy it. I had this crazy notion in my head that if I did, Addie would somehow come back to me." He grins. "For the longest time, I fought the developers that were trying to purchase the properties over there for years, but in the end, that entire area was torn down and rebuilt. "

"That's a shame."

"It is," he says as he runs his hands through his hair again. "I used to love going to see her. When she came to work for my parents, she'd make me leave the house so she could get her work done. If she had been my wife, if it could have been possible, she would have never had to work for anyone—if she didn't want to. I would have taken care of her. I would have loved her the way she deserved to be loved.

"I wish you could have seen her smile. I could listen to Addie talk for hours. I would have crossed the world to be with her. She was that special to me," he says as he walks back over to the chair and takes a seat.

I follow him and take a seat as well.

He waits for a few seconds. "You know, I always suspected that Addie was pregnant," he says, looking me directly in the eyes again. "It was the only logical explanation I could come up with after she and her mother left so suddenly. I questioned my parents about it just about every day, but they always acted like they didn't know anything. Those years without Addie were hard for me. It took me a long time to get over her, and yet I don't ever think I did."

I lean forward some in my chair. "A close friend of mine told me that we never really get over our first love. We just bury the feelings we had for them and hope that situations don't come up that cause us to have to dig them up again."

"Well, I guess this is a situation, isn't it?"

We both laugh.

"It is," I say.

He rubs his hands together. "It just dawned on me that I've got to figure out how I'm going to tell my wife all of this. She doesn't quite see things the way I do."

"You mean she's prejudiced?"

He places his leg on top of the other one and leans back in his seat. "She would say she's not."

"My adoptive mother was," I say, matter-of-factly. "She hated me because Addie was my mother. A black woman."

He glances at the floor before looking over at me. "That's sad to know. I'm sure growing up with her was tough."

"It was," I say, standing up.

"I can only imagine."

"I'm glad you can't, to be honest. Do you and your wife have children?"

"No. We have dogs. Go figure."

I smirk. "That's funny. Look, you don't have to tell your wife about me."

He leans forward and glances up at me. "Why not?"

I place my hands in my pockets, and I can feel the letter.

"Look, I just wanted to meet you. We don't have to take this any further than this. I have a father who, I have finally come to understand, loves me very much. I don't want to hurt him."

He stands up. "I respect that. However, I'm going to tell her because I want to be in your life. I've missed so much of it."

"That's funny. My father recently said something similar."

"He wasn't around for you growing up?"

I shift my body. "It's a long story." I pause as I pull my hands out of my pockets. "Look, you have a life. A wife. I live in New York. I'm on the road a lot. I have another tour coming up in a few months. We can just let things stay here."

"Is that what you want?"

"For now, yes."

He sighs but smiles as he glances at my hair. "You have my curly hair."

"Yeah, I'm just glad it isn't red."

He laughs. "You've got Addie's eyes though."

"Something from each of you."

"That's a good way to see it." He holds out his hand.

"It was good to meet you, Thomas," I say, taking his hand and giving it a firm shake.

"Please keep in touch."

"I'll try," I say as I begin to walk toward his office door.

"We've got to do more than just try."

I smile. "You're right," I say as I open the door and see Grace standing there with a notebook in hand.

"Do you mind?" she whispers, as she flips to a clean page and hands it to me. "I'm sorry. It's for my brother. He'd kill me if I didn't get your autograph."

"Sure," I say, surprised.

Opening the door to my rental car, it hits me as I pull the letter out of my pocket and place it inside my luggage.

What she meant...Don't be a caged butterfly.

Chapter Thirty-Three

"Man, I'm glad to hear your little trip to Winder was good," Bryan says as he and I sit in my kitchen, waiting for the coffee to percolate.

"I am too," I say as I get up to grab the bread and place it next to the toaster.

He looks around my kitchen. "Man, you know I come here just about every Saturday for breakfast, and I just realized that your kitchen is almost as big as my apartment."

I laugh. "I've told you a hundred times that you can move in here. This place is certainly big enough for the both of us."

He shakes his head. "Naw, I like my place. Plus, I know just about everybody in my neighborhood. You know what I mean?"

"Sure, but if you ever change your mind, just know that you are always welcomed here," I say as I grab a few cups from the cabinet and place them on the table. "You want some toast or something?"

"Just coffee is good for me this morning."

I placed a towel on the table and put the coffee pot on it.

"You know they just came out with those coffee pots that you plug into the wall. I got myself one."

"Yeah, I know. I still like the kind you put on the stove, now that I've mastered how to use one," I say as I take my seat.

He grins. "I'm surprised you ain't got yourself a cook and a housekeeper by now."

Shrugging my shoulders, I grin back at him. "Nope. Thanks to you, I've become rather accustomed to doing things myself."

We both laugh as we pour ourselves a cup of coffee.

"So did you look like him?" Bryan asks, suddenly.

I lean back in my chair. "Kind of. We're about the same height, and I noticed that our mannerisms are the same. He's got curly red hair, and his eyes are green, while mine isn't."

He looks me in the face and gives me a sly smile. "Hazel. You've got hazel eyes."

"Whatever, man."

"Good thing you didn't get red hair," he says as he takes a sip of his coffee.

"That's what I said." I was expecting him to laugh along with me, but he doesn't. He looks down at his watch.

"What's up? You late for something?" I ask, studying his face.

He leans back in his chair and looks around my kitchen again as if he's looking for something. Then he glances in my direction and places his hands on the table. "Look here, man, Simoné wants to see you."

"Why?" I say as casually as I can. I can see him staring at me, so I grab my cup and take a sip of my coffee. "She wants to join the band, doesn't she?" I finally ask.

He shrugs his shoulders and looks at his watch again. "That could be it."

"I don't know, Bryan. Using her in Chicago was one thing. Doing it on a permanent basis is another. It's taken me over four years to . . ."

"To bury her?"

"Yeah, I guess so," I say, looking down at the table. "I'm not sure if I can handle it. I really loved her, and now she's . . . she's getting married." I glance directly at him. "I think it's asking too much."

"I dig it. Really I do, but will you at least talk to her?"

I lean back in my seat again. "Can't you just tell her for me?"

"She's downstairs."

"What?" I say, standing up and glaring down at him.

"Don't look at me," he says, throwing his hands up in the air. "She insisted. You know how she is when she wants something."

"You mean to tell me that she's been downstairs in your car, this whole time?" I start to pace around.

He stands up. "Look here man, she thought it was best for me to gradually get into it. I'm just trying to make this thing happen. She's the one calling this thing. You know what I mean? I'm just the messenger."

I stop and stare at him. "I'm not sure I can do it."

He walks over toward me and places his hand on my shoulder. "It's Simoné. It seems to me that you and she still got things that need to be said, so you got to do this. Okay?"

I nod my head slowly. "Okay."

He takes a step back. "Cool. I'll go get her." He looks up at me. "It's going to be okay. You two are just going to talk. You can do this. It's like walking down the yellow brick road, you got me?"

I nod my head and watch him sprint toward the front door.

I can feel my heart beating quickly as run into my bedroom and grab another shirt, just before making a mad dash into the bathroom to quickly brush my teeth.

A few minutes later, I hear her voice.

"Hello? Timmy?"

"Have a seat. I'll be out in a second," I yell from the bathroom as I stand in front of the mirror trying to get the anxiousness on my face to disappear.

I place my hand on my chest and take a deep breath.

Just be calm.

It's only her.

The woman that I'm still in love with.

I click the light off and slowly walk out into my living room to find her sitting on my sofa.

With her legs crossed.

Skin exposed.

Looking . . . Looking beautiful.

I take a seat in a chair across from her and clear my throat as my eyes take her in.

All five years' worth.

"You cut your hair," I finally say.

I watch as her hand moves slowly to her hair.

"Yeah, just a little. I'm surprised you noticed."

"Really?" I ask, leaning forward and staring into her eyes.

She blushes and looks down. "You're right. I don't know why I said that. You always took in my details."

Our eyes dance like old times.

"That's because you had beautiful details to take in."

She moves to the edge of the sofa and leans forward. "Had?"

"You know what I mean."

She smiles softly. "Yeah, I do," she says as she takes a quick glance around. "This place is nice. It's big."

"That's what Bryan was just saying," I say, wishing my heart would settle down.

"I can't believe he's still living in that shack," she says as she folds her hands in her lap and I notice it.

The ring.

"So Bryan tells me that you're getting married," I say, glancing back up at her.

She moves her hand off to the side. "That was the plan."

I lean back in my chair and place one leg on top of the other. "Why do you say it like that? Don't you love him? That's what Bryan told me. That you're so in love that he's made you a better person."

"Timmy, don't."

"Don't what? I'm just asking a question."

"We both know that you're doing more than that."

I can tell that her eyes want to pull away from me, but I won't let them.

I'm afraid. Afraid that if I let her look away, that will be it.

"It's been five years. At this point, it's just a question. Really," I say to keep her attention. Keep her eyes moving to the music of mine.

"No, it isn't. Look, I came here to tell you something. Something I should have told you that night in the alley."

I look down. "I don't want to talk about that night," I whisper.

"I do."

I look at her, and I see the tears. "Why?" I ask.

"Because I hurt you."

There it is. The smell of pain. It's a poignant aroma. One that both of us have taken a good whiff of. "Look, you don't have to say that you're sorry just to be in the band."

A confused look comes upon her face. "Who told you I wanted to be in the band?"

I stare at her. "Then why are you here?" I say, leaning forward, searching her face for an answer.

"Like I said earlier, there's something I need to tell you . . . show you really."

I lean back. "I've already seen your ring."

She looks down at it. "I didn't come here to show you a ring."

I can hear the frustration in her voice, but I pretend. I pretend like I don't want to rip it off her finger. I act like I . . . like I don't still love her.

She stands up. "I'll be right back."

I look up at her. "Simoné, what's going on?"

"Just give me a minute. Please, Timmy. I'll be right back."

"Simoné."

"I have to do this. It's taken me five years to get up the courage, so let me do this."

I scratch my head. "Do what? What are you talking about?"

"Please, give me a few minutes. I'll be right back."

I stand up and watch her walk out my front door. I take a deep breath again and head into the kitchen for a cup of water.

A few minutes later, I hear my door open, and I see Bryan walking in with Simoné behind him. He moves to the side, and I look down.

I see the eyes of a little girl looking back into mine.

Simoné quickly moves and stoops down, turning the little girl to her. "Nina, sweetie, remember when mommy told you that you were going to meet someone special today?"

I watch the little girl nod her head.

"This man is that someone special." She stands up and turns the little girl toward me.

"Timmy, this is Nina. My daughter."

I smile and extend my hand toward her. "She looks just like you," I say.

Just as our fingers touch, the little girl's and mine, I hear Simoné. I understand the words that fall from her lips. The ones that cause my heart to feel the need to jump out of my skin and run down the road, butt-naked.

"Actually," Simoné says, pausing for a second. "She looks like both of us. She's your daughter, Timmy."

I ease back as the little girl continues to stare at me with big, beautiful hazel-brown eyes. I glance over at Bryan for confirmation, and he nods slowly.

We all stand there. Searching for words that don't seem to exist, for moments like this.

I walk over to the sofa and take a seat. I place my face in my hands and try to catch my breath. Then I look up at the little girl again and then at Simoné who is standing there—her eyes pleading with me to say something.

"How?" I finally say.

"What do you mean, how?"

"I mean . . . We haven't been together in five years."

She places her hand on the little girl's shoulders. "Nina is five. She's yours, Timmy."

I stand up again and slowly turn to Bryan. "You knew?"

"Look, man, this wasn't my secret to tell."

Anger. Disappointment. Fear. All flood my insides as I stare at him. "What do you mean it wasn't your secret to tell? Five years, man! Five years!"

Simoné moves toward me, but I reach out my hand to stop her.

"Don't blame him."

I glare at her, but then, then I look at the little girl, and the reality of her presence calms me.

Nina.

I sit down on the sofa and run my hands through my hair.

"Boney, can you take Nina back down to the car? Give Timmy and me a few minutes."

He nods and walks over to grab Nina's hand. "I'll take her home." He looks at me. "Timmy, look man, I know you're upset with me because I didn't tell you, but this here is really between the two of you. You two have got to work this out, so put your grown-man pants on and get at it."

I look at Simoné. She tries to smile.

I watch as Nina holds tightly to Bryan's hand.

"Come on, little girl. Let's go get some ice cream, okay?"

She looks into Bryan's eyes and then over at Simoné, who smiles at her.

Bryan looks down at me again. "You'll get Simoné home, right?"

I nod as he and Nina walk toward the door.

Simoné waves to Nina as they walk out, then she eases down into the chair across from me.

"My mother didn't want me to tell you," she says, a few seconds later.

"And you always do what your mother tells you, don't you?"

"Timmy, please."

I glare at her. "I want you to leave. I'll call you a cab."

"Timmy."

"Get out!" I say, standing up and looking her dead in the eyes.

"No!" She stands and moves in front of me. "It's taken me five years to get to this moment. Five long years."

"How do I know she's really mine?" I say, stepping back from her. "Bryan told me what your mother tried to do to him. That she got pregnant on purpose. Tried to trap him. Is that what you did?"

"No!" She moves back in front of me. "If it was, I would have told you that night, but I didn't because I didn't want you to think that. At the time, I didn't even know what my mother had tried with Boney, so you can't say that I did the same thing."

"Sure, I can. I've learned with you that the apple doesn't fall far from the tree. You know what I mean!"

"Timmy, stop it. Stop it!"

I see the tears flowing down her cheeks, and I want so badly to wipe them away. To touch her, but the rage inside of me won't let me. It won't let me feel her lips on top of mine.

"Please just leave, Simoné."

She moves even closer to me. The smell of her perfume travels up my nostrils.

"I'm not leaving. I came here not just for Nina, but for me as well. I came here for you. Every time I look at her, I see you. I remember how much . . . how much I loved you."

"You're lying!"

"No, I'm not. I love you. I loved you, then. I know I should have told you. I know I should have told you how I really felt."

"If you loved me, why did you do it? Why did you hurt me?"

"I don't know. I guess, back then, I did whatever my mother told me to do, and it cost me. It cost me you."

She reaches out for my hand, but I deny the touch. I look into her eyes, and I can see us in the park, so many years ago. I look away from her. "I trusted you. I loved you. Now you're standing here telling me that you love me? I don't believe you."

"Why would I be here if it wasn't true?"

"I don't know. I'm sure you and your mother have some end game."

"This is no game. My mother is not involved. In fact, when I told her this morning that I broke off the engagement with Derrick, she threatened to disown me. But I don't care. I've let her control me for too long. I want to be with you. These last five years have been hard. I can't get over you, and I don't want to try any longer. I want you, Timmy. I want you. Please. Please, just look at me. Look at me. I love you. I swear, I love you. I always have."

"These past years couldn't have been that hard," I say, as I reach for her hand and hold the ring up. "You got engaged."

She pulls her hand away and removes the ring, allowing it to drop on the floor. "My mother's doing."

We both stand there, staring at it.

"You know, when Bryan told me that you were getting married, I tried to play it off. I tried to pretend like I wasn't hurt by it, but all I could think about was him touching you. Him kissing you. It hurt just as much as it did that night."

She moves so close to me that I can smell the sweet aroma of the soap that she uses.

I step back and turn away from her. "I can't."

She stands behind me. I can feel her breath in my ear as she wraps her arms around me. "Timmy, I know you still love me. Bryan told me. He gave me hope. Hope that I didn't think could exist." She turns me around slowly. "My heart beats for you. Do you want to feel it?" she says, as she places my hand over her heart. I feel the warmth of her fingers. The thumping of her heart.

" No one makes my heart beat like this, except you. Tell me that you don't love me. Tell me that your heart doesn't beat just as strong for me still. Tell me I'm lying."

I reach up and touch her hair. I feel her body upon mine as we share an intimate space. When her lips touch mine, the battle of my heart reaches out for that familiar place. That place where all I want is her.

I pull back. "How do I know I can trust you this time?" I say as she moves back toward me.

"It's going to take time, I know. But I love you. I loved you from the moment we went out that night. You remember? We danced in the park. You held me close. Wrapping your arms around me. Kissing my neck. Since that night, I have never felt that way about anyone. That's why I couldn't do it. I couldn't marry someone else." She slips off her shoes and holds out her hand. "Dance with me."

"I don't want to dance."

She grabs my hands and wraps them around her waist. It feels good to hold her in my arms again. To caress her back. To get lost in her eyes.

She begins to sing, and the sound of her voice takes me back there again. I can feel the rain pouring down upon us. I can see the streetlights sparkling in her eyes.

I begin to move with her.

Slowly.

Gently.

Every step we take together, I fell my heart giving in.

"Simoné, I have missed you so much."

She places her head on my shoulder. "I'm sorry, I'm so sorry, but I'm here, and I'm never going anywhere. You're the one I want . . . It was always you."

She begins to sing again. I trace the movement of her mouth with my fingers as the tears fall from her face.

"Please be real this time," I whisper as I bring her close to me again.

"I am real. This is real," she says as she places her lips upon mine again.

As we continue to dance, I know.

I'd cross the world to be with her.

Chapter Thirty-Four

"Last night was crazy, huh?" Bryan asks, as he walks into my kitchen and grabs an apple off the counter.

"I'm still trying to process it all," I say as I measure out some coffee. "I still can't get over the fact that I have a daughter."

"Yeah, man, it's crazy, but that little girl is beautiful, and she's smart. I'm sure she gets it from her grandpa."

I glance over at him and grin. "Simoné and I talked about Nina and everything else, all night. Actually, she just left. I'm surprised you didn't see her."

"I took the stairs. Gotta watch my figure," he says, laughing as he leans up against the counter.

"Funny." I glance over at him and notice that's he's watching me carefully.

"What's up man, speak your mind. Ain't no one in this kitchen but the two of us," he says.

I pour myself a cup of coffee. "It's scary. I'm just not sure I know how to raise a daughter. Don't get me wrong—"

He sighs."I get where you're going. I know you'll love that little girl, but you regret getting in this type of situation so soon."

I nod my head slowly. "Exactly. I always thought Simoné and I would enjoy just being . . . married, before any kids came. You know what I mean?"

He smirks."Man, life ain't never like we imagine it to be. But look here, man, you got to remember that we all make mistakes." He takes a bite out of his apple. "So what you thinking now?"

I glance up at him. "What do you mean?"

"I mean, what you gonna do about this situation?"

"You asking if I'm going to ask Simoné to marry me?"

He doesn't respond. He just stands there watching me.

"Don't worry, man, I got my grown-man pants on. I'm going to take care of her and Nina. I promise you that."

He takes another bite of his apple. "Cool. I knew you would."

"I just don't want her to feel obligated to say yes, you know what I mean?"

He chuckles. "Man, please. That girl loves you." He tosses what's left of his apple in the trash and gives me this serious look. "Honestly, just between me and you, I think the only reason she agreed to marry that other cat was because of fear. She was afraid that you would never forgive her, and she didn't want to raise Nina alone. But her heart just wouldn't go through with it. She couldn't marry someone she didn't love. When she called me and told me that she finally wanted to come clean with you, I rushed her right over."

I grab my coffee cup and make my way over to the kitchen table. Bryan follows me after pouring himself a cup.

"I still wish you had told me," I say as I place a spoonful of sugar in my cup.

"I thought about it, but like I told you, that wasn't my secret to tell. It needed to come from her."

I lean back in my chair and take a sip of my coffee. "I need to get her a ring."

He shakes his head in disagreement. "I don't think she cares about that. She just wants to marry you. Shoot, I think Simoné would be happy if the two of you went to the courthouse tomorrow and made it happen."

"She deserves a wedding. Even if it's a small one."

"She deserves you, and you deserve her. That's all that really matters, man. Forget that other foolishness. You two have been miserable for five years without each other. That's long enough in my book. You feel me?"

"Yeah, I feel you. I wonder how her mother is handling this?"

"Look here, Jackie is going to be Jackie. She made it clear to Simoné that she ain't gonna have nothing to do with her if she marries you. As much as your adoptive mother hated you because you were black—

Jackie hates you just as much because she thinks you're white. I say let it stay that way.

"That way, she'll stay out of your lives. Jackie ain't no good for Simoné or for your daughter. She only wanted Simoné to talk you into signing with Fountain Records, so she could get a share of the royalties they promised her. Don't worry about Jackie, because she ain't worrying about you. Believe that." He stands up.

"Where you headed this morning?"

"I gotta run over to Sun City Records. They called me just as I was leaving my place, but I wanted to stop here first, make sure you were cool with everything." He looks me directly in the eyes. "You cool?"

I laugh. "Yeah, man, I'm cool. I think I'm going to hit those sheets for an hour or so, then I might take Simoné and Nina out for dinner later."

"Doing the family thing already...I dig it. Look here, I'll catch you three later. Kiss my grandbaby for me and think about the courthouse thing. I can set it up so that it's private. Let me know."

"Go ahead and set it up, but let me talk to Simoné about it tonight."

"That's what's up. You learning already."

Chapter Thirty-Five

My phone rings as I place the letter in my lap and reach over to pick up the receiver.

"Timmy, man, did I wake you?"

"I wasn't asleep. I was reading—it," I say, placing the letter off to the side.

"That's what, a hundred and one times now?"

I chuckle. "Something like that. I thought you were heading to the studio."

"I'm here," he says, but I can hear the slight hesitation in his voice.

"What's up? Is there something wrong with the last take we did for the new album?"

"Naw, that's cool. Look here, what exactly happened when you went to Winder, man?"

I sit up. "Nothing, except what I told you. Why? What's going on?"

"Man, I don't know how to tell you this, but it's in today's paper."

"What's in the paper?" I ask. Worried.

"Everything. Everything about you."

"What do you mean, everything about me?"

"I mean, everything about you. About you being black and about your birth mother being black. They're saying that you've been lying to the public."

I can feel my heart beating fast. "How? No one knows about that except me and you."

"Apparently, some girl in Winder—Grace, I think her name is—went to some of the tabloids and spilled the story. Man, she told it all."

"That's crazy, how could she . . ." Then I remember—

"Timmy, you there?"

"Yeah, I'm here," I faintly say.

"How could this little country girl have known about you?" he asks.

"She was there. Standing at the door."

"What do you mean?"

"When I opened the door that day, Grace was standing there with a notebook and pen. She must have been listening through the door and writing down what she heard."

"That's low. The things folks will do for some money."

"I can't believe she'd do this."

"Like I said, people are people and money makes some folks lose their minds. But look here, Jimmy wants you to come to the studio as soon as possible. I can send the car over to you."

I sit down on the edge of my bed, and I look at the wall in front of me. Holding the phone to my ear.

"Timmy, you still with me, man?"

"This is going to ruin my career. It's going to ruin everything. I knew this would happen. I knew I would never be happy."

My heart begins to race.

"Don't go dark on me, man. Don't sweat this. Okay?"

All I can think about is Simoné.

"Simoné is going to see that in the papers. She's going to know."

"You know she ain't going to care about that. She loves you. She ain't worried about you being black or white."

I stand up and place my hand on the wall to hold myself up. "But my career! How am I going to take care of her? How am I going to take care of Nina? My little girl . . ."

"Sun City Records got PR for this kind of stuff, man. I know they can put a spin on this. That's why Jimmy wants you to come in so we can get at it. He's bringing in the big guns to deal with this. I promise you that."

"I'm never going to escape her words," I say, holding my chest and trying to catch my breath.

"Whose words?"

"She didn't think I would amount to anything and now it's going to be true."

"Are you talking about Lena? Man, don't do this to yourself."

I punch the wall. "Everything I've worked so hard for will be gone. She'll have won. Everyone is going to see me as nothing but a fraud from this day forward. My music will mean nothing."

"Timmy, it's just a story. This kind of stuff happens to celebrities all the time. Like I said, Sun City will handle it. Trust me, man, it'll be okay. I ain't never lied to you."

I ease back down on my bed, and I sit there. Seeing her face.

Lena's face.

"I'm tired. I just want out," I whisper.

"What, you saying that you want out of the business?"

I pause. "I want out of life."

"Man, you can't mean that."

I can see her laughing at me as I struggle to hold the phone.

"I do. I tried to make it work, but it was never going to work out for me. I can see that now. It's my fault, really."

"It's not your fault. None of this is."

"It's my fault because I couldn't let it go. She tried to warn me."

"You couldn't let, what go? What are you talking about? Who tried to warn you?"

I glance over at the letter. "Addie. She tried to tell me to let it go. She tried to tell me not to let it cage me."

"Let what go? What is it that you need to let go?"

"The hatred."

"Look here, man, I promise you, this stuff in the papers, man, it ain't that bad. Just hold on. Don't do anything stupid. I'm coming to you. You hear me? I'm—"

I place the phone on the receiver and reach over to pick the letter up.

My eyes linger on the truth.

I'm never going to be free.

I'm always going to be...

...a caged butterfly.

Addie, please forgive me for not being the son you wanted me to be.

Part Three

Chapter Thirty-Six

*D*ear Diary,
　　When I was around five, I met my father.
　　I remember that day.
I remember our hands touching.

I only know him now through the pictures that hang on the walls of this apartment, the apartment that he owned, and through his records that Mama plays when she thinks I'm asleep.

About a year ago, Mama and I were standing in front of his grave, and I silently watched her remove the old flowers and put fresh flowers on it. I asked her why he took his own life. She wouldn't answer me, but Grandpa Bryan told me. He told me that the world embraced my father because they thought he was a white man who could play the mess out of what was considered black music.

Jazz.

Grandpa said that because my father looked white, the world was open to him. He could go and do anything. Play in places that most black jazz pianists couldn't. But when the world learned that my father was black and threatened to take everything he worked hard to achieve, he couldn't handle it.

That's why he left us.

Left us alone.

To me, he's a coward.

I'm going to really miss Grandpa Bryan. He's moving back to Chicago tomorrow to take care of his sister. He told Mama that New York holds too many bad memories for him.

I don't see Grandpa Livingston that much because he lives in Georgia. He writes sometimes. Sends me pictures of his dogs, but that's about it. He's an attorney. His wife left him some time ago.

It's just me and Mama.

We'd be poor if Grandpa Bryan didn't make arrangements with Sun City Records for my father's royalty checks to come to Mama. It was hard though since Mama and my father were never married.

Mama says that one day, the checks may stop and we may have to move. Leave this apartment. I hope that doesn't happen, since then I'd have nowhere to invite the girls with bright white skin from school over for doll parties.

The girls whose lives are perfect.

The girls who can do anything and become anything.

Because their hair is straight.

And their skin is white.

Like my father's was.

At school, I stand in the bathroom and watch them as they talk about their perfect lives and smile as they run combs through their perfect golden locks.

My hair is not like that.

My hair breaks brushes. Ruins combs and takes forever for Mama to get through it.

But it's long.

My nose is slender. Not wide.

My cheekbones are high.

That's something.

Something I can use.

When the day comes.

I wish I had their eyes.

Their eyes are blue. Sometimes green when the sun seems to shine through them.

But never hazel. Never dull. Never boring.

Even their dolls don't have hazel eyes.

I love their dolls, but Mama won't buy me one of them. She wants me to get the ugly one, and since I won't, I don't have a doll.

But tomorrow, that's going to change.

Tomorrow, I'm going to get a doll.

One with bright white skin.

One with blue eyes and golden locks.

I've been saving the money that Grandpa Taylor and Grandma Jean, who live in Chicago, send me sometimes.

Tomorrow is going to be the best day of my life.

Finally.

Chapter Thirty-Seven

ama walks into my room, surprised to find me already up. My teeth brushed. I had bathed and put on my skirt and top. Tied my shoes. Pulled my hair back in a ponytail and put my money in my purse. The pink one that Grandpa Bryan bought for me.

"I wish you'd get ready for school like that every morning. Sure would make the battles you and I go through each day non-existent," she says as she walks over and inspects me.

I jump off the bed. "Are we ready to go now?"

She looks down at her watch. "It's seven in the morning, little girl. The store doesn't open for another three hours."

"Oh." Disappointed, I climb back on my bed.

Mama sits down next to me and places her arm around my shoulders. "Since you're already dressed, why don't you go have your breakfast and then go practice? I had the piano tuned since you said it wasn't playing right."

I look up at her. "Mama, I don't need to practice. Grandpa Bryan said I got it."

She gives me a confused look. "Got what?"

"My father's gift," I say, matter-of-factly.

Her smile fades. I know she hates talking about him—my father. Too much pain in her heart, Grandpa Bryan always says.

I place my hand on top of hers. "Don't be sad, Mama. Grandpa said that I got your gift too. A little bit of both of you."

Her smile returns. "You sure do, baby girl. You sure do." She touches my cheek. "Now, go eat breakfast."

I run into the kitchen and have my usual bowl of cereal. Then I place the milk back in the refrigerator and the cereal box back in the bottom cabinet.

A few minutes later, I walk into the room with the piano in it and take a seat behind it. I look up and see my father's photo, staring back at me. Why didn't I get your skin instead of Mama's? Why couldn't you be strong like Mama is always telling me to be? Then you'd be here with us.

I hit a key on the piano and look back up at the photo.

Why did you leave me?

I place my hands on the keys and close my eyes. Then I play my mama's favorite—"Funny Valentine" by Ella Fitzgerald. Mama said that was the song my father fell in love with her on.

One day, I'm going to fall in love.

One day, I'm going to sing on stages.

Play for thousands.

One day, I'm going to have bright white skin.

Mama keeps telling me to love the skin I'm in. But I don't want my skin. I want the skin color that will make me famous.

Even more famous than my father.

Chapter Thirty-Eight

*T*he drive to the toy store is taking forever. I wanted to take the subway, but Mama insists on driving. She's always insisting on something.

"I really wanted to be there when the store opened," I say as I glance out my window.

Mama lets out a sigh. "We'll be there. As long as you get your doll, that's all that should matter."

I lean back in my seat and fold my arms together.

Mama glances over at me. "Stop that pouting. You know I hate that. Be a big girl. You hear me?"

I unfold my arms and sit up. "Yes, ma'am."

Mama smiles. "I wish I could talk you into getting a pretty little black doll once we get there."

"I told you that I don't want an ugly black doll."

Mama snatches her eyes over at me. Clearly upset but I try not to notice and continue to look out my window.

"Black dolls aren't ugly," she finally says.

"Yes, they are. They have nappy hair and big lips."

"Nina, black dolls are beautiful, just like you're beautiful. Don't you want a doll that looks like you?"

"No," I say, too sharply.

"No, what?" Mama says, trying not to reach over and give me a quick pop in the mouth for getting smart with her.

"No, ma'am."

She glances over at me and then blows her horn at some guy who tries to cut her off. "What's wrong with the doll I ordered for you? The one from Shindana Toys? I had that shipped all the way from Los Angeles, and you didn't even take it out of the box."

"That's because I didn't want it."

"Nina."

"Mama, can we just get my doll today? The one I want? You promised that if I saved the money, I could buy the doll I wanted."

She lets out a sigh, but I know my fight isn't over.

"You're right. We'll get the doll you want. But one day, I hope you come to love your beautiful black skin."

I don't say anything because I know. Even at eight years old, I know.

I will never come to love my black skin.

When Mama pulls into the parking lot of the toy store, I open the car door, but she grabs my arm and pulls me back.

"Nina, I have to park the car first. Don't ever do that again, you hear me?"

"Yes, ma'am."

"You always wait for me to park. Now, sit back."

She glances over at me to see if I have any type of expression on my face that might warrant a further discussion, but I do as I'm told. I dash out of the car the moment I'm sure it's stopped this time.

I run into the store, not waiting for Mama and head straight to the aisle where the dolls are.

My eyes move quickly. Scanning the faces of each one until I see it.

The one I've had my heart set on for months now. A doll I've seen the other girls bring to my doll parties.

I pull her down off the shelf and hold her in my hands.

I look up, and I see a sales clerk looking at me. She has on a red apron and a name badge that says, Angelica.

I hold my doll tighter as she walks over to me.

"We have some more dolls on the other end, ones that you might like better," she says with a smile.

I look down the aisle, and I see Mama walking down the aisle towards me.

"Thank you," I say to the sales clerk with the red apron on. "I have the one I want."

"You sure?"

I glare at her.

She bends down and looks me in the eyes.

"We do have black dolls. Our selection isn't that big, but we have a few. Come on, I'll show you." She tries to grab my doll out of my hand and force me to follow her down to the ugly dolls.

I don't move, and I won't let go of my doll. "Thank you, miss," I say again, glancing quickly at Mama. "I have the one I want."

Mama stands there staring at me. I know that if I say anything else, I'll get a pop on my bottom, so I try to just smile.

I really do.

The lady in the red apron walks down to the end with the ugly dolls and grabs one. She then comes back toward Mama and me. "This one is beautiful," she says, holding the doll out to me while reaching for the one that I'm holding. "She even has long hair like yours."

I take a few steps back. "Get away from me! I told you I don't want those ugly black dolls!"

The sales clerk glares at me, but I don't care.

"Nina!" Mama says as she quickly moves in front of me.

I look up and see the anger on Mama's face. "It's her fault, Mama," I say through tears. "You saw me trying to be polite like you taught me to be."

Mama reaches for my hand. "Come on. We'll talk about this in the car. Put that doll back."

I don't move. "Please, Mama, you promised. I didn't mean to yell at the lady. I wasn't trying to be mean."

The sales clerk moves toward Mama. "I'm sorry, ma'am. She's right. I was just trying to encourage her. It's my fault."

Mama looks down at me as I plead with her not to make me put my doll back through sniffles.

Mama sighs and puts her hand on my shoulder. "Stop crying, Nina. It's okay."

I cling to my doll. "I can keep her?"

Mama tries to smile as she reaches over and wipes the tears from my face. "Yes, you can keep her." She then turns toward the sales clerk. "I'm really sorry about all of this, she's been wanting this doll for a long time."

The sales clerk nods slowly, but she's still upset that I refused to take the ugly black doll.

"Nina, what do you say to the lady for yelling?"

I look over at the sales clerk and try to put a smile on my face. "I'm sorry, miss."

Chapter Thirty-Nine

"Mama, don't be mad at me," I say after I can't take the silence that sits between us.

"I'm not mad, just disappointed. I've tried so hard to help you to see how important it is to be happy with who you are."

"Where are we going?" I ask as I hold my doll. Looking up a few times to glance out the window.

Mama gives me a quick smile. "I want to show you something. We'll be there in about twenty minutes or so."

"That's forever," I say, anxious to get home and play with my doll.

Mama laughs. "It's not forever, Nina. You'll have plenty of time to play with your doll when we get home."

She clicks on the radio and starts to sing along with the music.

"I love this song," she says as she makes a right-hand turn and heads toward the expressway.

I lay my doll in my lap and drift off to sleep. When I wake up and look out the window, we're pulling up to a building.

"What part of New York is this?" I ask.

She laughs. "We're still in Manhattan. This is the New York Center building."

"What's in it?"

"Beauty."

I get out of the car and grab my doll.

"Leave it in the car," Mama says, pointing to the front seat.

"Please?"

She places her hands on her hips. "I mean it."

I sigh with disappointment but place my doll in the front seat and follow Mama to the side of the building.

She knocks on the door, and a black woman in a pink leotard and white tutu skirt opens the door. She bursts into a smile the moment she recognizes Mama.

"Simoné! Girl, I haven't seen you in forever."

"It has been quite some time, Jasmine."

I stand there, holding Mama's hand.

"Who do we have here?" the woman says, looking down at me.

Mama moves me in front of her. "Jasmine, this is my daughter, Nina Taylor. Nina, say hello."

"Hello," I whisper.

The woman laughs. "She's so cute, Simoné." She reaches out and tries to pinch my cheek, but I step back.

"I was hoping we could watch the dancers today," Mama says, glaring down at me.

The woman steps to the side to let us in. "Girl, anything for you. Come on in. You still singing at your mother's place?"

Mama frowns. "No. I haven't sung for anyone in years."

The lady nods her head like she has some insight as to why Mama stopped singing.

"Moved on from that, huh?"

"Yeah, motherhood can do that to you," Mama says.

They both look down at me.

"I understand. Come on, follow me."

Mama and I follow her over to a seat of chairs that are off to the side of the dance floor.

"You two can have a seat in these chairs. The dancers will be out in a minute. We were just about to get rehearsal started. We've got a show coming up. You and Nina should come and see us."

Mama and I take our seats.

"We will. Just let me know when and where." Mama says, just as the dancers begin to come in.

"So what did you think?" Mama asks as we walk back to the car.

"It was very nice," I say as I open my car door and climb inside.

Mama climbs in on the driver's side and turns toward me. "It was very nice, wasn't it. It was also kind of cool, don't you think?"

"Yeah, it was," I say, picking up my doll. Not sure what else she wants me to say about watching dark-skinned people with thick, nappy hair dance across a floor.

Mama reaches over and takes the doll from me and places it in the back seat.

I try not to show my disappointment for fear that if I do, I won't get a chance to play with it when we get home.

"Nina," Mama says to me, slowly. "I brought you here so you could see that being black doesn't mean you can't be successful. Those ladies and gentlemen have been a part of some of the biggest ballet and dance productions out there. They've even toured overseas. Each one of them is proud of their black skin, proud of their bodies, and they use both to create beauty. Just because you're black doesn't mean you can't do something that's beautiful. You understand?"

"Yes, ma'am," I whisper.

"Good. Let's go get some ice cream."

It's evening when Mama and I finally walk into the house. I rush into my room with my doll held tightly in hand as Mama follows me. She eases down on my bed.

I feel her disapproving eyes on me as I plop down on the floor in the middle of my room to comb my doll's hair.

"Mama, can I ask you something?"

"Sure, baby."

"If blacks can be successful, then why didn't my father think so? Wasn't he really black?"

I study her face, looking to see if she's angry that I asked her such a question.

She pats the bed for me to come over to her, so I stand up, holding my doll in my hand.

Mama points to my toy chest.

I glance over at it, not wanting to put my doll in it, but I do as I'm told and walk over to it, placing my doll on top.

Mama pulls the covers down and then helps me put on my pajamas. "Your father had a history of problems," she says as she tucks me in and sits on the edge of my bed.

"You mean he was crazy?"

Mama laughs. "No, why in the world would you think that?"

"That's what my teacher always says about crazy people when we're studying history, that they had a history of problems."

Mama laughs again. "Nina, she means that they had a history of mental problems."

"So my father had mental problems? That's what some of the girls say at school. They say that's why he killed himself."

Mama places her hand over her heart, and I notice tears in the corners of her eyes. "You listen to me. Your father was a loving and kind man. He wasn't crazy, and he didn't have mental problems. He had a rough life, as they say. He didn't find out he was black until he was in his twenties. It's true that he was afraid of people finding out, afraid of what he thought it would do to his career. But he wasn't crazy. He just gave up the fight."

"What fight?"

"Trying to be free."

"Free from what?" I ask, confused.

"His past. His feelings."

"What feelings?"

She rubs my cheek. "His hatred for his mother."

"Why did he hate his mother?"

"His mother wasn't a loving or kind person, and the things she did to him eventually caused him to—."

"Leave us?"

She nods slowly. I see a tear fall.

"Don't ever think badly of him. Okay?"

"Yes, ma'am." I reach up and wrap my arms around her neck.

She places a kiss on my forehead. "Come on, it's time for you to go to sleep. Tomorrow is Monday, and we both know how much you hate getting up for school." She smiles as she stands up, even though the tears are still falling down the sides of her cheeks.

Chapter Forty

"**N**ina, are you ready? You're going to be late for your performance."

"I'm coming."

"I'll meet you in the car. Hurry up!"

"I'm coming, I'm coming." I run to my dresser and look in the mirror. Not enough. I reach into my drawer and take out the makeup I keep hidden in the back. I dab more of the white powder on my face and make my way toward the door.

Mama already has the car warming up as I jump in. She stares at my face.

"What in the world is all over your face? Are you wearing makeup? We agreed—not until next year when you're eighteen," she says as she pulls the car out of the parking deck.

"This is my first real performance, outside of the stupid school stuff. I just want to do something special. Please let me wear it."

She glances over at me again. "Why do you have so much on? It makes you look . . . so light. There is no reason for you to look that light, young lady."

"All the girls are wearing their makeup like this tonight," I say as I pull down the passenger-side visor to look in the mirror.

I see the frown on mama's face out the corner of my eyes, but I ignore it.

"They can't be wearing that much?"

I close up the mirror and flip the visor back up. "They are," I say, smiling to try to win her over. "Besides, even if they aren't, it's only for one night. "

The frown on her face seems to deepen. "We'll talk about this later. I don't like you wearing that much. It's like you're trying to cover up your skin. Is that what you're trying to do?"

"Of course not. I told you, I just did it for tonight's performance. You know how heavy the lighting can be."

"That better be the reason."

"It is. What other reason could it be?" I say, a little too sharply.

She glances over at me quickly as she comes to a traffic light. "Don't get smart with me, young lady."

"I'm sorry, Mama."

She fringes a smile, but I know that she's still upset about the makeup.

"It's great that your friend Kelly was able to get you a part in this play. It will look good on your resume since it's a paying gig. Not many girls get a paying gig like this while they are in high school. "

I slowly nod my head in agreement. "It's cool."

I can feel my mother's eyes on me as we wait for the light to finally turn green.

I turn toward her. "I just wish it were bigger. I'm only doing one song. Kelly's role is bigger. They always give the bigger roles to the white—"

Mama shoots me a disapproving look as she moves through traffic. "Don't start, Nina. Kelly got a bigger role because she's an actress. This isn't a musical. It's a play."

"Yeah, I'm sure that's the reason," I say sarcastically as she turns into the parking lot of the small theater and parks the car.

"It is," she says with a frustrated sigh. "Where's your coat?" she asks as I jump out of the car.

"I didn't bring one since we're just running inside."

"Nina, it's winter."

"I'm going right inside." I spot Kelly near the front door and wave. "I'll see you when the show is over. Okay?"

"Hold on," Mama says as she walks to the trunk, pops it open and pulls out a coat. "Put it on."

"Can I go now?" I ask impatiently as I zip up the coat and glance over to see Kelly waving for me to hurry up.

Mama closes the trunk and places the car keys inside her purse. "Fine," she says, walking over towards me. "Have fun. Sing your heart out up there. I know you'll do great."

I smile at her and quickly head in Kelly's direction, glad that I don't have to hear one of my mother's never-ending lectures.

"That's a mighty big coat," Kelly says, laughing as I stand in front of her.

"You know my mother. Come on, let's get inside," I say as I begin pulling the coat off when the door closes behind us.

"You nervous?" Kelly asks as we walk into the women's dressing room.

"Nope," I say as I glance around and see all the women with skin that looks like Kelly's.

"I would be if I had to sing. You know I can't sing a lick," Kelly says, watching me as I sit in my chair watching women rush to change into their costumes.

"I can't believe you didn't get the lead singing spot, " Kelly says as she glances over at a tall woman with long blond hair that hangs down her back. "You're way better than her. I saw her audition."

"I know why I didn't get it," I say as I turn my chair around and face the mirror.

"Why?" Kelly asks while turning her own chair around.

Our eyes meet in the mirror as I reach up to touch my cheek.

"Never mind. Give me some of your makeup," I say, glancing over at her as she starts to pull her makeup out of her purse and place it on the counter.

She laughs as she hands me a small compact case. "I'm surprised your mother didn't get on you about wearing what you already have on."

I flip the case open and begin applying the foundation to my skin. "She tried. I told her I was just wearing it for tonight's performance."

"You better hope she doesn't find out that you put that much on when you get to school."

I hand her back the compact case and give her a sly smile. "She won't. I'm careful."

"Good, because your mother doesn't play. I hear most black mothers are that way."

I turn Kelly toward me. "What do you mean by that?"

"What? What did I say?" she asks after noticing the angry look on my face. "I didn't mean anything by that. Really. I'm just saying that black mothers are tougher than most white mothers. My mother couldn't care less how much makeup I wear."

I soften my face. "In my seventeen years of living, I've found that mothers are mothers, Kelly. Your mother is just special."

She chuckles as she puts the makeup compact in her purse. "Tell me about it."

She looks over at me and catches me staring again at the woman who got the lead singing role.

"Why don't you just do what I told you to do?" she says as she leans over and touches my hand to get my attention.

I turn my attention back to the mirror. "What? Start bleaching my skin? I don't know about that. I'm not sure it's safe."

Kelly moves her chair closer to me. "I wouldn't have told you about it if it wasn't safe. If you use that stuff, you won't have to put so much of my makeup on. Plus, you're not that black. "

I give her an 'I can't believe that just came out of your mouth' look.

"You know what I mean. I'm just saying that it wouldn't take much." She reaches over and touches my hand again. "Say you'll try it, for me."

I glance down the counter and see the woman putting her makeup on. "Maybe."

Kelly turns my chair toward hers. "Look, you're the one that always complaining about your . . . your skin problem," she says, glancing around to be sure no one is listening to us. "I know that's why you think you didn't get the lead. I'm not stupid. I know you. Why not give it a try?"

I glance down the counter at the woman again as she continues to put on her makeup.

"Okay," I finally say.

Kelly almost jumps out of her seat with excitement. "Seriously?" she asks, studying my face to be sure.

I sigh. "Where do I get it from?"

"I already have some."

I give her a questioning look. "How?"

"I got some from Barbara last week. Just in case."

"Just in case what?"

"Just in case you needed it," she says, smiling as she turns around and grabs her purse.

"Why would Barbara have something like that? I thought she was—"

Kelly gives me a devious smile "White with a perfect tan? Nope. She's been using it for years. Her mother gave it to her, gets it from a dermatologist. I told you it was safe."

I smile slowly as she pulls out a container and hands it to me.

We both stare at it for a moment.

"This will help get you started. Barbara said that she can get us more, but it will cost next time," Kelly quickly says as I open the container and give it a whiff.

"It stinks. What's in it?" I ask as I place the lid back on and turn it over to check out the ingredients.

"What do you care as long as it gets the job done?"

It was a good point. "How do I use it?" I ask, turning the container back around.

"Just put it on your face and the rest of your body every day. We'll be twins in no time. I promise."

I reach down for my purse and place the container in it. "How much is Barbara going to charge me to get more, once this runs out?"

I see the hesitation on Kelly's face. "How much?" I ask again, watching her facial expression closely.

She turns and looks in the mirror. "It's three hundred for a month's supply," she says too casually.

I turn my chair around to face the mirror. "Three hundred dollars! Where am I going to get that kind of money?"

"Lower your voice. Folks might think we're talking about drugs or something," Kelly whispers to me as she glances around the room again. "Just do what I do when I need money."

"Which is what?" I say, looking at her suspiciously.

"I grab it out of my mother's purse. She never notices it."

"I am not stealing money out of my mother's purse."

She lets out a sigh as if she can't understand why I won't even consider such a thing.

"If you want more of that, you will." I look over at the woman again. My heart feels like that little girl who didn't have the baby doll with bright white skin and blue eyes to bring to the sleepover. Kelly reaches over again and touches my hand. "Just take, like, twenty dollars each week, that way you'll have the money by the end of the month."

I stare at myself in the mirror. Looking into my hazel eyes and hating everything that they see. "I can't do that," I say with my mouth but knowing that deep down, at this moment, I was giving the thought more consideration than I ought to.

Kelly leans over and joins me in the mirror as we both stare at my unwanted complexion. "Look, this is what you wanted, isn't it?" she whispers to me.

"Yes," I mouth slowly.

I see another sly smile come upon her face. "Wait, I have the perfect answer!" she says, clapping her hands together as if she has just figured out how to commit the perfect crime.

"What?" I ask, hoping that it's something other than stealing from my mother or robbing a bank.

"Why don't you write to your grandfather? The one that you told me lives in Chicago. He's rich, right? And they send you money sometimes, right?"

We both look into the mirror with a ray of hope on our faces.

"They do."

Kelly claps her hands together again. "Then, there you go. You don't have to borrow it from your mother. Just tell him that you need it for some new singing lessons or something." She reaches into her purse and pulls out a small gift-wrapped box.

"What's this?" I say as she hands it to me.

"Something else to help with your transformation."

I open the box. "Where did you get these?"

"Don't worry about where I got them. Do you like them?"

"They're perfect." I reach over and give her a hug. "Thank you."

"No sweat. We're best friends, and that's what best friends do for each other. I figure once that cream starts working, those blue eye contacts will be the perfect finishing touch. We'll really be twins then."

I glance down at them again. "Now, make sure you hide both of those, we don't want your mother finding them. It'll be game over for sure."

We laugh as I put the contacts in the bottom of my purse, next to the container. "I'll hide everything in my closet, behind my shoes, when I get home."

I lean back in my chair. "Hey, what happens once this stuff starts to work? My mother will know."

"Just use some of her makeup to hide it. Once it really starts to work, there's nothing she can do about it."

"Perfect," I say as I clap my hands together just as the stage manager comes in and gives us a ten-minute warning.

I stand up and begin walking over to our costumes. "We need to get changed. As my Grandpa Bryan always says, 'Let's get at it.'"

Chapter Forty-One

"You did such an amazing job tonight!" Mama says as she pulls the car out of the theater parking lot.

"That's what you're supposed to say. You're my mother."

Mama quickly glances over at me as I sit staring out the window.

"True, but I still mean it. It was so beautiful to watch you up there."

I shrug my shoulders some. "It would have been better if I had gotten the lead. You heard the applause for that white girl. I know I sounded so much better than her."

"Yes, you sounded better. But at least you got a part," Mama says as she changes lanes.

"You and I both know that if I were white, I would have gotten that role. Maybe my father was right. Being white in the music industry is the way to go."

Mama quickly pulls the car over and turns it off. "Nina, what is this obsession that you have with being white?"

I look down at the car floor. "Don't give me the 'love the skin you're in' speech. Not tonight. That girl got that role strictly because of her skin color, or lack of it."

"There could have been other reasons why she got the part," Mama says, frustrated that I won't see it her way.

"Like what?" I ask, looking over at her.

She clears her throat, and I can see her searching quickly for a response.

"The part called for acting and singing. You only sing."

"Please, I could have done that role, and you know it."

Mama reaches over and grabs me by the shoulders. "Stop it! When are you going to learn?"

"What's there to learn?" I say, looking deep into her eyes.

"That you can be successful even being black. That you can do anything."

"That's not true and tonight was proof! Besides, how would you know? You never were successful. You never cut a record or did anything other than sing at your mother's club that's now nothing more than some run-down piece of crap. We're only living the way we're living because of my father, and he made that money because people thought he was white. I seriously doubt he would have gotten that far had people known he was a black man."

The sting of her hand caused my cheek to burn.

"Don't you ever talk to me like that and don't you ever talk about your father like that. Do you hear me!"

I didn't respond as tears streamed down my face.

"Nina."

"Yes, ma'am."

Mama leans back in her seat for a few minutes and stares out the window.

"I'm sorry," I whisper, but we both know it's a lie.

Chapter Forty-Two

"My mother and I got into another big fight last night."

"Why?" Kelly asks, sitting up in her bed.

I look over at her through the rather large mirror that's just above her dresser. "You know why. She wants me to stop with the skin bleaching."

"It's too late for that now. You look like a white girl with a perfect tan."

I turn around and smile. "Thanks to the new stuff that Barbara was able to get me. That stuff was expensive, though."

"It was worth it, wasn't it? I mean look at you," Kelly says, getting off her bed and walking over to me. "Honestly, I think it's time to put those contacts in."

We both stare at my face in the mirror, my eyes loving everything they see.

"I'm going to have to get some new ones. The ones you gave me dried out."

She leans over my shoulders to move her bangs out of her face. "That's an easy fix. Are you going to dye your hair?"

I glance at her golden blond hair. "I was thinking about it."

"What color?" she asks, slyly.

I grin. "You know what color."

"Golden blond?"

"You know it," I say, snapping my fingers in the air.

She reaches into a drawer and pulls out a box. "Here."

I look at the front of the box and almost scream. "This is perfect."

Kelly pats me on the shoulders. "I knew it would be. Let's go use it now." She grabs my hand and pulls me to her bathroom. "Are we still good for getting the apartment after graduation?" she asks as she hands me a couple of towels.

"Yeah, we're still good. My mother is not happy that I'm not going to college," I say as I open the box and begin mixing the color. I glance up and see a look of concern on her face. "We're getting it. Don't worry."

She smiles as she pulls out the chair from her vanity and I take a seat.

"How's your mother taking the news that you're moving out and not going to college?" I ask as I begin to part my hair and apply the color to it.

She walks over to her tub and sits on the edge of it. "You know my mother. She doesn't care what I do as long as I don't interfere with her life. She's gone most of the time, and whenever she's home, she's out with her friends, spending all my father's money."

I stop and glance over at her. "When was the last time you saw him?"

"My father? I talk to him about once a month, but he travels a lot. I don't really care about the traveling as long as he keeps sending me those checks," she says, winking at me. "You better keep moving. You don't want to have green hair."

"Girl, you're a mess."

"Just keeping it real."

"Oh, so we're talking like we're hip now?"

She giggles. "Just throwing a little 1980s culture your way."

"I see. Do you need me to get you a big gold chain or something?"

"What, you don't think that white girls have any culture?"

"Is that what that is?"

She stands up and tries to pose like LL Cool J.

I scream out laughing. "Don't do that. Ever."

She sits back down on the tub. "I don't know what you're talking about. LL and I go way back. In fact, he's going to be my baby's daddy."

I laugh even harder. "What am I going to do with you?"

She starts rubbing her stomach. "I'm starving. Do you want something from downstairs? I can have the cook make us something."

"Didn't we just eat about three hours ago?" I ask as I glance in the mirror and try to imagine my hair blond.

"Your point?"

I turn the water in her sink on. "I don't know how you do it. You can eat anything and not gain an ounce, while I watch everything I put in my mouth."

She laughs as she walks over to help me wash the color out. "Girl, have you seen my mother? She's as fat as a cow."

"Your mother is not that big, Kelly. She's like what, a size eight or something?" I ask as I bend over in the sink and she begins to rinse the color out.

"That's like, plus-size in all the fashion magazines. I eat, but I have my ways of not ending up looking like her. I mean, no one is going to hire a fat actress."

I turn the water off as she hands me a towel to wrap around my head. "What do you mean, you have your ways? I hope you're not doing what some of the girls at school are doing?"

"Girl, you know I don't do drugs. At least, not yet anyway." She looks at me and laughs as she opens up a drawer and pulls out her blow dryer.

"I know you're not stupid enough to ever do drugs. You know what I'm talking about," I say, watching her facial expression as I plug the dryer in.

She walks back over and takes a seat on the edge of the tub again. "Look, it's not like I do it all the time. Just when I overeat."

"Kelly."

"Don't Kelly me. Besides, you're not one to talk. You're bleaching your skin to look like me, and I'm doing what I do to stay looking like me."

"It's not the same. You could really hurt yourself doing that."

"Bleaching your skin is just as bad," she says, motioning for me to turn the dryer on.

"I thought you told me that stuff was safe."

"It was. It is. Kind of. I mean, it's been working for you. You haven't had any nasty side effects. Just some peeling skin sometimes, but nothing major, right?"

I try to smile, but the thought of what she's doing scares me. "Be careful. You're the only best friend I've got."

"I know. That's sad."

"Whatever."

We both begin to laugh.

"I'm calling the cook. I want pancakes, and you need to get to drying your hair so we can see if we're finally twins or not."

"Pancakes at this time of the night?"

"Girl, you know he makes a mean set of pancakes."

"It's almost ten o'clock."

"Pancakes are good at any hour in my book. You in or not?"

"Yeah, go ahead," I say as she gets up and begins walking back into her bedroom.

"Hey, you spending the night?"

"Yeah, so don't snore or put your feet in my face this time," I say as I turn the dryer on.

We both laugh.

Two hours later, I pull the covers back at the foot of her bed and climb in.

"It looks just like mine," she says as she slides into the bed and sits up against the headboard.

I reach up and touch my hair. "I know. I love it."

She clicks off the light.

"Finally," I whisper in the darkness.

Chapter Forty-Three

"So this is the Bronx," Kelly says as we walk into our new apartment. She looks around and bursts out laughing. "I feel like I'm on welfare or something. My shoe closet was bigger than this place."

I look around as well. "I love it because it's ours."

She closes the door as we step farther inside. "You're right. It's ours. At least this neighborhood is nice. They say Woodlawn is an up-and-coming neighborhood."

We both plopped down on the floor.

"I'm just glad it has two bedrooms, so I don't have to listen to you snore," I say, grinning over at her.

She reaches over and pinches me. "I hope we can get some furniture soon. You know I'm not used to living the poor life."

I reach over and pinch her back. "We're not poor. We're living . . . thrifty."

"Girl, you and I both know that I have never done . . . thrifty." She glances at the small kitchen area. "We have got to get some paint. These white walls have got to go."

"Kelly."

She smiles. "Calm down. I'm just pointing out the obvious. You know I could call my father."

I shake my head. "No. You promised. We're going to do this on our own. Remember?"

"Yeah, but we need a sofa at least. All we have is our beds, a refrigerator, a stove that looks like it barely works, and a little table that the overweight landlord with a bald spot in the center of his head gave us since he thought you were so pretty," she says, giving me the side-eye.

I reach over and touch her hand. "Stop that. We can do this. Besides, I have some of my graduation money left over. I can get the sofa. Trust me."

She glances around again. "I trust you," she says reaching into her purse. "Here, take this and get us some real furniture." She pushes a handful of money towards me. "It's my graduation money."

I shake my head because I know she's lying. "I'm not taking that. We agreed that we would split everything. When I can afford it, we'll get more furniture. Right now, we'll just get the sofa. Okay?"

She shoots me a disapproving look and puts the money back in her purse. "I can pay for it all, you know, including a much bigger place."

I reach over and touch her hand again. "That's not the point. We agreed that we would find work and use whatever we made from our gigs to buy what we need. Let's stick to that. Promise me."

She looks away from me.

"Kelly . . . promise me."

She lets out a heavy sigh. "Fine. But, you better find a gig and quick. This place is so small, it's depressing."

I stand up and pull her up. "It's not depressing. It's our home. Yours and mine. Besides, I may have already found a gig."

She grabs my arm. "What? When? How?"

I grin. "Stop with all the questions. It's just an audition. I saw a flyer and called. They booked me for an audition tomorrow. It's a jazz musical, I think." I notice the expression on her face change. "What's with the look, I thought you would be more excited."

"I'm excited. I just thought…"

I place my hands on my hips. "You thought that you would be the one to get a gig first. Well, you still might be. Like I said, it's just an audition."

She pretends to fix her clothes from sitting on the floor. "I'm happy for you, really I am. It's wonderful," she says, looking up at me and trying to put on a smile. "You found us a great but small apartment. You got us that wonderful table in our tiny kitchen, and now, you've found a gig. It's all working out. We're on our way," she says, winking at me.

I try not to show how hurt I am by her words, but I've never been able to hide my feelings very well from her.

She walks over and takes my hands off my hips. "Look, don't pay any attention to me. You know how I am sometimes. I really am happy for you. Honestly." She claps her hands together again as if she's trying to convince herself of her own words. "I know you'll get it that gig. No one can sing jazz better than you. You were born with the gift. I'm sure that once they realize who your father was, you'll get the part easily."

I take a step back from her. "I'm not going to tell them who my father is."

She starts to walk toward one of the bedrooms. "Sure you won't."

"I mean that, Kelly. Whatever gig I land, I'm going to land it on my own. Off my own name and my own talent."

She gives me a strange look. "Don't forget the transformation. I'm sure that will help, as well." She stops at the doorway of one of the bedrooms. "I want whichever one of these is the biggest."

I shake my head in dismay. "Sometimes I forget how spoiled rotten you can act."

She laughs as she opens the door of the bedroom and flips on the light. "This must be the smaller one."

It's my turn to laugh now. "Actually, they're both the same size," I say. "I tried to get you to come and look at it before we signed the lease."

She takes a peek around the room. "Well, this one has a window. Does the other one have a window?"

I fold my arms. "No, it doesn't."

She grins. "Perfect. Then, I'll take this one."

We both laugh.

Chapter Forty-Four

"What are you singing today?" asks a woman that I can hear but can't see, as I sit behind a piano that appears to be older than I am.

"I'll be performing 'Here Comes The Sun' by—"

"We know who it's by," says a man. "You can begin now."

"Right," I whisper as I take a deep breath and rest my hands on the keys.

I see my mother standing in front of me as I hit the first note. I know that if she were here, she'd tell me to pick a spot in front of me and focus.

Not on the people.

Not on my fears.

When you sing, she'd say—"The people disappear, and your fears fade off into the darkness. All that's left is the music. Allow it to mix with your heartbeat. Allow it to stir in your soul. Then open your mouth.

"Pull from your gut.

"Pull from your pain.

"Find your joy.

"Don't feel for the keys, let the music guide you. Let it come to your rescue. It will always save you. It will always be there. Focus."

I listen to her words as I remember the look on her face as I walked to our front door with my packed suitcases.

I remember the tears that streamed down her face.

The ones I tried to ignore were there.

I remember the pain in her heart.

The pain that I know I put there.

But there was joy.

It was faint. Somewhere off in the distance.

I saw it when she smiled.

She smiled because I was going after my dream.

That's why I love her.

My mother.

My fingers stop, and I wait.

I wait for a clap. For applause.

For a sign.

Something that tells me that my feet are on the right path.

The path to my dream.

There is nothing as I move from behind the piano and walk off the stage toward the exit door.

"That was amazing."

I turn around, and I see a tall, slender black man staring back at me.

"Not too many people can sing and play the piano like that. Where did you learn that?" he asks as he takes a few steps toward me.

"I practice."

"That's obvious, but that kind of performance doesn't come from practice, it comes from here." He reaches over and touches my heart.

I take a step back.

"I'm sorry, I'm Edgar," he says, extending his hand.

I shake his hand. "I'm Nina. Nina Taylor."

"I see."

I look at him questioningly. "You see what?"

"I see why you sang a Nina Simoné song. It was a good choice, by the way."

"It's a jazz musical, so I sang a jazz song."

"True, but the type of song you sing is just as important as how you sing it."

"You must be an expert?" I say, annoyed.

"Some people say that I am."

"Look, I have to go. It was nice meeting you . . ."

"Edgar."

"Right, Edgar."

He reaches out and gently grabs my arm. "Seriously, you play the piano and sing like you've got some true soul in your heart. I don't know many white girls who can pull that off. I'm hard to impress, and you, Ms. Nina, impressed me. You been sneaking off to Harlem when your parents aren't looking or something?"

I look down at his arm as he slowly removes it. Did he just call me a white girl?

"Like I said, I practice, and I happen to love jazz."

"Jazz is easy to love." He smiles, and I notice how warm and kind it is. "Well, I won't hold you up. Like you said a minute ago, you have to go. Unless you want to grab a cup of coffee or something?" he asks, still smiling at me as if he's sure I will say yes.

"Thanks, but no thank you. It was nice . . ."

"Meeting me?"

"Something like that," I say, eager to leave.

He takes a few steps back from me. "So you think you'll get a callback?"

"I doubt it."

He places his hands in his pockets. "That's honesty. Why do you think that?"

"I just do," I say, glancing back at the exit door.

"Have some belief in yourself. That's the only way people are going to believe in you."

I turn back toward him. "You sound like my mother."

"She must be a super smart and attractive woman."

I reach out my hand. "Bye, Edgar."

"Bye, Nina," he says, taking my hand and giving it a quick shake.

Chapter Forty-Five

Walking into our apartment, I see Kelly on the phone, so I move into the kitchen area, grab a glass from out of a box we still haven't unpacked, and rinse it off.

"I see they got the phone working. That was fast," I say as Kelly hangs up and walks over towards me with a big grin on her face.

"Yeah and just in time," she says, pulling out a chair and taking a seat.

"Just in time for what?" I ask, joining her at our small, hand-me-down table, that I know she hates as much as I do.

"For them to call," she says with a devious smile on her face.

"For who to call?"

"Some guy named Edgar," she says, watching me carefully.

I frown. "I don't know why he would have called. I didn't give him the number."

"It's called a callback. But, in your case, it's apparently called . . . you got the part."

I jump up. "You're kidding me. I can't believe it."

"Believe it. First audition. First part. Only you, Nina," she says, getting up and walking toward the bedroom she claimed as her own.

"Did he say when I should come back?" I say, trying hard to hold in my excitement.

"He said to come by on Monday, and someone will be there to give you the script."

I lean over and brace myself using the table. "I can't believe that I was so rude to him. He tried to take me out for coffee, but I turned him down."

"Well, he obviously didn't notice or care. In fact, he sounded . . . quite interested in you."

I move toward her. "Don't say it like that. I'm just getting started in my career. I'm not trying to start anything else. Besides, he was—"

"Black?"

"I was going to say . . . older."

"Oh, that changes things. Sort of."

I grab her hand. "Kelly, he thought I was white."

"Shut up!" she says, leaning against the wall.

I start grinning like a little girl. "It's true."

"Like I said before, it's all working out."

I frown and lean against the wall beside her.

"I'm not salty. I mean it. You worked hard to get here, and now here you are. I guess I better start pounding the New York pavement for my own gig, huh? I can't have you becoming famous before me."

I turn toward her. "Kelly, this isn't a contest."

She smiles. "I'm messing with you. Stop being so serious. You just landed your first gig. We need to go out and celebrate."

We start to scream like schoolgirls.

"I knew my mother was wrong," I say as we plop down on the floor.

"What do you mean?" she says, stretching her legs out.

"She's been trying to convince me that I can make it as I was as a black woman, but I seriously doubt that I would have gotten this part had I shown up as one."

"You're probably right. I'm sure the blond hair did it," she says, grinning.

"Shut up."

She jumps up. "Come on, let's go celebrate."

"I'm broke, remember?"

She pulls me up. "I'll loan you some money. You're a working girl now, remember?"

I smile. "That's right."

Kelly hugs me. "I'm sorry for being salty."

"You'll find something. I know it."

"I better," she says grabbing my hand and pulling me toward the front door. "We've got to grab something to eat while we're out. It's dinnertime, and I'm starving."

I stop her. "Just promise me you'll keep it down this time."

"That depends on how much I celebrate tonight. Come on, lighten up. Don't spoil this moment."

Chapter Forty-Six

"**N**ina, get up," Kelly says, standing over me.

"What time is it?" I say, slowly opening one eye.

"Time for you to get your butt to your first rehearsal."

I jump up and look at my clock. "Oh, no! I'll never make it in time."

"You'll make if you get going, like, now."

Kelly moves out of the way as I sprint into the bathroom. Ten minutes later, I run back into my bedroom, searching for something to put on.

"Here, put these on." She tosses me a pair of jeans and a shirt.

"Thanks," I say, grabbing them from her.

"I still can't believe that within two weeks of us moving into this apartment, you're already rushing out for your first gig and one that is paying—and well at that."

"I know. I thought I was going to throw up all over myself when they told me how much. I really like the script though," I say as I throw the jeans and shirt on.

"Yeah, that script was obviously written by a very talented individual. Not like that high school crap we had to do."

"It's even better than that one gig you got us last year." I glance over and see a small hint of anger on her face and instantly wish I could take back my words.

"You got paid for it, didn't you?"

I smile. "You know what I mean."

She sighs. "Yeah, I do. Hurry up, you've got to get out of here."

I slide on my shoes, grab my purse, and start rushing toward the front door.

"It doesn't look like I'm ever going to land a gig," she says, frowning.

"You will. It's only been a couple of weeks." I say, quickly unlocking the door.

"I've auditioned for almost ten parts, and not one of them has called back. Not one. It's depressing."

"I gotta go. Something will come, just believe—"

"Don't you dare say to just believe in me."

"It's true," I say, stepping out into the hallway.

"Go."

"By the way, where were you last night?" I ask, quickly.

"I was hanging out with some friends."

"What friends? We don't know anyone around here."

"You don't. Now get going and stop acting like my mother." She sticks her tongue out at me and closes the door.

Thirty minutes and a crowded train later, I run into the theater, soaking wet from the heat and looking for a seat in the back row.

"Nina, so glad you could join us."

I look up and see Edgar on the stage.

He frowns as I take my seat.

"For those who don't know me—"

Everyone laughs.

Except for me.

"Okay, so most of you know who I am, but for those who don't, I want to say welcome. My name is Edgar Omar Jamison. I've written and directed over twenty Broadway musicals that have been featured in some of today's leading industry-related magazines and newspapers."

My mouth falls open.

"Today is all about getting to know each other, so you can relax. The next six weeks, however, will not be like today. They will be filled with hard work and long hours. I expect the best because I will give you the best of me. Critics will come, boasting their critical talk. Negativity will be in the air. Such is the case with most things in life. But in the end, this Broadway production will be one that people remember."

I place my hand over my mouth so that no one hears me gasp. Broadway production!

"Each of you was selected because of your talent, not necessarily because of your experience. That's why the auditions were advertised the way they were. Using simple, old-school flyers, as they say. It's something we've done in the past with excellent results. I love raw talent, and I love working directly with natural talent. That's why many of you got a personal phone call from me. I love hearing the hunger in your voices. The excitement. The eagerness.

"As the saying goes . . . don't leave home without it."

Everyone laughs.

He moves his hands to quiet us down. "Now, let's be real. When this production opens, people will come to see talent. To see a performance. It's what they paid for. Give them every penny of their money. Don't be stingy. Don't save some for yourself.

"It's not fair. They paid for it. Give it to them.

"When this production is over, if you didn't have experience, you will have it. If you did have experience, you will add to it. Talent is what I want here. Deliver it."

I see his eyes searching through the dim light until I feel them on me.

"Be here on time. Every day." He smiles as I sink down into my seat. "Know your lines. You've had two weeks, so you should be off-book by now. We will not be feeding lines to anyone starting next week. If you are a singer, sing. If you are an actor, act. Know your part like you know your skin. Does everyone understand?"

Everyone shouts at the same time that they understand. But I sit there. Watching him. Being in awe and feeling foolish for treating him the way I did the first time we met.

"Good. If you don't, there's the door." He points to an exit door on the side of the stage. "No hard feelings. I'm sure there's some low-paying Off-Broadway production that would love to have you."

I watch as confidence carries him off the stage and one of the stage managers steps out.

Chapter Forty-Seven

"N ina."

I turn around and see Edgar standing at the end of the hallway by the dressing rooms.

"Congratulations, Ms. Nina Taylor."

I walk over to him. "Why did you say it like that?'

"Like what?"

"Like you were putting emphasis on my last name."

"It was on your first name, actually."

Feeling foolish, once again. I look away. "Is there something to your last name?"

I turn my attention back to him quickly. "No, I just—" I look down. "I'm sorry, I didn't realize who you were that day at the audition."

"It's okay. You're new to this, and besides, I like meeting people who don't know who I am. That way I get to see them as they truly are."

"I wish I had made a better impression."

He places his hands in his pockets and leans up against the wall. "I saw what I needed to."

"Which was what?"

"Like I said today—talent. It's what got you the part."

I catch myself looking into his eyes. Searching them. Hoping they will tell me how I should take his words.

"Stop," he says.

"Stop what?"

"Stop trying to determine how to read into what I just said."

"I wasn't—"

He grins at me. "Yes, you were. Anyway, I came looking for you because I want you to find Stan. He handles the music. As we go along, we may change some of the songs you perform so that they fit your style. Stan and I will be working closely with you. After you see Stan, go see Debra. She's our acting coach, and she's one of the best in the business. She'll get you where you need to be. I want you to go to her after we finish rehearsals each day. Are you okay with that?"

"Yes," I say while trying not to look completely taken in.

Taken in by his belief in me.

"Good. You're our star for this production. You understand that? You understand what that means?"

I look him in the eyes. Searching for his confidence so that I can draw from it. "It means I'll have to bust my butt to deliver."

He gives me that warm and kind smile of his again.

"Exactly. Glad to see you read that right." He starts to walk away.

"Edgar?"

He stops and turns back around.

"Thank you for believing in me," I say.

"Someone had to."

Chapter Forty-Eight

"How has working with Debra been these past few weeks?" Edgar asks as he walks out of the theater and finds me sitting on the steps, looking over my lines.

"Rough, but a great experience. I'm learning a lot."

He laughs as he takes a seat next to me, placing his briefcase between us. "Yeah, she can be that way, but only when she feels something good will come out of all her hard work."

I close my script and look over at him. "Then she must really see something good in me."

He smirks as he glances up at the sky for a second and then back to me. "Trust me, if she didn't, she would have told me so. Stan and I have been very impressed with you as well. So has the rest of the cast. They all seem to really like you."

A leaf floats down and lands in front of us.

"The fall wind is coming in," I say, reaching down and picking it up.

"Yeah, the trees of New York are shaking their leaves at us."

I join him in a light banter of laughs.

"You should laugh more. It looks good on you."

Not knowing how to respond, I look down at my leaf.

"You want to go for a walk?" he asks, seeing the nervousness on my face as I look down the street. "It's just a walk. I'm not asking you to marry me or something. Trust me, you're way too young for me. I'm not trying to be thrown in jail. I've taken a walk with many other singers and actors. Nothing at all meant by it. I promise."

I let out a sigh of relief. "I was beginning to wonder."

He stands up and grabs his briefcase. "Sorry if I gave you that impression. I'm just trying to get to know you more."

"I love New York at this time of the year," I say, as we walk down the stairs and onto the sidewalk.

"Have you lived here all your life?"

"I have. My father is from Chicago, but he moved to New York when he was eighteen. My mother has always lived here. I doubt that she would ever live anywhere else."

"Your father . . . Timmy Taylor, the jazz pianist, right?"

I stop. "How did you know?"

"I didn't when we met at the auditions. But a friend of mine was there the first day of rehearsals, and she recognized the name, and you, for that matter. Jasmine's a ballet dancer. Apparently, you two met when you were younger. She said that your mother brought you to watch them dance one day.

"Jasmine will be helping me with the choreography. She also mentioned that she knew your mother when she sang at a jazz club. I got the impression that they go way back," he says, searching my face for a reaction to his revelation. "Why didn't you tell me yourself?"

I look around. Fighting the anger and fear that I feel inside. "I didn't tell you because I really didn't want anyone to know."

He nods slightly. "I get that. You wanted to make it based on your own name." He smiles and tries to put my mind and fears at ease. "Don't worry, I'm the only one that knows. At least now I know where the talent comes from. Your father was amazing, and according to Jasmine, your mother can really blow, as they say."

"Yeah, I think I remember Jasmine. My mother took me to see her in order to teach me a lesson."

"A lesson about being black and seeing the beautiful things that we as black people can accomplish?" He looks me deep in the eyes again.

I start walking.

"You are black, aren't you?" he says, as he walks at my side.

"By the world's definition, I guess."

"What definition is that?"

"The one that says that I'm black even though my father's real father wasn't. And since we're speaking the truth here, my father killed himself because he didn't want people to know that he was . . . black."

"He could pass for white. He did pass for white, actually."

"I know."

We stop, and I watch as people move around us.

"I've seen pictures of him. But that isn't the case with you. And that doesn't explain why you bleach your skin. Why are you trying to be something you're not?"

I start walking again. "Who says I bleach my skin?"

"Jasmine told me that when she saw you years ago, you clearly looked like a young black girl, not at all like you do today."

"Your friend seems to be telling all my business," I say, heading back toward the theater.

He reaches out and stops me. "Look, Nina, you're talented. You don't have to try to be something you're not. Just be you. You want so badly to make it on your own name, but you aren't willing to try making it in your own skin and on your own talent. No one will see what you've accomplished if they feel that you got there like . . ."

"Like this?" I say, turning and looking at him face-to-face.

"Exactly. If it comes out that you've been bleaching your skin, people will call you a fraud. They won't respect you or your talent. White people will disown you for trying to look like them, and black people will disown you for trying to deny your black heritage. You'll never be free of that. People will always remember that about you. Is that what you want?"

I look around again as the tears start to flow down from my fake blue eyes. Mixing in with the bleach, the makeup, and the delusions.

Falling into my dye-colored blond hair.

"Nina." He reaches for my hand. "You can trust me. Do you want people to remember you as a fraud or as a remarkable young lady with talent and determination?"

"I don't know," I say with quivering lips. "I just wanted to make it. I didn't want to have to struggle so much because of my skin color. It's not fair."

"It's not. Ask any black person on this street or around the world, and they will tell you that." He reaches over and wipes the tears from my face.

"My father . . . my father was able to accomplish what he did because people thought he was white. He made it. He was big in his time, and he wasn't even out of his twenties. I just want to make it like he did, and I don't think I can get there as a...as a black person."

"Your father was born the way he looked. True, he could have stated that he was black, but to my knowledge, he didn't even know that until his career had already taken off. So there would have been some forgiveness from the public. It would have taken some time, I believe, but had he just addressed it, people would have accepted him because he had true talent."

"That wasn't a chance he was willing to take," I say, matter-of-factly.

"The truth still came out. Killing himself didn't change that. I'm sorry to put it like that, but that's the reality of the matter."

"You want reality? Here's reality for you . . . He was a coward. A coward who left us." An older woman walking by us looks up, but I don't care. I don't care if she heard me.

Edgar waits until the older woman is out of hearing range.

"Nina, I'm not going to stand here and tell you that it's easy to make it being black. It's downright hard. I know," he says, pointing to himself. "I've had to work harder than most. There aren't many blacks doing what I'm doing in this industry, right now. There aren't many who have made it to this level. But I did it by staying true to who I am. A black man with talent. I can write. I can direct. I let the world see that. That's what I give them, and I let them decide if they want to accept it or not."

He touches my face. "Stop the bleaching. Be you."

"I don't know if I want to. Maybe I like who I am. Maybe I like how I look."

"You don't. I see it in your eyes. The eyes don't lie. They tell you a lot about a person. All one has to do is be willing to listen with their heart, instead of judging with their mind."

"You aren't going to kick me out of the production, are you?" I ask as the reality of that outcome comes to the surface.

"Of course not. Like I said, you got this part based on your raw talent. Nothing else. That's what we saw that day. That's what I heard at the auditions. We're presenting you as a woman. Not as a white woman who can sing jazz with soul. Just as a woman who can sing jazz with meaning. If you looked black, we still would present you that way."

I look at him and try to smile but am still not convinced that I'll have a job once we get back to the theater.

"Stop reading into my words, Nina. You bring what I need for this production. Your voice. And man, can you play that piano! It's like butter. Your fingers just seem to glide over the keys, and the music you make when you sing, it's like pure, raw sweetness."

His smile starts to dismiss my fears as we begin walking again.

"Thank you," I say, reaching the theater.

"For not firing you or for helping you to see that you should be happy with the skin you're in?"

I look into his eyes, and I see my mother staring back at me.

"Maybe both," I say.

Chapter Forty-Nine

"**K**elly," I say as I walk into her bathroom to find her sprawled out on the floor, holding her stomach. "Are you okay?"

She looks up at me with tears in her eyes. "Yeah. I'll be all right. Sometimes the reality of what girls have to go through to not look like their mothers is too real." She reaches her hand out. "Help me up."

I grab it and help her to her feet. "I thought you told me that you were done doing this."

She wipes her eyes. "I never said that I was done doing this. I simply said that I wouldn't do it as much. There's a difference."

I take a seat on her tub and look her over. "You've got to stop this. It could kill you."

"Stop being so dramatic. I swear you're letting your little bit of success go to your head. For the last two months, maybe more, all you do is try to tell me what to do. It's getting old, don't you think?"

I stand up and place my hands on my hips. "I'm not trying to tell you what to do. I'm just worried."

"Oh goodness, there goes the hands on the hips—just like a mother. Well, guess what Nina, I left my mother at her own house. Don't forget that."

"Kelly—"

"Stop it. I mean it. I'm not a little girl. My mother doesn't live here. She's off doing exactly what she always does—living her life." She walks slowly toward the door, using the wall to steady herself.

"Where are you going?" I ask slowly. Knowing that I'm treading on thin ice with her, but the friend inside of me just can't let things be.

"Out with my friends." She shoots me over a nasty look. "Don't worry, I'll be home before my curfew."

"About those friends of yours . . ."

She stops and stares me down. "What about them?"

"I hear . . . I hear that they do drugs and that they drink a lot . Maybe you shouldn't—"

"Maybe I shouldn't what?"

I pause. "Maybe you shouldn't hang out with them so much."

She starts to laugh as she leans up against the door. "Who else am I going to hang with? You're off at rehearsals just about every day. I have nothing else to do. No one is calling me for auditions because apparently, I can't act. So I go out. I'm nineteen. I'm free to do as I want. Just remember that."

"Maybe you could start taking acting lessons." I see the fire in her eyes, and I want to slap myself for allowing those words to fall from my lips.

"Get out!"

Chapter Fifty

I unbutton my coat as I walk into the coffee shop and spot Edgar sitting by the window.

He looks up and waves me over.

"Preview show on Thursday and then the opening on Friday. You ready?" he asks as I take a seat.

"Ask me again on Monday," I say, searching the restaurant for a waitress.

He grins. "I'm glad I finally got you to have a cup of coffee with me."

"You know, when you first asked me, I thought you were trying to—"

"Hit on you? Isn't that how the young folks say it these days?"

"Close enough," I say with a bit of light laughter.

"Honestly, when I heard you play at the audition that day, I just wanted to know where that came from. You played and sang with such passion, I couldn't help but get my butt out of my seat and almost chase you down. I'm sorry again if it came out the wrong way."

"It's okay, now that I know," I say as I spot a waitress and signal for a cup of coffee.

"There are three things in life that I consider my favorites. Talent, music, and the stage."

My favorite things. His words take me back. "My mother used to say that my father's favorite things were music and her smile."

Edgar leans back in his chair. "Your father was something. I have a few of his albums. In fact, ever since I met you, I find myself playing them all the time. Do you ever listen to any of them?"

I look out the window, and I swear I can see him behind the piano, smiling back at me. "My mother listens to them all the time."

"You should too, you know. He is so much a part of who you are."

"My Grandpa Bryan says that I have a little bit of him and my mother in me. He calls it the gift."

"Was your grandfather in the music business?"

I smile as I think about Grandpa Bryan. I miss him so much. "He was my father's manager. He was the one who got my father his record deal. They were the best of friends."

The waitress brings my coffee over and a glass of water. I grab the water quickly and take a sip.

"It's hard talking about your father, isn't it?"

I take another sip of my water. "I met him once. I was so young I barely remember it," I say, looking down at my hands. "But I remember his touch. We shook hands the day my mother introduced us. I was five years old."

"I'd love to meet your mother. Is she coming to the show?"

"My mother and I don't talk much," I say, finally taking a sip of my coffee. "But I'm sure you already know that."

His sly smile tells me I'm right.

"Why not?" he asks, as the waitress comes over and tops off his coffee.

"It's a long story." I place my hand on top of my cup to indicate to the waitress that I'm not ready for a refill.

He places a few spoonfuls of sugar in his cup and gives his coffee a quick stir before looking over at me. It's a look that I'm familiar with. One that used to come from my mother and means that he's about to go into a lecture.

He starts slowly.

"Look, I'm in my forties. Not an old man yet, but old enough to know that you need your family. I didn't have any until I was fifteen. I was raised on the streets, as they say. Lived out of garbage cans and ate when I made enough money washing people's car windows. It wasn't until one day I met this one woman who took me in. She wrote plays for Broadway, best-selling books, and even wrote a few movie scripts that became major hits at the box office. She taught me everything about the stage. Everything I know about how the stage should flow. How it should feel. She became my family until she died."

"I'm sorry to hear that," I say, knowing that the lecture is not finished.

"She cared about me, and I suspect your mother cares about you."

"How do you know that my mother cares for me?"

"You weren't living on the street, were you? You didn't grow up hungry, did you? You had a coat when you needed it, didn't you? When you needed a hug, I'm sure she was always there to give you one."

I look away from him, remembering that winter night that she took the coat out of the car and made me put it on.

Remembering the time she took me to meet Jasmine.

Remembering the things she always tried to teach me.

Remembering all the times, she tried to be what she was supposed to be. My mother.

"I've said some pretty ugly things to my mother over the years."

He reaches over the table and grabs my hand.

"I don't mean anything by this, but you should call her. Invite her to the show. I'm sure there isn't a daughter in this world that doesn't regret mouthing off at her mother at some point in her life."

"Maybe."

He pulls his hand away and takes another sip of his coffee.

"Edgar, why do you spend so much time with me? I don't see you doing this with anyone else in the cast."

He grins as he leans back in his chair. "This industry can be a dog-eat-dog world, as they say. They see talent like yours, and they try to use it until they bleed you dry. I've seen it happen plenty of times. I'd hate to see that happen to you. Besides, like I told you, someone took me in and taught me everything I know. I'm just paying it forward."

"Have you paid it forward with others?" I say, looking at him questioningly.

"Of course. I've helped many others, actually. Had coffee with them too, if I thought they were worth the high cost of coffee here in New York." He gives me a wink.

"Glad you think I'm worth it."

"You should be."

I laugh. "Says the man oozing with confidence in me."

"Stop that, Nina."

I see the concerned look on his face.

"What? What did I do?"

"You keep caging yourself in doubt. In feeling that you're not good enough. You want to know why I spend so much time with you? It's because I know that if I don't, you'll let that wonderful and amazing raw talent that is flowing through your veins dry up, instead of setting it free. I can't let that happen. You understand me?"

I glance out the window again and whisper, "I do."

Chapter Fifty-One

*m*y eyes are heavy as I struggle to look over my lines for the last time.

Finally, after not being able to recite another word or sing another note, I toss the script on the coffee table that Kelly purchased a few weeks ago and lean my head back on the sofa.

I can't get Edgar's words out of my head.

All of them.

I touch my skin.

It feels rough like the bleach has removed every ounce of softness. I pull myself off the sofa and walk over to the gold mirror that hangs on our wall.

Another item that Kelly purchased, without waiting for me.

I pull a handful of hair around so that it lays on my shoulder. The blond color is faded, and the hair looks tired from having it permed more often than I should.

Where are you, Nina?

Where is the real you?

I hear the door opening and look over to see Kelly stumbling in.

"You're just getting home? It's four in the morning."

"Girl, you have got to stop trying to treat me like a child," she says, staggering over to the sofa and plopping herself down on it. "I'm grown."

I look her over. Her eyes are bloodshot red. "I was worried."

"Yeah, you've been saying that now, like, every day. I keep trying to tell you that it's getting old." She glances down at the coffee table and sees my script.

"I'm going to bed," she says, trying to stand. "Shouldn't you be in bed too, Mommy? It's four in the morning." She laughs, tripping over the chair as she pushes past me. "Running last minute lines, huh? You want me to help you? No wait, you need a real actress to do that," she says, making it to her bedroom door. "How ironic this all turned out to be."

"What are you talking about?"

"You. You never even wanted to be an actress and look at you now—you're going to be a famous singer and actress." She moves her hands in the air like she was opening a show or something. "I think you lied to me. I think you only got this part because you told them about your famous father."

"I told you I didn't."

"Well, I don't believe you," she shouts, stumbling back to the sofa and plopping down on it. She looks up at me. "Look at Nina Taylor. The wannabe white girl. The daughter of the man who didn't want to be black, so he killed himself. Funny how the apple didn't fall far from the tree."

"That's enough!" I say, walking toward my bedroom.

"Truth hurts, doesn't it? Is that why you're leaving? You can't handle it, huh? I remember . . . I remember when we were back in high school . . ."

I stop and stare at her. Anger boiling. Hands on hips.

"I remember when all you ever talked about was being like me. Well, look how the tables have turned. Here am I struggling to be like you. Maybe I ought to dye my skin black. Maybe then I'll get a part. What do you think? You think that will work? I mean, if you can pretend to be a white girl and land a role like the one you've got, then I should be able to pretend that I'm a black girl. Isn't that how it works? We can just pretend."

"I'm going to bed and you should as well."

"Yes, Mama. Isn't that what you call your mother? Mama? Tell me, do all black girls say that? I really need to know if I'm going to become a black girl."

"Kelly!"

"Stop yelling at me." She stands up and lays her hand on her forehead. "My head hurts. Maybe I did drink too much. You know I can fix that." She winks at me and uses the wall to make it to her bedroom door again. "I-I just gotta say one last thing before I go in here and throw up."

"I think you've said enough."

"No, I don't think so, because we're friends, and friends tell each other the truth, isn't that right?"

"What else could you possibly have to say?"

"Just that I think you treat your mother like dirt. You really do. You're ungrateful. Here you have a mother who loves you. One who cares. And you couldn't care less. Did you know that she came by? Two weeks ago. Said you wouldn't take any of her calls, so she came to see you. My mother has never been here. She's never even called. Even now, she doesn't care whether I live or die. She's just glad I'm out of the house.

"It's a shame you can't see what you have. Yeah, you got some big role in some fancy production, but you still don't have anything. You're a fake. Everything about you is fake. I know, I provided it all for you. Right down to that wannabe blond hair color. One day, people are going to see it, and I'm going to make sure of it."

I walk over to her.

Not remembering the laughs we've shared. Not caring about the secrets or the promises to be friends forever.

"Like father, like daughter," she says with a challenging smirk upon her face.

I raise my hand.

I feel her skin underneath it as the tears stream down my face.

Chapter Fifty-Two

I hear someone screaming.
I sit up quickly in my bed.
I hear it again.
And then, again.
It's Kelly.
I jump out of bed and run into her bedroom. Flipping on the light. My eyes racing toward her bed.
I hear it again.
It's coming from the bathroom.
I run to the door and grab the handle.
It's locked.
I start banging on it.
"What is it? What's wrong?" I ask, through the door.
"Call an ambulance."
My hands shake as I dial 9-1-1.
A woman answers. "9-1-1, what's your emergency?"
"I live in the Woodlawn neighborhood. The Pincer building. Level 3, apartment H. Something is wrong with my friend. Please send someone."
"Can you tell me what's wrong with her?"
"I don't know. I was sleeping, and then I just heard her screaming. Please, just send someone."
"We have an ambulance on the way. Can you tell me how old your friend is?"
"She's nineteen. Please hurry."
"The ambulance will be there in a few minutes. Are there any pets in the apartment?"

"No." I hear a thump.

I let the phone drop and run to the bathroom door. I push on it until it opens.

"Kelly?"

Chapter Fifty-Three

*T*here's a clock on the wall of the hospital waiting room that reads 10 am.

Three hours it's been, and I feel like I could pull my hair out, waiting for the doctor to come and tell me what's going on with Kelly.

Just as I stand up to stretch, I see Kelly's mother rushing down the hallway wearing six-inch heels and holding tight to her gold Gucci bag.

I give her wave and watch as she tries to speed-walk her way over to me.

"What happened?"

I shake my head. "I don't know yet. The doctor hasn't come out."

She shifts her purse from one hand to the other. "What do you mean, the doctor hasn't come out yet? You called me over three hours ago."

"Has it been that long?" I say, upset that she's just getting here, but not completely surprised.

She looks around the waiting room and stares for a second at a chair as if she is afraid to sit on it. Afraid she'll get her all-black outfit dirty. "The driver was stuck in traffic. Took us forever to get here."

I know that really means that she was shopping.

"Can you do me a favor and go get me a coffee or something?" she says, picking up a magazine from the table next to us to use as a seat protector.

I watch as she picks up two more and makes sure they're covering the seat thoroughly before sitting down.

"Sure. I need to find a pay phone anyway."

"Well, bring me back my coffee before you make your call. Actually, you know, I just picked up the newest Motorola 8000 portable phone. They call this thing 'The Brick,' and boy, does it feel like one," she says, pulling the phone out of her purse. "In fact, after purchasing this thing, I had to go and buy a new purse just so I could have something to put it in. That's why I'm just getting here."

I fake a smile. "I'll go grab your coffee."

"Oh look, here comes a doctor down the hallway. Is that Kelly's doctor?" she asks, standing up, her necklaces dangling.

I look down the hallway. "I don't know. We could try asking him."

She quickly sticks the phone back in her purse and rushes up to him. I follow behind her.

"Excuse me, can you tell me what is going on with my baby girl? Her name is Kelly Sheldon. Blond-haired young girl with blue eyes, like her father." She stops and stares at me for a second before turning her attention back to the doctor. "Whatever it is, just do what you have to. Money isn't a problem."

"You're her mother?"

"I am," she says, extending her hand with its perfectly polished pink fingernails.

"Maybe we should have a seat."

The doctor and I watch as she adjusts the magazines again before sitting down.

"Mrs—?"

"Donna. Donna Sheldon."

He sits down and I keep standing.

"Mrs. Sheldon, I don't know if you know this, but your daughter has a severe eating disorder. She's been engaging in self-induced vomiting, and that's what's causing the severe pain and blood in her stomach. We also found drugs in her system."

She stands up quickly, almost knocking me down. "What? That's not true! My daughter would never do such a thing. Maybe I need to have her taken to another hospital. One that is more competent."

I grab her hand. "It's true, Mrs. Sheldon. She's been doing it for a while. I tried to get her to stop."

She pulls away from me. "And you didn't tell anyone? Why didn't you tell me? What kind of friend are you?"

"Mrs. Sheldon, I tried to—" I see the anger in her eyes.

"Never mind. After today, you and Kelly's friendship is over. It's bad enough you're trying to look like her." She looks me up and down. "I don't want you near my daughter. You're the one that probably got my poor baby started."

"I didn't."

She turns her attention back to the doctor again, ignoring me as much as possible. "What's going to happen to my daughter? You do whatever it takes. Her father will pay the bill. Money is no problem."

The doctor glances over at me as I wipe away the tears. He pulls a Kleenex out of his coat pocket and hands it to me.

"She doesn't need that," Mrs. Sheldon says, slapping the tissue so that it falls to the floor. "My Kelly wouldn't be in here if it wasn't for her. She's always been a bad influence. I've told Kelly that often."

The doctor reaches in his pocket, grabs my hand, and places another Kleenex in it.

I wipe my nose as he smiles at me before facing Mrs. Sheldon again.

"We're taking good care of Kelly, but she's going to need counseling and a good treatment center that specializes in eating disorders after she leaves here. I can have a nurse provide you with some brochures."

"I'll find a treatment center for her. Like I said, money isn't an object. Just get her better. I'll be back tomorrow morning, will she be ready to check out then?"

"We'd like to keep her here under observation for a couple of days, just to be safe."

"Fine. Whatever you think is best," she says, as she looks over at me. "Just so we're clear, Doctor, I don't want this girl around my daughter. Make sure every nurse knows that."

The doctor looks in my direction. "I'm afraid we're going to have to ask you to leave." He calls over a nurse.

"Can you assist this young lady? Help her get home or something?" The nurse nods.

Mrs. Sheldon steps in front of the doctor, addressing the nurse. "I don't want her near my daughter. You make sure every nurse knows it."

The nurse glances at me and nods again.

Chapter Fifty-Four

Afraid.

That's what I feel in my toes. In my hands. In my heart as I stand in front of my mother's apartment.

Afraid to knock on the door.

Afraid to use my key.

Afraid to look her in the eye and admit how much I had messed up and how much she had been right.

Just as I go to put my key in the lock, she opens the door and immediately pulls me to her.

"Nina."

We both stand there looking at each other with tears in our eyes.

"Hi, Mama."

"Hi, baby," she says as she hugs me again before moving inside. "Let me make us a cup of tea."

I close the door and follow her into the kitchen.

My mother is beautiful. Her skin. Her eyes. Everything about her is beautiful. I see this now as I sit at the kitchen table, watching her move around the kitchen. It's like seeing her for the first time.

Seeing her strength through a new lens of life.

Her wisdom, through a new sense of appreciation.

"I'm sorry, Mama."

She fills the familiar coffee pot with water and places it on the stove before walking over to me. She takes my hands into her own. "I've missed you," she whispers.

I start to bawl as she pulls me to her and wraps me in the comfort of her motherly love. The touch of her hands reminds me how much I missed her as well.

After a few moments, she pulls back and wipes the tears from my cheeks, and I regret that she has to touch them. That she has to see the lack of the real gift that she gave me.

The color of her skin.

We hear the water boiling, so she walks over to the stove and turns it off.

"You still have that coffee pot?"

"Your father loved it. We keep the things that the people we love also loved. It's how it is. At least for me, anyway," she says, taking a seat at the table.

I reach over and touch her hand. "I just left the hospital. I had to call an ambulance to have Kelly rushed to the hospital."

"Why? What happened?" she asks with concern but relieved that it wasn't me in the hospital.

"She was screaming, Mama. Her bathroom door was locked and—."

She rushes over to me and wraps me in her arms again. "Whatever it is, she's going to be alright."

She gives me a few minutes to try to calm down.

"Can you tell me what happened?" she says as she walks over to one of the kitchen drawers, pulls out a few tissues and hands them to me.

I take one and blow my nose.

"Kelly is bulimic. She's been practicing self-induced vomiting for a while," I finally say, as Mama leans up against the counter.

"Did you know she was doing this?"

In all my shame, I nod my head slowly.

"Did they say that she will be okay?"

I nod again.

She lets out a sigh of relief as she reaches into the cabinet to grab two cups and then reaches into a drawer to get spoons.

"They are keeping her until Friday, for observation," I say as Mama pours the hot water into the cups. "To make matters worse, Mrs. Sheldon is blaming me for all of this. She even ordered the nurses not to allow me to see Kelly."

"She's upset that you didn't tell her or me, for that matter." She begins placing the cups and spoons on the table and sits.

I look down at the table. "Kelly will have to go to a treatment center once she gets out," I say, putting a few teaspoons of sugar in my cup.

Mama blows on her tea before taking a sip. "Eating disorders are serious. She could cause severe damage to her organs, and if she keeps doing it and doesn't get the help she needs, it could kill her."

She looks me in the eyes.

"I don't do it. I never have," I say quickly, understanding the reason for the intense scrutiny.

She takes another sip of her tea and then smiles. "I'm glad to hear that. How are rehearsals coming along?"

From across the table, my mother sees the humiliation in my eyes for not being the one to tell her that I got the gig in the first place.

"I'm so—"

She reaches over and touches my hand. "I didn't ask you that to shame you for not being the one to tell me. I asked you because I'm happy for you. Let's start from there."

I nod my head like the little girl that I feel like, fighting the tears, once again. "The rehearsals are finally over. The preview show opens . . . tomorrow," I say, barely getting it out.

Mama gets up and walks over to a drawer, pulls out an envelope, and then places it in front of me. Grinning.

I look down at it.

"Go ahead. Open it."

I pick it up and open it slowly. My eyes widening as I see the name of the musical on the tickets. I look up and see mama's eyes beaming with happiness.

"I got them a couple of weeks ago after I stopped by your apartment and Kelly told me about it. All your grandpas are coming, as well. I'm so happy for you, Nina."

I can't hold back the tears any longer as I lay the tickets on the table and rush over to give her a hug.

"Please forgive me, Mama. Please forgive me."

She holds me tight.

Chapter Fifty-Five

"What is belief?" Edgar asks as he moves to the center of the stage.

The same stage that I will perform on, in just a few hours.

"It's more than a feeling. It's more than a word. You can't buy it. In fact, there isn't enough money in the world that can help you get it. Why? Because it lives down here. In your gut. It travels up here. In your heart. And it breathes here. In your mind. It captures your soul, and only you can let it go. So don't. Hold on. Hold on, I tell you. Hold on like it's life. Because it is. Without belief, you aren't living. You're just going through the motions.

"Live, people. Walk in your belief.

"Each of you must step out on this stage tonight, and the world must not only see your talent, but they must also see your belief. Your belief in yourselves.

"Don't let them take it away. Hold on to it.

"Know that anything can happen tonight. It's the stage. The stage is imperfect. With the stage comes missed lines, missed cues, lighting that might not work. The list could go on. That's okay. Hold on to your belief. No matter what happens. Don't let it go.

"Show the world your belief.

"By now, the meaning of the word—belief, should be in your pores. Its essence should be what people breathe in when they see and feel your presence on this stage.

"Take a whiff. Do you smell it? It's the belief that I have in each of you.

"Thank you."

The applause was something I hope to never forget.

Chapter Fifty-Six

I hear nothing but the beat of my heart as the curtains slowly open.

I feel the keys of the piano telling me that they're ready for me as I reach down and touch them.

I feel the vibe of the keys as if they are sending me a scent.

A scent that smells like pure rhythm.

A scent that only I can take in.

It's not a scent like candy canes and young girl's dreams.

This scent is grown.

It has passion in its bones.

It's flowing determination into my nostrils and showering me with zeal.

I feel like I'm bathing in it as it flows down to the tips of my fingers.

It's dripping from my lips and caressing my lungs with its aroma— opening them wide to send my voice into the crispness of the air.

Even with my eyes closed, I can see the dancers on stage. Telling the story that I sing.

The horn enters.

Then the heavy call of the drum.

The dancers respond as they move in poetic harmony.

The saxophone calls out to me, and the violin makes known its presence.

The story is being told through movement.

Through arms, feet, and twirls that bring grace to the stage and draw in the audience.

Scene by scene, I feel this.

Even when the action begins and the story unfolds.

The story of a woman.

She's searching for a taste of freedom that she finds hidden in the corners of music. In the depths of something unknown.

She beats her chest from grief. Wipes her eyes from heartache. But she stands strong. The music she sings comforts her. Tells her that she's not alone.

She searches for what to call it. Searches for how to name it.

She finds love through it. It's under the surface. Trapped in the melody. She etches it out, and little by little, it takes on a form.

The form of jazz.

She's like a woman giving birth.

Bringing forth chords and keys.

She will become known as the mother of jazz.

The mother of rhythm.

The last scene erupts.

The dancers stop.

The actors stand still.

The lights fade to black.

The applause can be heard and felt.

Chapter Fifty-Seven

"*N*ina." I look down the small and crowded hallway that's behind the stage and see Grandpa Bryan moving towards me. "Grandpa Bryan!"

The moment we reach each other, he wraps his arms around me and kisses me on the cheek. "You were. . ." He steps back and looks into my eyes with a beam of pride. "Exactly as I always knew you would be. I didn't know you could act. Where did that come from?"

I can't wipe the smile off my face as I stare at him. "Practice, and a lot of it. I'm so sorry to hear about Aunt Margaret," I say, stepping a bit closer to him so that only he can hear me.

"I was just glad to be with her when it mattered most. But let's not talk about that tonight." His warm smile reminds me how much I have missed him. "Your acting was something else. I think you can do something with that. You know what I mean?" He winks at me.

I laugh. "Yes, Grandpa Bryan, I know exactly what you mean. I'm just glad tonight is over, although the real show is tomorrow and we still have three more weeks of shows to go after that."

"You were amazing out there, little lady," Grandpa Livingston says, walking up. "It was definitely worth the trip from Atlanta."

I step from around Grandpa Bryan to give him a hug.

"Hey, do I get one of those?" Grandpa Taylor says, and he and Grandma Jean make their way through the crowd with flowers in their hands.

I take a step back and look at each of their faces. "This night has been like a dream come true for me. I can't thank each of you enough for coming."

Mama walks up with a few dozen roses in hand.

"Mama, look who found me," I say, feeling like I'm walking on a cloud of joy and excitement.

"The show was beautiful, and you were just as beautiful. I'm so proud of you," she says, handing me the flowers.

"The media is here," Edgar says as makes his way toward us.

I see him, and Mama make eye contact.

"Edgar, this is my mother—Simoné."

He extends his hand. "I've heard so much about you. Jasmine is a friend of mine."

Mama smiles. "Jasmine and I go way back," she says.

"That's what she told me, but she didn't say how beautiful you are."

I watch Mama blush as Grandpa Bryan steps up.

"Edgar, this is my Grandpa Bryan."

"I've heard of you, Mr. Edgar. I can see why people enjoy your work. The show was amazing. The guy you had on bass was pretty good as well."

"Boney Bass Bryan. Man, you are a legend."

Grandpa Bryan smiles widely as they exchange handshakes.

"Edgar, let me introduce you to the rest of my family," I say, as I see the look of awe upon Edgar's face.

"You were great out there tonight. I told you all you had to do was believe," Edgar says to me.

"And click her heels three times."

"Grandpa Bryan!"

Everyone laughs.

"Come on, Nina. We need to get going. The media is waiting to interview you and the rest of crew," Edgar says.

"What am I supposed to say to the media?" I ask, stepping close to Mama.

She takes my hand.

"Just smile and answer their questions," Grandpa Bryan says. "We'll wait for you in the foyer."

I nod, nervously.

"I'll come with you," Mama says.

I sigh in relief as we follow Edgar down the hallway.

Chapter Fifty-Eight

*L*ights and reporters.

That's all I see as Edgar, and I step up on the platform. He takes the empty chair in the center and indicates that I should take the one next to him.

Mama finds a seat in the back as the reporters waste no time firing questions at each of us.

One of the reporters stands up and moves closer to the platform when Edgar selects her.

"Sylvia Jackson, as you know, Mr. Jamison, with the New York Times."

"Glad to have you with us again, Ms. Jackson."

"Thank you, Mr. Jamison. It was an amazing preview show tonight. I'm sure opening night tomorrow will be even better," she says with a recorder in one hand.

I see Mama sit up in her seat.

"Mr. Jamison, the song that opened the show tonight sounded familiar. May I ask where it came from?"

"The music was written and performed by one of my favorite jazz pianists, Mr. Timmy Taylor."

"And the name of the young lady who performed it? For the record."

I see Mama stand up.

"Our lead actress, Ms. Nina Taylor."

"Is it true that she's the daughter of the late Mr. Timmy Taylor who committed suicide after being exposed for trying to pass as a white man?"

Mama begins to move.

"Ms. Taylor is our lead actress. That's all I can comment on."

She looks directly at me. "Ms. Taylor, are you the daughter of Mr. Timmy Taylor?"

"Yes," I slowly whisper in the microphone. My knees knocking together under the table as Mama steps up on the platform.

A member of the cast that's sitting next to me gets up and allows Mama to take their seat.

Cameras begin snapping pictures of the two of us.

"My sources tell me that you bleach your skin. Any comment about the truth of that? Are you ashamed of your black heritage?"

Edgar leans into his microphone. "Ms. Jackson, we're here to talk about the amazing job each of these actors did tonight, and that's all. I think you've asked more than the allowed number of questions today."

Ignoring him, she keeps her eyes focused on me. "Ms. Taylor, is it true?"

Mama places her hand on top of her microphone. "You don't have to respond," she whispers to me.

I look in my mother's eyes, and I see that little black girl in the toy store holding her white doll tightly in her hands as if it was the most beautiful thing she'd ever seen staring back at me.

I see my mother's facial expression that day.

The looks of disappointment.

The look of fear.

I reach out and touch my mother's cheek as a tear falls down her face. "Love the skin you're in," I whisper to her.

I turn my attention back to the reporter. Allowing all my fears to slip off into the darkness.

"Yes, it's true," I say into the microphone. "I started bleaching my skin when I was in high school. Not that long ago, actually. I wanted to be something else. Someone else. I wanted to be white." I reach up and touch my cheek. "You're right Ms. Jackson, I was ashamed of my black heritage."

"Why is that?" Ms. Jackson asks, holding her recorder up closer to the platform.

"I was convinced that being white was the key to success, but my mother and Edgar have helped me to see that that isn't the case. It's my talent and my belief in myself that will make me successful in all the ways that really matter. Most importantly, to myself."

I look down at my hands. "Inner beauty. That's a phrase that, after today, I look forward to embracing."

"I just have one last question for you," she says.

I stand up. Mama stands too. She wraps her arm around me as we walk off the platform.

"That will be all the interviews for today," Edgar says, as he and the rest of the cast follow behind us.

Chapter Fifty-Nine

"**M**ama," I say, opening the door of my apartment. "Good morning. Did you get any sleep?" I shake my head.

"I came by to bring you something."

I step aside to let her in. "I hope it's not the paper," I say, yawning and glancing down at the box in her hands.

"It's not, but I did read a few of them this morning."

I fight to hold back the tears as she tries to soften the reality of the situation with a motherly smile.

"Come on, let's put some coffee on," she says as we make our way into the kitchen area, putting the box and her purse on the table. "Where do you keep your coffee?"

I point to a cabinet by the refrigerator. "Grandpa Bryan just left. I'm surprised you didn't see him in the hallway. He was at my door before the sun came up. Afraid I would do something —"

Mama turns around, holding the coffee can in her hands. "Something like your father did?"

I see the sadness in her eyes, and I walk over and hug her.

"To be honest, I can't say that it didn't cross my mind as well," she says, placing the coffee can on the counter.

I touch her cheek the way she used to do me when I was a little girl. "I'm okay, Mama. Really. It's going to be rough until things die down, but like Edgar said to me this morning, on the phone . . . at least most of the articles mentioned that they really thought I put on a great performance." I give her a strong smile. "I've got to keep moving forward. We've got the show to do tonight. I'm just going to focus on that."

She returns my hug. "I am so proud of you, but I wouldn't be surprised if tonight's show sells out by the time it opens. Unfortunately, bad publicity is sometimes a good thing in that industry."

"What's in the box?" I say as we both wipe away tears.

"Something for you," she says, grinning.

"Can I open it?" I ask, eager to get to a happier mood.

"Sure."

I wipe my eyes again and open the box. "It's my father's coffee pot."

"I want you to have it. It was his favorite, as you know."

I pull it out of the box and place the box on the floor. "I know, but you love this coffee pot. I can't take it."

"Of course you can," she says, reaching for it. I hand it to her and take a seat at the table.

"That table looks as old as I am."

"It probably is. The landlord gave it to us," I say with a slight chuckle.

"That was nice of him."

"He thought I was cute."

"I see." She turns on the faucet and adds the water into the coffee pot. "Let me show you how to measure out the coffee for it."

I laugh. "Mama, I've seen you do it for years."

"You're right." She smiles as she measures out the coffee and places it in the coffee pot. "You need a new stove. This one is as old as that table," she says, finally sitting down.

"Yeah, Kelly and I were getting there." I sigh as I look around. "I doubt that she'll be coming back. We had a big fight before I had to rush her to the hospital. I'm pretty sure our friendship is over."

"I hate to say that it's probably for the best." She reaches over and touches my hand. "How are you going to be able to afford this place by yourself?"

"I'll make it work," I say, catching a slight look of disappointment on her face. Knowing that she was really hinting for me to move back home. "I was thinking about asking Grandpa Bryan to come and stay, now that he's back."

"That would be nice," she says quickly. Relieved that I won't be staying here alone, but I can tell that there's something else on her mind as she glances down at her purse.

"Mama, you okay?"

She gives me an unconvincing nod.

The coffee pot starts to percolate, so I get up and grab us a couple of cups, placing them on the table with cream and sugar. My eyes watching Mama. Waiting for her to say something.

"You going to tell me what's going on?" I say as I pour the coffee.

She lets out a sigh and then looks over at me with a smile. "I was so proud of you last night. The way you handled that reporter. The things that you said."

"I meant them," I say as I add some sugar to my coffee.

"I know you did. You've grown up so much." She glances down at her purse again.

"Is there something in your purse that you want to give me?" I ask as I too glance over at it.

"There is," she says, opening it slowly and pulling out an envelope. "I want you to have this."

"Mama, I don't need any money," I say, refusing to accept it.

She chuckles. "It's not money."

I take it, noticing my father's name on the outside. "Is this a letter that you wrote to my father?" I ask curiously because it doesn't look like her handwriting.

"It's a letter that your father's birth mother wrote to him, just before she died."

I stare down at it as it rests in my hand. "She died right after giving birth to him, right?"

"That's right," she says, picking up her coffee cup and taking a long sip. "I know that you might not have time to read it, with the show and everything else that's going on, but I hope you'll take some time, once the show is over, to read it."

I lay the envelope on the table and take a sip of my coffee. "How many times have you read it?"

"Enough to know it by heart," she says, standing up. "I better get going so you can try and finally get some sleep." She glances down at the envelope.

I walk over and hug her. "I love you, Mama."

She reaches out and touches my cheek. "I love you too. Now try to get some sleep. Even if it's just for a few hours."

I nod and walk her to the door.

Chapter Sixty

Walking to the back of the theater, I see Grandpa Bryan standing there, talking to Edgar. The moment their eyes meet mine, I know something is wrong.

"What's going on?" I ask as Grandpa Bryan walks over to me

"Nina, it's your mother. She's in the hospital. She was hit by a car," he says.

I drop the bag that I'm carrying to the ground. "What? What happened?" I ask, fearing the worst.

"Witnesses said that a car came out of nowhere as she was pulling out into an intersection."

I take a step back from him and gasp. "She isn't . . ."

Tears fall from his face as he reaches out and grabs my hand.

"I ain't gonna lie to you, baby girl, it ain't looking too good, but she's fighting," he says painfully.

I pull my hand away and stare at him in disbelief. Then I glance at Edgar as Grandpa Bryan's words register in mind.

"Don't worry about the show," Edgar says. "Just go." He picks my bag up and hands it to me.

Grandpa Bryan reaches over and wipes the tears away. "I'll go get the car."

Chapter Sixty-One

Breathe.

That's what I keep telling myself as Grandpa Bryan hits the expressway.

I glance out the window, but all I can see are—moments.

Moments when Mama wiped my tears away.

Moments when she looked into my eyes and smiled.

Grandpa Bryan glances over at me. "We're almost there."

I don't respond. I watch the world pass by in a blur. A world that wouldn't be the same without being about to share my moments with her.

With my mother.

The car comes to a stop, and I jump out and run into the hospital. My heart beating.

Tears flowing as I rush over to the nurses' station.

"Simoné Daniels, please. She's my mother," I say as a nurse with kind eyes quickly scans a chart.

"She's still in surgery," she says as Grandpa Bryan makes his way inside and over to me.

"Let's go to the waiting room," he says, "it's down the hallway." He grabs my hand, and I can feel him trembling.

"When did this happen?" I ask as we reach the waiting room and find a seat in the corner.

"When she was just a couple of blocks from your apartment. I was at her place when the police knocked on the door. They said that they had tried to call." He looks down at the floor. "I had laid down for a nap. I didn't hear the phone." His voice begins to fade as the tears return.

I reach over and wrap my arms around him. "It's okay, Grandpa Bryan. Mama is going to be okay."

She has to be.

"Did they catch the person who hit her?" I ask.

He looks down the hallway.

"Grandpa Bryan?"

He stands up.

I follow his eyes and see an older woman making her way toward the waiting room. She looks like an older version of Mama.

"Is that?"

"Your Grandmother. Jackie," he says, clearing his throat and wiping his face.

I stand as she walks into the waiting room with a cane in hand.

"Jackie. You got my message," Grandpa Bryan says to her.

"Finally, but yes. What happened?"

"She was in a car accident. She's still in surgery," Grandpa Bryan says. "You want to sit?"

She shakes her head. "Did they find the person responsible?" she asks, leaning against her cane.

"It was a kid. Police believe the driver was drunk," Grandpa Bryan says as he glances at me.

"It's been a long time since I've seen you," she says, looking me up and down.

"Hi, Grandma Jackie."

"You trying to look like your father? Such a shame," she says to me, shaking her head in disgust.

"Jackie, this ain't the place," Grandpa Bryan sternly says as he takes my hand.

She glares at him. "Did the kid that hit my daughter get hurt? What are the police saying?"

"Banged up a bit but nothing major."

"I hope the police are pressing charges. If they don't, I will," she says, shifting her weight.

"The police are still getting all the facts," Grandpa Bryan says to her while giving my hand a gentle squeeze. "Why don't you take my seat, Jackie?"

Out of the corner of my eye, I see Kelly's mother coming down the hallway. I pull my hand away from Grandpa Bryan and make my way over to her, just as she enters the waiting room.

"Mrs. Sheldon," I say, as she scans the waiting room for a seat that she feels she can sit in. "How is Kelly? Is she still getting out today?"

"What do you mean, is she getting out today? She had to be brought back in here today, and by the police, at that."

"Why?" I ask slowly. My legs trembling as my mind starts to . . .

"That crazy girl checked herself out last night, went off with some low-down people she calls friends, and got herself drunk or high, I'm not sure which one, probably both. Then, to make matters worse, she gets into some fender-bender going back to that place you call an apartment this morning."

Time stops as I watch her lips move.

I see Grandpa Bryan moving toward me.

"You okay?" she says as I stand there with my hands shaking. "You look white as a piece of linen."

"Did you just say . . . Did you just say that Kelly hit someone?"

"Weren't you listening? You on drugs too? That's probably how Kelly—"

"Who did she hit?" I ask, forcing my hands to stay at my sides.

"Some woman. I don't know much about it. The police just keep asking her questions, which is why we're still here, and they won't tell me how much longer that's going to go on."

I feel the rage.

It's in my toes.

Traveling up through my bones.

Grandpa Bryan moves between us, reaching out to me.

"It was Kelly," I whisper as I look into his eyes.

"It was her daughter, Kelly."

He grabs me and pulls me close to him as I see Grandma Jackie moving toward us.

"My mother is in here because Kelly hit her. Kelly hit my mother, Grandpa Bryan."

He pulls me closer.

"How dare you blame Kelly?" Mrs. Sheldon says, glaring at me.

I pull away from Grandpa Bryan. "How dare I blame Kelly? Do you hear yourself? Wake up! It was Kelly! It was your daughter! I know it!"

I lash out at her, but Grandma Jackie sticks out her cane to hold me back.

Mrs. Sheldon takes a few steps back from me. "She—"

I point my finger at her. "Don't! Don't you dare say she didn't do it. She did it! I hope they lock her up! You hear me? I will make sure they do!" I get in her face. "My Grandpa Livingston is an attorney. My Grandpa Taylor is rich, so money is no problem."

Grandpa Bryan reaches out and tries to pull me away from her, but I won't move.

"I'm sure it wasn't Kelly," Mrs. Sheldon says looking into my blazing red eyes.

The doctor walks into the waiting room, just as my hand goes up into the air. I recognize him instantly as the one that treated Kelly a couple of days ago.

I search his face as my hand slowly comes back to my side.

"I'm sorry," he says."We did everything we could."

I feel the floor shake as I scream.

Chapter Sixty-Two

Nina-1996

Grandpa Bryan removes his oxygen mask and tries to sit up. "So you finally did it, huh?"

I get up from my chair and rush over to fix his pillow. "How is that?"

"It's good. Stop fussing over this old man and answer my question," he says.

I take a seat on the edge of his hospital bed and face him. "Yes, Grandpa Bryan, I finally went to see her. It's taken me ten years, but I finally did it. You know what I mean?"

He smiles and places the oxygen mask back on for a second. Taking a few deep breaths as he continues to look me in the eyes.

"You know you shouldn't be talking," I say.

He removes his mask again. "Why? I'm gonna die anyway. I'd rather use my last breath to talk to my granddaughter."

I touch his hand because it's all I can do to keep myself from crying.

"How's my man, Edgar?"

"He's good. He's been such a great friend over the years."

"We all need them," he says.

"Yes, we do."

He looks over at the window, and I can see the past in his eyes. "I'm sure my father felt like you were a good friend to him," I say.

His face lights up as he looks back at me. "Yeah, your father was like my brother from a different mother."

"Grandpa Bryan, you still got jokes."

"I ain't dead yet. Close though," he says, grinning.

"Don't say that."

His trembling hand reaches out and touches mine. "I've been reading about you in the papers. Your mother would have been so proud of you. Winning all those awards from them big movies you're doing."

I wipe a tear away. "I miss her every day, Grandpa Bryan. I'd give anything just to have a moment with her again."

"She always believed in you. She believed that you would give the world something it could use."

I look into his eyes again and smile. "You read the letter?"

"A long time ago. Your mother let me read it, right after your father died. It helped. Butterflies ain't never looked the same to me since. Crazy, ain't it?"

I smile at him. "Not crazy at all, Grandpa Bryan. I think that letter was an inspiration to anyone who read it. It made me realize that I was carrying hatred in my soul—for her. For Kelly."

"That's why you went to see her?" he asks, struggling to put his oxygen mask back on.

"Here, let me help you with that." I wait for him to take a few deep breaths. "Better?"

"Yes."

"Yes, that letter is why I went to go see her. It took me ten years to read it, to be honest. Mama gave it to me the day she was . . . she was killed." I stand up and walk over to the window. I look at life moving down below. People having moments and I let out a sigh.

"Nina."

I turn back and look at Grandpa Bryan. "I'm sorry." I sit back down on the edge of his hospital bed again. Wiping more tears away. "That letter—It made me see the ugliness of hatred and the need to forgive.

"The need to forgive Kelly. The need to forgive me.

"I realized that if I didn't do either of them, then I would continue to carry around that ugliness, on the inside." I touch his cheek. "I wanted to be free, Grandpa. I didn't want to be . . .

"a caged butterfly."

The End

CPSIA information can be obtained
at www.ICGtesting.com
Printed in the USA
BVHW032137050219
539593BV00001B/44/P